LOCH

NESS

MONSTERS

IN

ATLANTIS?

BY

DANIEL JASON

Matthew

Wolverine's

Atlantis

North Atlantic
Current

Canary
Current

SARGASSO
SEA
ATLANTIS

Gulf
Stream

North Equatorial
Current

complimentary first edition to Robert W Murray of Clan Murray

Sweet dreams always!

LOCH NESS MONSTERS IN ATLANTIS?

a novel by
Daniel Jason

Daniel N Jason 12/25/02

Edited by
Linda Morgado

Illustrations by
Robert Buchanan

Time Dancer Press
Houston, Texas

Loch Ness Monsters in Atlantis?

© 2002 by Daniel Jason
All rights reserved
TimeDancer Press
ISBN 0-9659470-3-3

No part of this work may be reproduced or
distributed by any means without the express
written permission of the publisher.

This is a work of fiction. While some similarities may
exist between characters, events, and locations within
the story and actual persons, places, and circumstances,
the reader is advised that extensive liberties were taken
during the creative process, and these similarities are
purely coincidental.

Dedicated to Dyslexia, a Gift That 15% of the US population possess

Dyslexia is a language-based learning disability. Dyslexia refers to a cluster of symptoms, which result in people having difficulties with specific language skills, particularly reading. I was born a Dyslexic, but didn't realize the fact until adulthood.

My grandparents were so amazed at my reasoning from 2 years old to 5 years old that my grandfather, David Mc Roberts, had visions of me graduating from Harvard.

Then, I started Kindergarten and coming home one day, I asked my grandfather if Harvard was as hard as kindergarten?

A dyslexic sees everything in pictures and we see situations in 27 different ways within 1 second. School was a living nightmare. The letters turned on their side, upside down and slanted. I had to decipher these letters into real pictures. You cannot see *a, the, so, but.* In other words, these do not translate into pictures. They forced me to read aloud causing me to sweat and stutter. It was worse than having a tooth pulled without gas.

The multiplication tables took me months to learn. One high point was my grandfather and the rest of my family. They taught me high self-respect and that I could accomplish any goal that I set my mind to do. A dyslexic must have either parental support or great teachers to acquire high self esteem. I was fortunate to have both. My family, the McRoberts were Scots-Irish and great story tellers. My aunts and uncles talked to me on an adult level, so I developed college level vocabulary in Grade School. This confused my teachers because my vocabulary was extensive but I could barely read. They tested me and found my imagination and reasoning was close to college level. But they didn't have a clue about Dyslexia. When I told them that the letters turned upside down, they looked at me strange and then they checked my eyes. I started wearing glasses and kept my mouth shut on the letters.

In high school I focused on sports (runner and High jumper) and I lettered 4 straight years in High School.

College was great but Vietnam came up and I spent three years in the Army. I finished my tour of active duty in the First Cavalry in Vietnam.

Then back to college and a Bachelor of Science in Business Degree from California State University of Los Angeles.

I married and my ex-wife read to me about Dyslexia. After I realized I had Dyslexia, only then could I attack the problem.

I thank God that I have Dyslexia, it gives me a vivid colorful imagination. I love being in the entertainment business because Writers are the foundation of all movies.

WHICH CAME FIRST, THE BOOK OR THE MOVIE?

APPRECIATION TO INSPIRING PEOPLE AND MY GOD

Deepti Bireddy is a wiz on the computer. Her design of our website gave Time Dancer Press a home to be proud of on the Internet. She was able to install (within a month) credit card sales through PayPals on the website. Something, Time Dancer Press had failed for three years to accomplish.

Linda Morgado did the creative editing of this novel. Her diligence to detail and subtle changes create more vibrant pictures for the reader. Time Dancer Press chose Linda Morgado out of forty other applicants for the work of creative editor. Her easy-going style and meticulous attention to detail made her a pleasure to work with and gives our boss, our readers, a five star novel.

Robert Buchanan is a very recent discovery. His drawing of my golden retriever, Casanova on the back cover, is awesome. The picture captures the true spirit of Casanova's trustworthiness, enthusiasm, and love for this book. Robert takes the time to research the subject before he draws. His drawings are intense and photographic, so look for more of his drawings in Time Dancer Press's future novels.

My golden retriever, **Casanova** for helping me with the tough scenes through mental telepathy. He inspired the series, on my website www.danieljason.com , " Confessions of a Texas golden retriever in front of the air conditioner." He has a Scottish sense of humor and never meets a doggy biscuit he doesn't like. He is a true friend and a great companion.

George Lucas whose spectacular movies give delight to hundreds of millions of people inspired me to write. I look forward to the time that George will make this book a great movie that will entertain the next generation. Yes, George, I await your call.

My God for creating in me, dyslexia, and the determination to succeed. If, there were ten thousand other gods, still, I would seek out my God to worship only Him. **Praise God.**

TABLE OF CONTENTS

Chapter   Page

Chapter 1

Kraken's Attack

Gentle waves bob the ship up and down upon a clear turquoise sea. Two fishing lines meander from the stern of a pristine white ship, which is flying an American flag and a Texas flag. Matthew Wolverine sits with a loose grip on his deep-sea rod, in the stern of the ship, as his stare bores deep into the turquoise waters. The tensions of months of business worries have tightened his neck and shoulder muscles as hard as ice. Unconsciously, he succumbs to the sea's tranquility. Now, these tensions slowly evaporate into the air. As his mind drifts to his family, Matthew angles his head over his shoulder to speak bluntly to his chief financial officer, "Scotty, my family and I need a sabbatical from the pressure of the oil business. I need to rejuvenate my marriage and just be a dad to my children. My business is an all-consuming mistress that sucks away all my time. She steals every second of my conscious thoughts. Shalee and my children are sick of my constant business worries and so am I. Raquelle is no longer Daddy's little girl. She is a teenager and is rebellious. Now, we have heated altercations daily. My son, Eric, is noticing girls. There is so much I haven't taught him. This next year is crucial to them, so I want my mistress to become your mistress for one glorious year. But I must warn you that, once you commit to her, her beauty quickly fades, as she manipulates your life. She demands all your thoughts and can't be left alone, even for a short time, or she gets mischievous." Then his eyes drift back to the water.

Scotty Terrier's mind mulls this candid talk like a piece of tough gristle. Ambition, in Scotty's mind, uncoils slowly, like a snake about to swallow a plump field mouse. Finally, after all these years, his decisions will be the final corporate word. Scotty's mouth salivates with the sweetness of Texas oil power, but one wrong word could break his boss's euphoria. Scotty's tongue gently slides over his lips; then, at a leisurely pace, he speaks, "Shalee is a loyal wife. Her sensual long, blue-black hair surrounds her to-die-for bedroom eyes. You are the envy of every oil executive I know and, if I had a wife with a body like Shalee's, then your mistress wouldn't stand a chance." Scotty squints his eyes, as he bites his lip. Did he speak too freely to his boss?

With a side-ways glance, Matthew appraises his employee. Scotty Terrier is short, stocky, and as muscular as a gorilla. He is the only accountant Matthew knows, that works out one hour in the company gym, lifting weights, before starting the business day. Like a Scottish terrier, he is intelligent and loyal. Matthew detects no lust in Scotty's voice for his wife, only a tinge of envy mixed with an inner gnawing for power. Matthew shakes his head; Scotty is just stating the truth about his boss's wife. The allure of the mistress of business power beguiled Scotty from the first moment he joined Matthew's corporation. Scotty had completed his daily workout and was working when Matthew arrived at the office and he was still working when Matthew left the office. Matthew fed that desire by rapidly promoting Scotty to chief financial officer in less than ten years. Scotty didn't have time for any of his romances to blossom into love and marriage.

Matthew knows that the mistress of business power is subtle and that, over the years, that mistress subtly filled his mind with anxiety over the oil business. His mistress insidiously wormed her way into Matthew's every thought. His jaw clenches, as his mouth dries, "So, will you run my business, from this ship, for one year?"

Scotty's forehead wrinkles, as he blurts out, "Why can't I run the business from Houston?"

Matthew's eyes narrow and fill with tenacity, "She is still my mistress and I want to be sure that you don't kill her!"

Shalee emerges from below the deck in a one piece, skin-tight, leopard print bathing suit. Her voice is pleasant but commands an immediate response, "What is this about a mistress, Matthew?"

Matthew turns to witness Shalee's emerald eyes flash to reinforce her question. With the sun at her back, a blue tinge shimmers from Shalee's black hair to ring her upper body in a sapphire aurora. Angelic luster radiates toward Matthew and Scotty. Both men involuntarily take a deep breath. Matthew smiles, "Shalee, you put Helen of Troy to shame."

With an impish smirk, Shalee presses her interrogation, "Don't change the subject. What is this about a mistress?"

Matthew methodically gives her body the once-over. She stands with feet shoulder-width apart and hands on her hips, as she unconsciously draws in a breath that embellishes her bosom. His eyes scan her high cheekbones, small nose, luscious lips, full, firm, round breasts, tiny waist and long smooth legs. She locks into his body language that shows how he hungers for her body. His smile broadens as his eyes convey to her that she is a solid ten. After two children and many years of marriage, Matthew still cherishes her beauty. His eyes ignite her passion, but she knows the allures of his mistress, so she strives to keep his illusion of her as the ultimate beauty a reality--at least in her husband's mind. Matthew gives her a come hither look, as he states matter-of-factly, "The only mistress you will ever compete against is my business, but she is about to become Scotty's mistress for a year. Isn't that right, Scotty?"

Scotty grunts as Shalee saunters toward Matthew. Her long black hair extends down her back, to cloak her buttocks. As she sensually descends to sit on Matthew's lap, with her back toward Scotty, Matthew, with years of practice, skillfully shifts her hair from her back, over her left shoulder, to drape her left breast. His right hand deftly glides upon her silky mane from behind her neck, over her left shoulder, then down her chest. Shalee gazes, intensely, into Matthew's aquamarine eyes, as she purrs. Delicate, gentle caresses impart his amorous nature into her body and she covets each stroke. She crosses her legs. Her husband knows how to please her. His caresses take her to the seventh heaven. This is the granite that anchors their love.

Scotty bites his lower lip, as he grabs his fishing pole. His knuckles turn white from the pressure of his grip, then he shifts his gaze to his left, away from Matthew and Shalee. His boss, in Scotty's opinion, shows physical affection for his wife, too openly, around others.

Raquelle and Eric emerge upon the deck to witness their father embrace their mother in a deep French kiss. This scene of affection is so frequent, in their family, that the children learned early in life to stealthily observe their parents without disturbing them. They only had to see their father's temper explode once, to learn that it is something you avoid at all cost. Their mother's wantonness grows after each caress, which unleashes more passionate kisses from their father. History will repeat itself and, in a short while, they will retire below the deck to consummate their passion.

Raquelle and Eric discreetly turn their backs to their parents. Eric looks at the deck, then releases a deep sigh, "I never see any of my friend's parents that openly affectionate but, then, none of their mothers look like Mom."

Raquelle leans on the rail, looking into the water and she

3

fantasizes, "Dad's caresses are so smooth, sensual, and adept. His slightest touch sends Mom into rapture for hours. I wish he would let me date."

Eric breaks into a wide grin, "Heck, you're just fifteen and your birthday is not for another month. Maybe, when you're a high school senior, Dad will let you date. Now, let's have some fun and do some diving."

They both turn to descend below the deck to change into their diving gear. They try not to disturb the people working at their computers, but one employee suddenly bolts from his chair, clutching a piece of paper, and plows directly into Raquelle and Eric. The worker doesn't apologize, but continues to push roughly past them to ascend the stairs.

As they change, their mother's shout reverberates through the interior of the ship, "It's always a business crisis that takes priority, instead of me! I can't compete with your mistress. I want one year of marriage where you give me your full attention! I am going diving with the children and, when I surface, you decide what is most important to you--me or that mistress you call your business--but remember, we are Texans and, under Texas law, half of everything we worked for is mine. I will rip your mistress in half before I let her win you!"

Shalee storms below the deck, pounds on the cabin door and orders the children out, so she can change. As Eric opens the door, the scowl on his mother's face causes him to recoil in surprise. She roughly grabs his shoulder to toss him out and slams the door so hard, the whole ship vibrates. From inside the cabin, she orders them to get their spear guns because something in the water is going to die. She quickly changes into a dark blue bathing suit and they hurry on deck to strap on their tanks, flippers, face masks, and weight belts; then they grab their spearguns and jump into the water. As the three press deeper into the water, Matthew descends below the deck to quickly draw up a power of attorney, giving Scotty full control of all Matthew's businesses for one year--but only from this ship. Scotty stands, nervously, on the deck, rigid and with clammy hands. Matthew signs the paper, has an employee notarize his signature, then calls Scotty below the deck to meekly put the power of attorney into his moist hands.

"Sometimes my wife has to use a cattle prod to make me get my priorities straight. Like we on earth, I sometimes forget that it is the sun that gives life. If the sun goes supernova, then the earth dies.

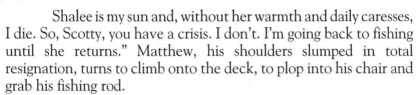

Shalee is my sun and, without her warmth and daily caresses, I die. So, Scotty, you have a crisis. I don't. I'm going back to fishing until she returns." Matthew, his shoulders slumped in total resignation, turns to climb onto the deck, to plop into his chair and grab his fishing rod.

Descending deeper in the water, her spear gun in front of her, Shalee speeds ahead of her children. Her face and stomach burn with anger. She spies a large cave opening, wavers for only a moment, then rushes inside the cave. The sunlight filters through the cave's entrance, as she swims deeper inside, then stops because something tugs at her mind that this cave is eerie. Cautiously, she moves close to the right side of the cave to survey the wall. A gentle current pushes against her body. Shalee reaches for the wall, but is stopped by a clear thick coating that encases it. She scans the walls and, in every direction, this thick coating blankets them. She brushes the wall with her right hand and it effortlessly slides down. No rocks or bumps protrude from the walls, just this glass coating.

With the sunlight filtering in, this cavern reminds Shalee of a missile silo she once visited in Nebraska. Even in this warm water, goose bumps spring up over her body. She shivers and squints into the darkness of the cave's recesses. Her children tread water, just inside the cave's entrance. They see their mother's back and tanks quiver and they tighten their holds on their spear guns. Shalee's intuition alerts of impending danger, so she spins around to face her children. Holding her spear gun in her left hand, she raises both hands, pushing them away from her body, signaling for them to stay out of the cave. Then her right hand urgently gives them the thumbs up to surface. Behind both Raquelle's and Eric's face masks, their eyes begin to bulge and, spontaneously, they raise their spear guns toward their mother and fire simultaneously.

The shockwaves of their heinous act paralyze her body and her heart skips a beat. Her mind races as to why her children would want to kill her. In this moment of confusion, the spears pass inches from Shalee's right arm. Instantly, the water violently vibrates, as two enormous tentacles appear on each side of Shalee. She only notices the tip of the tentacle to her right, but this apparition of terror jump-starts her legs. Like an electric beater on high, Shalee's fins involuntarily propel her straight up to the top of the cave. She breaks water and her fingers claw at the glass wall. She flounders in the water, trying to get a grip on this glass. Then her hand grasps a hold and she scrambles up onto a ledge. Breathing heavily, she points her spear gun at the water. Her whole body quivers in fear and she hopes that this is a nightmare from which she will immediately awake, preferably in Matthew's arms. Suddenly, the whole top of this cavern explodes in light.

Meanwhile, Raquelle and Eric beat a hasty retreat out of the cave, as tentacles flutter behind them. A school of large fish swims in front of the cave's entrance and Raquelle and Eric head into it. The fish scatter, but not before two are snagged by the two long tentacles. The children surface and quickly climb onto the ship. Their shouts bring their father flying out of his chair. Discussion centers on the size of the squid. Eric places it squarely at one-third as big as their ship. Matthew changes into diving gear, then dons his tanks. They search for extra spear guns and spears with which to load them. Matthew orders Scotty to remain over this spot until they return. Then Matthew, Raquelle and Eric plunge overboard, each carrying a double-spear gun.

From the side of the cavern top, directly opposite Shalee, come the sounds of movement. She squints to observe a large hole in the wall on the opposite side of the cavern. Two figures emerge from this tunnel, then stop to methodically inspect the circular ledge around the water. She imagines this may be a secret U.S. submarine base, but these men aren't in military uniform. Their red shirts and pants shimmer like a snake's skin. They have shoulder length black hair and gigantic swords hang from their sides. They spot Shalee and break into a trot toward her. Like an injured bird, with serpents slithering down upon her, Shalee frantically searches the sides of the cavern for an escape.

There is no other opening and the water holds the terror of the squid. She fears the squid more than man, so she turns to fight the two men. The men rush upon her and her eyes become riveted to their eyes. Their eyes are yellow with black vertical slits. Shalee's stomach tightens as she raises her spear gun. The men ignore her threat and speed up their run. Over the years, Matthew drilled into her mind that, if you must kill a man, you wait until you can't miss. She waits until the first man is only a few strides away, then squeezes the trigger. She aims for his stomach and the barb of the spear bites deep and he goes down on his knees. The other man strides past his fallen mate, as Shalee tries to thrust the spear gun into his stomach but, because she is still wearing scuba tanks, her mobility is limited. He wrenches her weapon from her hands, then smashes his open hand across her face. Shalee slams into the ground, then into oblivion.

To stop the vicious pain, the wounded man pulls the barb of the spear out of his stomach. Now, a gaping hole oozes black blood, thick as crude oil. His hands cover his stomach. The black blood oozes slowly to coat his hands. The wounded man looks down and the sight of so much black blood causes him to faint.

The second man removes Shalee's tanks, facemask and fins, then ties her hands. He roughly snatches her off the ground to stretch open her right eyelid, "Emerald eyes! What a sacrifice to the Red Serpent! This will mean the high priesthood for me!" The man hoists Shalee over his shoulder, then turns to inspect his bleeding comrade. A pool of sticky ooze grows beside the unconscious man. The man carrying Shalee erupts into maniacal laughter that fills the cavern, then he delivers one exuberant kick to sail the wounded man over the ledge and into the water. The man hovers for a moment on the surface of the pond. Then, gradually, he sinks. His massive sword speeds his descent toward the cave guardian's lair at the bottom of the water. On the top of the pond, a small black spot appears.

The scent of human blood in the water causes the squid to turn a dark gray and head back toward the cave. As the man descends, the water revives him. The squid enters the cave--wary, mantle first. The man lands right on top of the squid's eye and the squid jets to the bottom of the cave. The turbulent water from the squid's funnel pushes the man out of the cave's entrance and into the sunlight. He looks up to spy the bottom of a pristine white ship overhead, then furiously strokes to swim for its safety. The strong scent of human blood flows from the wounded man, incensing the squid, as it turns bright red, then spurts out of the cave after its next meal. Water vibrates around the man as he kicks harder, but still glances down. Ten tentacles extend toward the man. These tentacles have suckers. Some of the suckers have a ring of chitinous teeth. The two longest tentacles enfold the man. The suckers bite into the man's flesh and he screams, but this only expels the air from his lungs in a flurry of huge bubbles, which rush for the surface. The longest tentacles drag him downward to the squid's buccal cavity. Like a giant parrot's beak, the coal-black upper beak opens and closes into the lower beak. The squid's tongue is a radula, a chitinous ribbon with backward razors of sharp teeth. The squid takes its first bite from the man's stomach wound and a cloud of black goo slowly conceals the squid's mantle, leaving only the tentacles visible in the water.

Matthew, Raquelle and Eric pause at the cave's entrance to

witness this calamity, then they enter the cave. Raquelle and Eric swim, almost touching their dad. Matthew hates crowding, but he understands their need for protection. They surface at the top of the cavern, as a satisfied squid returns to the cave bottom. Matthew scurries up onto the ledge, then shouts for Shalee. The sound of footsteps echoes from a hole in the far end of the dome. Matthew flings his tanks, flippers and facemask to the ground, then he plucks up his spear gun to sprint for the opening.

Matthew reaches the opening, but he cautiously proceeds into the tunnel. The tunnel is restrictive and not illuminated, but it is not long. From the other entrance, a lone warrior draws his sword as he moves into the tunnel toward Matthew. The illumination from the other cavern shows Matthew only a black silhouette approaching. With the speed of a shark attack, Matthew swings his spear gun to eye level and fires. The twang of the released spear resonates inside the tunnel as the metallic shaft bores into the silhouette's Adam's apple. Involuntarily, the warrior releases his sword so both his hands can grasp the projectile, which now protrudes from his neck. Like a hungry wolf on a fallen moose, Matthew instantly clears the distance between them to grasp the sword, as the warrior pitches face down into the dirt.

Meanwhile, still swimming in the water, Eric finds a crack in the coating and pulls with all his might, to scale the ledge. Instead, a large sheet of the clear coating, in the shape of a gigantic arrowhead, breaks off the wall and plunges into the water. This jagged break, with some scalpel-sharp edges descends, point first, straight toward the resting squid at the bottom of the cavern. The squid has eight tentacles snug beside its body, as two short tentacles float across the cavern floor. The broken piece slices through the two short arms. The squid grabs it with one short tentacle, but its edges bite deep into the wrapping tentacle. The squid thrashes its tentacle to release the break but it holds fast. The squid's body changes from a translucent silvery-gray to bright red, as it jets to the illuminated top of the cavern and the origin of its pain.

Finally, Eric scales the ledge, then quickly removes his tanks, face mask, and flippers. Next, he extends his left hand to his sister. Raquelle clutches Eric's left hand for support. She gets a handhold then she swings her right leg up onto the ledge. Eric notices, way down in the water, a large red object approaching fast. He recognizes a squid's mantle and he panics. With his right hand, he violently seizes a handful of his sister's backside. His fingernails dig deep into her flesh, as he flings her body onto the ledge. She screams in pain, then flips off her tanks and flippers, as she jumps up, ready to beat her brother to a bloody pulp.

Waters explode, and splash over the ledge, as a now dark-maroon squid bobs in a thrashing pool of water. Its eyes transmit the coldness of arctic wind. Eric grinds his teeth and scoops up his spear gun. He doesn't aim, but just fires toward the squid. His first spear sails over the water, but drops harmlessly in front of the maroon monster. The squid lashes the arm, which is still clutching the broken piece of coating, against the wall, a short distance from Eric and Raquelle. The break shatters into slivers that penetrate deeper into the tentacle. The squid changes to scarlet. With spear guns in hand, Eric and Raquelle make a mad dash toward the cave opening and the safety of their father. As they race along the ledge, the squid glides through the water leaving an ammonia and blood trail, but its bloodthirsty stare never leaves its prey.

Matthew now firmly grasps the sword's hilt, as he emerges from the tunnel, into a giant cavern. The cavern is full of men in loose leg chains, clinging to picks and shovels, just standing there, dumbfounded. Then light beams flash over Matthew's head to explode into the wall; these explosions shower him with dirt. Other light beams flash to his right and rock fragments burst from the wall. Matthew dives into the dirt to his left. He crawls to the edge of the small plateau outside the tunnel's entrance. He looks down the slope to see what weapons fire these light beams. At the lowest point in the cavern is a small lake where three jet-black submarines are being loaded. A cargo compartment in the front sub has a bluish-green haze of thick powder floating above it. The warriors beside this submarine have their right arms pointed up toward Matthew, and they press on something that is attached to their right wrists and a flash of white light, from each device, leaps toward Matthew. Each weapon appears to fire only once, since the warrior immediately draws his sword, but each holds back until every man fires his weapon. Matthew thanks God that they are lousy marksmen. The light flashes cease, so these warriors reluctantly start to climb up the hill toward Matthew.

The warrior carrying Shalee over his shoulder had hit the dirt halfway down the hill to let his soldiers finish off Matthew with their shots. With Matthew unharmed, the man rises to hoist Shalee over his shoulder. Then he bulldozes down the hill, through his slow-climbing troops, past the first two subs and boards the last one. Matthew leaps up to return to the tunnel to search the dead warrior's wrist for this light beam weapon. A rapid examination reveals the wrist weapon and he removes it. A large arrow sits on top of a red crystal. Matthew reasons that it is strictly point, push, and shoot. He straps it on his wrist, as Raquelle and Eric, still carrying their spear guns, both race past him to emerge from the tunnel. They turn to scream at him that the squid is coming into the tunnel to eat them. The slapping of its tentacles on the floor and wall reverberates inside the tunnel, as the squid gets its grip and pulls its mantle up out of the water.

Shalee awakes to raise her head toward Matthew, then she fills the cavern with a desperate cry for help, as she descends into the submarine. A slave in chains beside the sub stares into Shalee's emerald eyes. Matthew takes aim with the wrist weapon, at the front of the submarine, but hesitates. Matthew's inner voice kicks in as it analyzes the coming fight. If Matthew fires at the submarine, he will cripple it but, with his children between him and the charging warriors, they will be his first casualties. The squid's thrusting tentacles now exit Matthew's side of the tunnel. He fights a two-front war that he can't win. He can't put his children behind him, because they would be instantly crushed to death in those massive tentacles. A still small voice inside Matthew orders him into action, as he whirls around to fire his light beam, through the tunnel, into the glowing eye of the squid. The squid's mantle rests on the ledge horizontal to the tunnel's entrance and the beam enters its right eye and proceeds through the mantle, as it bursts a gigantic hole in the top of its head. The hole swiftly dumps all the squid's life fluid into the pond in the other cavern.

As the tentacles fall lifeless, the fear of the squid leaves Raquelle and Eric. They simultaneously bolt behind their father. Matthew scoots to the edge of the small plateau to meet the charging warriors, as he yells down to the slaves to fight for their freedom. Matthew, Raquelle and Eric fire their spear guns into the onslaught. Two quick kills, then Raquelle fires again, causing one wounded warrior. The slave closest to the first sub turns to shout that O has been captured and that they must rescue O. The men in chains jerk their heads around at the mention of O, and they rush their guards. First, they bury their pickaxes deep into the chests of their guards. Then, pickaxes and shovels swing overhead, as the slaves plow into the side of the advancing column of warriors.

Matthew's sword slices through the lead warrior's forearm, then into his neck, as the submarine holding Shalee submerges.

Matthew acts like a berserk cat, with claws mutilating any hated dogs within reach. His blade slices through hands, arms, heads and knees until it, and he, are covered in black ooze. The children and Matthew have fought halfway down the hill. The captains on the two remaining submarines witness the slaughter of their warriors and command their crews to pour out and help their comrades to victory.

Matthew sees the outpouring of the crews from the subs and orders Eric and Raquelle to turn and run back up to the plateau. Each of them grabs a sword as they ascend the hill. The light weight of the swords surprises both Eric and Raquelle, but then, they are running on adrenaline now. With swords held high, they race up the hill to the plateau. Then Matthew turns to sprint up the hill, as the warriors, like angry bees, swarm behind him. Matthew reaches the top of the hill and turns to yell at the prisoners to attack the submarine captains. With Eric at his right and Raquelle at his left, Matthew forms the head of their "V" attack, and they wade into the swarm of approaching warriors. Eric strains every muscle to swing his sword. It bounces off his opponent's sword. Eric is strong for a twelve-year-old, but he is no match for a warrior, so he is pushed backwards. Therefore, he changes tactics and slices at his opponent's knees. The warrior recoils in pain and Matthew finishes him off. Matthew shouts "Knees!" in Raquelle's direction. She switches techniques and goes for the warrior's knees.

The prisoners smell freedom. With every fiber in their bodies, they leap upon their captors' backs and bite deep into their enemy's necks. The death screams of their captors reverberate through the cavern. The captains of both submarines aim their wrist weapons to fire at these prisoners on the backs of their crews. The blast kills many prisoners and crewmen, but the remaining prisoners grab daggers and swords from the dead and turn to hurl the daggers at the two captains, who are standing on their subs' decks. While the majority of the daggers hit the subs, some find their marks and the two captains slump dead on the decks of their respective ships.

A deep, guttural boom explodes from a prisoner and the other prisoners follow suit. The cavern shakes with this proclamation of victory. For a split second, the guards stop fighting Matthew and turn to witness their escape subs now manned by dead captains.

Matthew doesn't hesitate to lop off three guards' heads before they can turn around again. He wades into the mass of stunned warriors. The battle lasts only a short time longer, as no prisoner shows mercy to his guards.

Eric and Raquelle stick close to their father's side as they make their way to the first sub. The last scream of a dying guard slowly fades as Matthew, Eric and Raquelle reach the water. They clean off the black ooze, then climb the gangplank to arrive at the first dead captain's body. Matthew searches the body for keys and removes them from the dead captain's neck.

The prisoners in chains gather into a crowd in front of the gangplank to see what these three champions will do. Matthew hands the keys to Raquelle, with instructions to leisurely unlock each leg chain, as he calls the men on board and talks to them. He looks for the oldest prisoner. Then he motions for him to come on board. This man has a long gray beard down to his belly button, stringy hair and is coated in bluish-green dust. Raquelle stops breathing to escape the prisoner's stench.

As she slowly unfastens each leg lock, her father speaks, "My wife was kidnapped in the submarine that escaped. My children and I have fought to free you and we ask your loyalty and help to rescue her."

Matthew extends his hands, palms upward, toward the unwashed man. Tears fill the old man's eyes, as he falls upon Matthew's chest. Matthew gently strokes his matted gray hair, as he reassures him that he is free. Raquelle and Eric exchange glances because the man's rank stench doesn't seem to affect their father.

After a few minutes, the old man pulls back to stammer, "Years ago, I gave up hope of ever seeing my beloved Atlantis again! Whatever God you serve and whatever quests you send me on, know that I will faithfully serve you. Only, let us first return to Atlantis!"

Matthew wonders if this man is delusional, but he plays along, "Can you get these two subs to Atlantis?"

The old man straightens up to his full stature and nods, then he turns to march smartly down the gangplank, to announce to his fellow prisoners that they are to return to Atlantis. From inside every prisoner comes a deep guttural cry, which booms until the roar fills the cavern. Raquelle and Eric cover their ears with their hands. After the din dies down, Matthew orders each prisoner, individually, to board the submarine so he can gain his fidelity, as Raquelle removes his chains. There are over fifty prisoners, so this takes some time. After the last prisoner is unchained, Matthew commands them to strip the dead guards and leave their clothing and weapons beside the water. The prisoners start stripping the bodies.

The old man boards, first one submarine, then the other, and drags the two captains' bodies off each sub to strip them. He orders some of the other prisoners to carry the bodies to the plateau. Then he flings off his rags and plunges into the water. He grabs a handful of sand and aggressively scrubs his body and hair until all the blue-green dust floats away. The other prisoners follow suit by neatly piling their new clothes beside the water and jumping in. The men laugh and splash each other until each is clean. Matthew's eyes narrow as he watches this scene. He notices that the other prisoners wait until the old man exits the water before they, themselves, go out to dry and dress. The old man puts on the captain's uniform with the self-assurance of a Marine. He picks up the other captain's uniform, then he turns to march straight up the gangplank to Matthew. "My name is Eli. I was the first captain of the fleet of Atlantis before my capture by Abaddon (the city of destruction). You and your son have aquamarine eyes. Only men of the ruling nobility of Atlantis have such eyes. The rest of the Atlantians have deep, dark blue eyes. Emerald eyes are so rare that a female with emerald eyes can only marry a male of the ruling nobility. Your daughter's crystalline emerald eyes radiate elegance. Are your wife's eyes as lucid emerald as your daughter's?"

Matthew nods vigorously.

Eli swallows hard, "Then she is a rare prize! She is O. The Red Serpent will swallow her whole, after he has covered Abaddon with his red tide."

The lids of Matthew's eyes tighten as his face becomes granite, "Then we must conquer Abaddon and rescue my wife. How long before the next tide?"

Eli shakes his head, "I have been in the mines for years. We must return to Atlantis for that answer, but these subs are filled with Bluegreen. It is the fuel that powers every machine within the Sargasso Sea and brings our nobility happiness when they boil it and drink it hot."

Chapter 2

Is Atlantis Real?

Matthew's new navy first pulls the squid through the tunnel into the sub's cavern, then half of them carry their captors' naked bodies through the tunnel and fling them down into the waters of the other cavern; they spit on these bodies as they sink. The bodies sink quickly to the bottom, but they leave a thick black scum covering the pond.

The other half of the navy uses daggers to cut the rings of chitinous teeth from the squid's tentacles. Three men hack away at the giant "parrot beak" of the squid's mouth. They free it and take it to the water to scrape away any skin on the beak. As Eli and Matthew talk, each man walks the gangplank to reverently bring a ring of teeth, from the suckers of the squid's tentacles, up onto the deck. Each man kneels before Matthew, then solemnly places his offering in a pile at Matthew's feet. The smell of ammonia almost knocks Raquelle and Eric off their feet, so they move to the bow of the sub.

Matthew's reconnaissance training causes him to analyze their actions, after which he begins to take steps to win their hearts. The three men, who worked on the squid's beak, march up the gangplank, cradling the two halves of the beak in their hands, and shouting, "Kraken's beak!"

Even in this light, the beak shines like newly mined coal. Matthew holds the two halves of the beak high over his head. "This Kraken thought it would eat my flesh and hold you in slavery. This beak shows that we have mastery over every Kraken in the sea and none of them will ever again keep you as slaves. Eli led you to attack your captors from behind and, in hand-to-hand combat, you killed them all. Eli, I give you the lower half of the Kraken's beak for your bravery and I command you to give one of these rings of teeth to each of these brave warriors, to be worn around his neck, as a sign of his extreme bravery, to the people of Atlantis. Upon our arrival, we must proceed to rescue my wife."

Eli cautiously cups his hands in front of him to receive his award. He clasps it with the gentleness with which you hold a newborn baby. Then his chest begins to rise with pride. It reminds Matthew of World War II films he has seen, in which a Marine receives the Medal of Honor. Eli, with his left hand, clutches the half

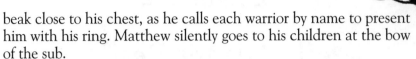

beak close to his chest, as he calls each warrior by name to present him with his ring. Matthew silently goes to his children at the bow of the sub.

Meanwhile, Scotty Terrier is going nuts, waiting for the Wolverine family to surface. He has a morbid fear of sharks, but he dons scuba gear and descends into the water. As he goes deeper, two sharks blaze past him. He swallows hard and tightens his grip on his spear gun. As he approaches the sea floor, the petrified diver looks in all directions for more sharks. After he turns halfway around, he looks toward the cave, but all he sees are a hundred sharks in a feeding frenzy. Their tail fins are wagging so fast that a huge cloud of black gunk totally obstructs the cave's entrance. As more, and larger, sharks race very close past Scotty, he fires at a two-foot shark and hits it. As it thrashes in the water, a twelve-foot shark, without missing a beat, opens its mouth and gulps the two-foot shark. The large shark chews twice, then spits out the harpoon. Scotty turns white and starts to shake. He rises slowly to the ship, as he ponders that power of attorney. He reasons that Matthew is just missing and, after he boards the ship, he heads below. He faxes the power of attorney to the Houston headquarters and he is in control, for one year, as long as he stays on this ship. There will be some changes in Matthew's businesses.

Eli presents the last ring, then makes sure all the cargo holds are full of Bluegreen. He approaches Matthew and asks permission to cast off for Atlantis. Matthew wants to swim to the surface, and his ship, through the other pond, but Eli informs him that, by now, a shark's feeding frenzy seals the other cave's entrance. Matthew nods, "Eric, Raquelle, into the sub."

The subs look like giant squids, with long, torpedo-shaped bodies. In the center, are two enormous half-spheres, which look like eyes, one on each side and ten tentacles--eight short and two very long tentacles, extending from the rear.

Eli calls to the second sub, "Follow me to Atlantis, but not too close. We don't want them to think we are attacking."

He, then, enters the first sub, "Rig for dive. Dive. Chief Engineer, plot a course for Atlantis."

The subs descend for several minutes, then they turn to exit a small opening in the side of a trench. The two subs proceed in darkness, then Eli orders a clear exterior. The hull of the sub magically becomes transparent. Matthew, Eric and Raquelle gasp, then they blurt out, "How is this possible?"

Eli smiles, "Abaddon models their submarines after the Kraken. This sub moves by using a jet of water, forced through a siphon in the rear. We can travel through the ocean in silver, clear, maroon, red, pink, or scarlet. The ten tentacles are connected to our cargo of Bluegreen and, if we are attacked, the Bluegreen is shot out through all ten tentacles, to mask our escape. In this sub, our enemies are the sperm whales. In Atlantis, we model our subs after the sperm whale, but use jets of water, for propulsion, like these do. Matthew, pass me your wrist weapon and I will recharge it." Matthew takes off the wrist weapon and gives it to Eli, then they go up to the very front of the sub where Eli shuts off all lighting to that section.

Matthew, Eric and Raquelle move to the front of the sub. Their stomachs tighten, as they see the blackness rushing past. Eric steps forward to touch the hull. "Dad, the hull is warm. There isn't any light from the surface, but the hull is warm."

Raquelle points, "Look at that--glowing fish!"

Matthew sits down on the floor to lean against the hull. It is warm, as the soothing water rushes by. Raquelle and Eric snuggle against their father. Matthew clears his throat, "I was proud of both of you for fighting those warriors."

Eric shivers, "Dad, I was scared. That Kraken coming after us... His tentacles were so close and so big! I ran so hard that my legs ache, but I didn't know if he would grab us in the cave. Then you killed him, but those men immediately attacked us. I fought them until my arms cramped. They were so strong and they wanted to kill us."

Raquelle chimes in, "Dad, that was not like my fencing classes. Even with all my best moves, those men would have killed me, if it hadn't been for you! I was afraid we wouldn't win."

Matthew swallows hard and pulls his children tighter, "I am very proud of both of you. It took real courage to fight those warriors. I know you were scared, but you fought, and that is what counts. A Wolverine fights, no matter what the battle or the outcome.

When our great ancestor, Angus, arrived in Maine, he was on a lost Viking ship with a spent crew. The Vikings looked to Angus to get them some food. Then, on shore, five Indian warriors appeared. Angus grabbed his sword and dagger and walked out to greet them. These Indians were suspicious. They had never seen such a large canoe--or a man in a kilt. Angus motioned that he needed food. The Indians saw the starving sailors in the Viking ship struggle just to sit up. Each sailor's eyes were sunken and their hollow cheeks suggested that they would all be dead in three days. The Indians sized up this muscular man and his strange clothes. His broad sword and dagger matched his hardened warrior's face. Angus pounded on his chest and spoke, 'Wolverine.' The Indians' ears perked up and they repeated, 'Wolverine'. They pointed to a nearby hill and made a sign for food back to Angus. He nodded his head, then trudged up the hill. There was a light snow on the ground. Angus stopped before he reached the top of the hill and knelt to crawl on his belly to the crest of the hill. The Indians did the same and they all peered over the hill.

As they looked over the hilltop, a herd of deer, with one buck and four does, was grazing about thirty feet away. An Indian put an arrow in his bow, then quickly rose to shoot the nearest doe. The arrow hit her just above the heart and the herd started to scatter. Blood spurted from the wound, but she took off running with the herd. The leader pointed to the valley and shouted, 'Wolverine!' Then all the Indians burst out laughing.

Angus shook his head, pulled his dagger, and he raced down the hill. The herd scampered into the woods and the doe made it to a pile of rock within ten feet of the forest, then her legs spread wide and she dropped with a loud thud. Her blood poured over the rocks. She rose to hobble three more steps, then crashed into the snow. She was dead before she hit the ground. Out of the rocks, came a blackish-brown bear-like head with a big nose, sniffing the air. A mass of fur with a light brown stripe extending down both its cheeks, it wondered out on short, bowed legs. It sniffed the air, then it climbed up on the rocks. It licked the blood, spotted the doe and scurried toward it. As Angus ran, he replaced his dagger in his belt and drew his sword. Within ten feet of the doe, he stopped and the wolverine turned, with its teeth bared. The teeth were yellow and long, the fur rose on its back and its bushy tail stuck straight up, as it gave a low growl. The Indians on the hill were shouting, 'Wolverine! Wolverine!"

Angus had never seen a wolverine and he instantly developed more appreciation for his name. This animal looked like it would have Angus for a snack and the doe for the main course. The wolverine's eyes narrowed, as Angus prepared to attack. Out of the forest, charged two growling black bears. The wolverine and Angus turned to face the charging bears. The Indians on the hilltop froze solid, for a moment, to watch the massacre.

Angus plunged his sword into the bear's belly, as the charging bear raked his right claw across Angus's left side. Angus pulled his dagger, then whirled to face his attacker.

The wolverine leaped into the air, just as the black bear charged on all fours, for the throat of his adversary. The wolverine did a one hundred eighty-degree turn in the air and raked his claws into the neck, then the back, of the black bear as he slid down to the ground. The bear swung around, howling in pain, using his forearm to launch the wolverine into the air. It sailed straight into the center of Angus's back, and they both fell into the snow. The muzzle of the wolverine touched Angus's face and Angus could smell the stench of rotten meat on its breath. The wolverine looked into Angus's right eye and winked. Then, the animal was up like a shot. He charged the black bear but, as the bear swung his mighty right paw to extinguish his enemy, the wolverine screeched to a halt, for a split second. As the bear's right paw neared the ground, the wolverine leaped for the bear's right back leg and buried his right front claws into it. As he swung his body fully around, the wolverine raked the bear's back leg with his hind claws, then released his hold to sprint for the forest. The black bear bellowed with pain and tried to turn to pursue his attacker, but he fell. The tendons in his right hind leg had been severed, and his blood gushed into a pool on the ground.

The other bear heard the pain in her mate's growls and turned to help him. Angus seized this moment to leap on the bear's back and plunged his dagger deep into her throat. He thrust again and again until the bear fell to the ground and still he drove his dagger into her throat, until his strength was gone and he dropped the dagger and rolled off the bear, to land on his stomach, in the snow.

The other bear turned to crawl to his mate; the wolverine leaped on his back and buried his razor-sharp teeth into the back of his neck, until he felt the vertebrae crunch in his mouth. The black bear whimpered, then died.

The Indians were now cheering for the wolverine, from a safe distance on top of the hill. The sounds of 'Wolverine!' filled the valley. Angus lay, spent, beside the female bear. His eyes were closed and he waited for the wolverine to kill him. Soft muffled growls pierced the air and Angus cautiously opened his eyes. The wolverine was standing on its hind legs, as its front paws gyrated back and forth. Then its hind legs started to shuffle and its rump twirled from side to side. Its tail swung along with its rump and Angus swore it was dancing. The front paws moved faster, as it leapt upon the black bear that it killed. It danced from the bear's legs up to its head, then it

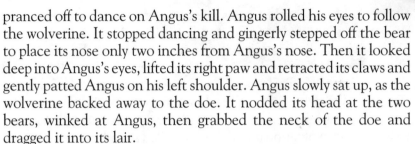

pranced off to dance on Angus's kill. Angus rolled his eyes to follow the wolverine. It stopped dancing and gingerly stepped off the bear to place its nose only two inches from Angus's nose. Then it looked deep into Angus's eyes, lifted its right paw and retracted its claws and gently patted Angus on his left shoulder. Angus slowly sat up, as the wolverine backed away to the doe. It nodded its head at the two bears, winked at Angus, then grabbed the neck of the doe and dragged it into its lair.

The Indians watched until the doe disappeared into the wolverine's lair. They quietly came to Angus. They pointed to him and mouthed the word, 'Wolverine'. Angus rose, then the Indians and Angus picked up one bear. They carried it thirty feet, then stopped to drop it. They went back for the other bear and carried this bear thirty feet past the first. They leap-frogged the bears until they crested the hill. Then three Indians quickly skinned the bears, as the other two gathered branches to start a fire. The Indians roasted the bear meat over a blazing fire. The smell of roasting bear drifted toward the water's edge and drew all the sailors out of the ship. One brave went to his village for more food and two wolverine pelts. Many Indians returned to the fire with food and the sailors ate their fill. The brave that carried the wolverine pelts pointed to the two bearskins, then offered the wolverine pelts in exchange. Angus nodded and received the wolverine pelts. As he touched them, he noticed the smooth hairs. He returned to Scotland and showed the Wolverine pelts to our clan." Matthew looks down at Eric and Raquelle and they are fast asleep. This is their favorite bedtime story. He does not notice Eli standing in the hatchway. He just stares at the water rushing by and the hypnotic flow soon has him asleep. Their sleep is calming and restful for hours so, when they awake, they are energized. They rise and return to the control section of the sub.

Eli studies a map, then he looks up and motions the three of them to join him. He first hands Matthew his wrist weapon and a dagger, then he slowly speaks, "Have any of you heard of the Sargasso Sea?" Matthew and the children shake their heads. Eli points to the map, "In the middle of the Atlantic Ocean, two thousand miles long and one thousand miles wide, is the Sargasso Sea. To the east, the Canary current travels west, to become the north equatorial current, which travels northwest, to become the Gulf Stream, then eastward, to become the north Atlantic current. This surrounds our desert in the sea. We planted golden-brown algae; this seaweed is called Sargassum, and it gives the sea its name. This seaweed kept many

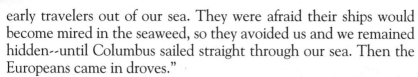

early travelers out of our sea. They were afraid their ships would become mired in the seaweed, so they avoided us and we remained hidden--until Columbus sailed straight through our sea. Then the Europeans came in droves."

Matthew points to the Sargasso Sea on the map, "So this was Atlantis. Well, how did it sink and how are you able to live under the water?" Eli strokes his chin, "It started just after the great flood. God had destroyed everyone but Noah and his family. After about three hundred years, a perfect female baby was born. She was so beautiful that, when people looked at her, they raised their hands to their mouths and said, "O." So her mother named her O. She was a genius and she had visions from God. She was terrified of rain and floods. Her father was a successful fisherman. From the time she could walk, she helped him on his fishing boats and she designed stronger nets and stronger boats. This quadrupled the fish they caught and their wealth increased. Soon her father had more than fifty ships. She matured and word of her beauty spread to many countries. The craftsmen closely guarded the secrets of glass, iron, copper, gold, silver, and other metals at that time. From far and wide, they came to seek her as a mate. She had a vision that, far to the west, lay an island that was as fruitful as the Garden of Eden. She convinced her father to use the craftsmen to build sailing ships that would take them to this island and, afterward, within twenty moons, she would choose her mate. Each craftsman felt that O would choose him, so he worked his heart out. She had a vision and spread the rumor that the most handsome men lived on this island, but she would only allow the most beautiful girls to accompany her there. The ships were built and the day they were to sail arrived. O chose one thousand girls out of all the girls that had assembled and they all sailed west."

Matthew interrupts, "How could they build that many ships and why would the fathers let their daughters leave?"

Eli studies Matthew's worried brow, as Raquelle holds her father a little tighter, "They cut down many forests to build the ships and a girl, at that time, as in some parts of Atlantis today, was a burden on her father. So, for ten large fish to each family, O purchased the right to choose a girl for her trip. These fathers needed sons to work the land or to fish and, since all the beautiful girls were leaving with O, even the ugly girls, that were left, could bring sons-in-law into their families. So this fleet of ships sailed west and weather smiled on them; there was no rain and they had a gentle westerly breeze. They landed on the eastern shore of Atlantis in less than six months, without losing a single ship. Fruit trees, fully loaded, greeted them close to the beach when they landed. The fish lay in shallow ponds when the tide went out and Dodo birds came right up to them without fear. Food, on Atlantis, was plentiful.

O had them immediately search the island for building materials. They found limestone, marble, and granite. The quarrying of the granite was done for dimension stones for blocks and slabs. Their first quarries of pure marble, which is white with a translucence a hand's breadth deep, were used for our first buildings. Each building had granite foundations and white marble floors. Then they constructed colossal buildings, with sparkling wide columns to support massive roofs and thick walls, close to the beaches. These buildings shone like pearls under both the sun and the moon. They became beacons to all ships coming to Atlantis. At high noon, the blaze of the white buildings could be seen from ten miles at sea. The sailors guided their ships into the glow, until they reached our harbor. O had all the craftsmen work together and share their secrets. As I said, she was a captivating woman and no man could resist her requests. The tradesmen soon discovered that, by working together, their creativity blossomed. As a result of their cooperation, they discovered a clear glass that is almost impenetrable."

Matthew bursts in, "How is this possible?"

Eli takes a long look at Matthew, Eric and Raquelle, "You were not born in Atlantis. The secrets of Atlantis are not for surface dwellers. I will tell you what we do, but not how we do it. I owe each of you my life, but the secrets of Atlantis stay with Atlantians!"

Matthew nods his head, "Just tell us what you can, then."

Eli smiles, "O built palaces, homes for the craftsmen, and docks for our harbors; fruit trees continued to produce in abundance and they feasted on Dodo birds, whenever they were hungry. Life was good for that first two years, but it came to an end because O would not choose a mate. Many of the sailors took wives from the other women. Our fleet of ships grew and we sailed west to colonize the Yucatan. Some of the craftsmen got tired of waiting for O to make a choice and took wives of the other females. The discovery, in the middle of the island of Atlantis, of fields of precious stones, silver, and gold caused more dissatisfaction. O seized control of all the fields. She was generous with the wealth, but all of it came from her hand and some people began to grumble. The flow of wealth became abundant among our craftsmen and sailors, so some boats sailed east to Greece. We could grow grapes but they would not ferment into wine on

Atlantis. The people on the Greek islands were warm, friendly and had a lot of delicious wines. Our sailors drank too much and told them of the paradise that they had found to the west and of our white marble buildings that shone, like beacons, to ships in sunlight or moonlight for ten miles. Some Greek boys and men volunteered as sailors, just to see Atlantis. They marveled at our buildings, harbors, and fruit trees and the Dodo birds that just came up to you and made it so easy to get your dinner. They returned to their Greek islands with tales of the wonders of Atlantis. Trade with these Greek islands escalated until many took Greek wives to settle in Atlantis. Our population grew and we were happy until the Red Serpent appeared from the west end of Atlantis.

He was over thirty feet in length and weighed over a ton. Twenty very strong men, all with serpent eyes, carried him on a litter. Six other men, also with serpent eyes, led this train, and each man carried a tray of sparkling jewels. They marched eastward, at night, at a slow pace, camping beside water each morning. The Red Serpent must daily immerse in fresh water or his skin will crack and he will bleed to death. Word spread that these jewels were presents for the queen of Atlantis. When they reached the palace, the Red Serpent slithered off the litter, at the foot of the palace steps, to await O's summons. His men, with the six trays of sparkling jewels, ascended the stairs to gain entrance to the palace. The trays of jewels were placed at her feet. She reached for a handful and ran her hands through blood red rubies, deep, rich blue diamonds, and green emeralds, as she hastily summoned the Red Serpent to appear before her. He slithered up the stairs and into the palace. You must understand that she invited him into the palace.

Aye, she invited destruction into her palace. Snakes are sly, crafty, and demonic. The Red Serpent is their lord and he may have been the same serpent that deceived Eve in the Garden of Eden. We do not know, because his origin is obscure. With a hiss, he spoke our language, all the while flattering O on her beauty. He stated, matter-of-factly, that these jewels could only slightly enhance her beauty, but that he would be happy to help her pick out just the right settings in gold and silver, for his jewels, to heighten her grandeur. O had never thought of herself as queen, but the Red Serpent planted the seed and he and his men watered it daily. He boasted of finer jewelry in his castle on the west end of Atlantis and said that she was welcome to come to view his wealth at any time. O thanked the Serpent for his gift and gave him a building close to the palace to house him and his men.

Early each morning, the Red Serpent slithered through the streets, followed by his men, with their snake eyes, and he joyfully greeted every craftsman. The craftsmen feared him, but he offered the services of his men as free labor, for that day, if they had a need. Who can resist free help? The Red Serpent carefully became part of our daily life in Atlantis, and some of our people became his servants. His jewelry, gold, and silver flowed from the west with more of his snake-eyed men. He purchased land, built harbors, and visited O daily. She became dependent on his advice. Snakeskin is pleasant to the touch and what went on between them, I do not know, but he returned to the fresh water lake close to the palace, each day, before noon, to bathe in the fresh water. This is our lake of birth. The lake guardians, porpoises, and the Atlantic and European Eels give birth in our lake, even today. But, each day, after the Red Serpent swam in our lake of birth, we found baby porpoises and eels dead and mutilated. Atlantians turned a blind eye to this murder.

The Red Serpent purchased land at our east harbor's entrance, started building projects, built our navy, then started a secret project. Tons and tons of gold arrived from the west. Sand piled high on his secret project site. A huge furnace melted, into a liquid, the tons of gold, then poured this liquid into the sand model. The pile of sand rose over one hundred ten feet. This took ten years, until, on the night before O's thirtieth birthday, the Red Serpent had all his servants remove the sand. When O rose the next morning and looked into the harbor, she and all of Atlantis stared at the back of a one hundred-foot burnished gold statue of a nude O, with arms outstretched to the sea to welcome returning sailors. It was anatomically correct and coated with almost-impenetrable glass from head to toes. Our craftsmen had learned the secret of this glass. The Red Serpent and his men built a huge fire to sacrifice animals, porpoises, and two lake guardians to the statue of O. They proclaimed that this statue was a goddess. Most Atlantians were repulsed by these sacrifices, but some joined in to sacrifice to the statue of the goddess O. Up to this point, God had blessed Atlantis but, with these new developments, He became incensed and we got a prophetic message, 'Atlantis will be destroyed in one year. Flee or die!'

Over the next year, some of the healers and builders in Atlantis took their wealth and boarded their ships. Half sailed to Egypt and half to the Yucatan. The ones that sailed to Egypt became their healers and, eventually priests to the Pharaohs.

Our builders designed and built the great pyramids. The greatest navy the world has ever known, shrank to one-tenth its former size.

Afterward, the Red Serpent left for ten months. O had nightmares, her vision was of the destruction of Atlantis by flooding. Her father took command of the people that were left and ordered that bubbles be constructed over all the buildings, and especially, over the lake of birth. The craftsmen worked day and night with this almost-impenetrable glass to enclose areas one mile wide and over one hundred feet high. They started at the beach and worked inland to the middle of Atlantis. They left a space of one-half mile between each bubble. Corridors of glass ten feet wide and ten feet high connected the bubbles. There were hermetically sealed glass doors at both ends of each corridor, so that each bubble was independent.

Then they discovered how to get oxygen into the bubbles. Our craftsmen modeled their device after the fish; it was a small device that fit into the mouths of Atlantians and acted as a gill. All this developed while the Red Serpent was away. When he returned, he was furious. The glass covered none of his buildings. He clashed with O's father. The Serpent informed her that only he could save her. Cold rain started to fall that night. O chose the Red Serpent as her savior. She left with him. The cold rain quickly soaked her to the bone and she began to shake violently. The Serpent suggested that, if she didn't wish to get sick from the rain, she ride in the back of his mouth. There is space in the back of his mouth that is dry. O was wet and cold, and maybe she wasn't thinking clearly, so she nodded. The Red Serpent opened his mouth and she walked inside.

Notice that she did this of her own free will. Her father saw her enter the Serpent's mouth and went berserk. Sword in hand, he took the palace guard and approached the Red Serpent. He ordered the Serpent to release his daughter. It only stuck out its forked tongue, and smiled. His men drew their swords and waded into the midst of the palace guards. The guards were thrown back, but they started shouting that the Red Serpent had killed O. The craftsmen, sailors and other men of Atlantis rushed to the palace, where they hacked and bludgeoned the Serpent's guards into a bloody pulp. He slithered, as fast as he could, for the nearest lake. The men of Atlantis got close enough to slice his tail with their swords but, as he descended into the lake, he turned his skin clear. At the back of the Red Serpent's throat is a sac, which contained O, who was pounding on the snake's skin, trying to break free. The Serpent smiled, stuck

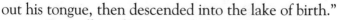

out his tongue, then descended into the lake of birth."

Raquelle and Eric sit with their mouths wide open. Eric drops his shoulders and shakes his head, "So did O ever get out?"

Eli is slow to respond, "The Red Serpent drains the life force out of humans. That is the reason that his servants have blood that is black. He drains their blood, over a period of time, to replace it with his venom. When their blood becomes over fifty percent venom, they develop snake eyes. She never made it out."

Matthew's forehead knots, "So the Red Serpent won't eat Shalee unless she willingly goes into his mouth?"

Eli takes a deep breath, "All bets are off, when the Red Serpent releases the red tide. He becomes famished and must replenish his red blood supply by draining ten men per day, for one month but he starts this cycle with a female sacrifice, which is eaten whole. That will be your Shalee."

Matthew scans the interior of the sub, a full three hundred sixty degrees. "Don't any of these machines tell you when the next red tide will occur?"

A sailor, with shoulder length blond hair, speaks, "Aye, I have checked the computer and the next red tide is in eleven months!"

Chapter 3

Cold to the Bone

Having been in total darkness for two days, Shalee now fights to untie her hands and feet. At last, the knot loosens and she unties her hands, then her feet. Her hands feel each wall from top to bottom. One side is a locked hatch; the other side is the hull of the sub. Her hands slide over smooth seamless glass. Suddenly her room blazes with light. It takes a minute for her eyes to adjust. With her back to the hatch, she stares out a large concave window. The blunt face of an oarfish glances in at Shalee. Like a flounder, it is flat, but it uses its pectoral fins to wiggle, rather than swim, by the window. The oarfish swims so comically that Shalee wonders if this is a bad dream. The oarfish takes a few seconds to pass and Shalee calculates it to be over twenty-five feet long.

Suddenly, the light goes out. Someone has a weird sense of humor. Shalee tries the hatch. It is still locked and the room is getting colder. She sits down and folds her arms because of the chill. She rubs her hands briskly up and down her arms to warm herself. It only helps a little. She wishes she had more on than her blue bathing suit. Soon, she hears a sucking sound coming from the window. She fears that the window may have a rupture. The lights flash on, after a minute, and Shalee sees a small row of lethal teeth attached to the window. The light scares the thing and it jets away. A small vampire squid with eyes the color of a blue jay's feathers and two horns in brown skin, speeds away. A chill of fear, rather than cold, runs down Shalee's back. She swallows hard, then the sub starts to descend at a forty-five-degree angle and the light goes off.

The cold increases to steal the heat from Shalee's body. She rubs her legs and arms, but to no avail. Her eyes grow heavy from the cold. She realizes that she has hypothermia. Her captors are diabolical. It doesn't matter that her hands and legs are free. They can slowly kill her with the coldness. Shalee spies two flowing lights, way down in the black water. As the sub approaches the lights, they become clearer. They are two streams of magma, a half mile apart, flowing out of a mountain side. The magma shows a hole in the side of the mountain and the sub proceeds into the hole. The light in Shalee's room comes on and she sees an eye, as large as her head, staring through the portal at her. Her head spins, then she faints. The sub proceeds into the hole and starts to rise. In a short time, the sub breaks the surface of the water; this is a glass dome harbor.

Vipurr slowly opens the hatch. Shalee lies, unconscious, on the floor. He smirks and turns to the captain beside him, "How stupid these surface dwellers are; she thought she could escape by untying her hands and feet, when all I had to do was shut down the heat."

The captain reaches down to prop open Shalee's right eyelid, "She has emerald eyes, all right, so I want a piece of the price you get from the high priest for this sacrifice."

Vipurr widens his eyelids, so his snake eyes protrude; his mouth opens wide, as his forked tongue curls out, "I won't sell her to the high priest, but I will personally give her to the Red Serpent, then ask for the position of high priest. As for you, the loss of two subs filled with Bluegreen means you deserve to be digested, slowly, in the stomach of the Red Serpent; but, be loyal to me and, as high priest, I will spare your life."

The captain looks at the forked tongue of Vipurr. His transformation is over half-way complete and, even as high priest, the Red Serpent will drink his blood and replace it with venom so that, in a few years, when the transformation is complete he will be a small, slithering black snake. The captain only nods, as he picks Shalee up, and they both exit the sub.

The faint smells of brimstone wafts through the air. The yellow dock churns with small black snakes. Vipurr walks into the mass of snakes and they rub against his legs. He caresses their heads and smiles at them. The captain swallows hard, as he wades into the serpents. Some of them hiss at Shalee--or are they hissing at the captain? The captain, as a child, had the Red Serpent drink his blood. That was the first time--and the last. The captain spent as much time away from Abaddon as he could. These snakes could only smell a faint trace of the Red Serpent's venom in his blood, and they didn't like it.

Vipurr turns toward the snakes hissing behind him, just as one bares its fangs and prepares to strike Shalee's hand. Vipurr points the dial on his wrist at the serpent's head and presses the trigger. Like a surgical knife, it cuts the serpent's head off just behind its mouth. The snake falls into the salt water as Vipurr booms out, "This is my emerald-eyed sacrifice to the Red Serpent. Do you really want to drink before your master drinks?"

Snakes scramble over each other to get out of the way. Some fall off the dock, into the salt water, and the sizzle of their skin blistering causes a hum in the air. Vipurr thinks aloud, "…one of the drawbacks of total conversion. I need to stay away from salt water."

The captain has a clear path and he bolts ahead of Vipurr toward a massive ebony marble structure in the shape of a coiled serpent. This ebony marble shines like fresh-cut coal and, like the white stone in Atlantis, is lustrous to a depth of six inches. This giant black serpent structure drinks in the sunshine to radiate heat inside its coils. A dome, over a mile in circumference and two hundred feet high, covers the ebony building. The entrance is a snake's head with one eye filled with rubies and the other eye filled with emeralds. Two huge fangs, with twenty feet between them, tower one hundred feet to the roof of the serpent's mouth and two small fangs, both five feet in length, with a space of five feet between them, sit in the front of the mouth between those massive fangs. The captain slows his pace and Vipurr catches up, then pulls ahead. A trail of black serpents slithers after Vipurr, but stops before the giant fangs.

Vipurr halts at the right fang of the building, kisses it, then enters the building. The captain does the same. The interior walls are covered in pea-size blue diamonds, a large fresh water pool occupies the center of the dome and, at the far end, is a coiled gold serpent statue. The gold in this statue weighs over one hundred tons. The golden serpent's head extends over the pool, with its mouth wide open and its tongue in full extension. Vipurr reaches into the water and splashes it back and forth. Then he waits. Soon the surface of the water ripples. A red head with a lashing black tongue breaks the water and the Red Serpent scrambles up the coils of the golden shrine until it emerges on the statue's outstretched tongue. The Red Serpent spies the woman, then scans the interior of the building. It perceives no danger, so it slowly slithers down from the shrine to face Vipurr.

He bows, "I bring you an emerald-eyed sacrifice for the red tide--in exchange for a high priest position?" The Red Serpent's tongue licks over Vipurr's shoulders and he bows lower and places his hands on top of his head, elbows in front. The Serpent raises his head high and bares his fangs. The large fangs pass behind Vipurr's arms. Between the two large fangs are two small fangs. The small fangs bore into the muscles at the base of the willing victim's neck. The Red Serpent drinks three sips of his servant's blood, then withdraws the small fangs, as he inserts the tip of one large fang into Vipurr's left shoulder muscle and releases three drops of venom. Convulsions seize Vipurr's body. He is wriggling on the floor as he visibly shrinks.

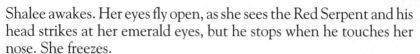

Shalee awakes. Her eyes fly open, as she sees the Red Serpent and his head strikes at her emerald eyes, but he stops when he touches her nose. She freezes.

From behind the golden statue, appears an opening in the wall and two men, wearing long red coats, made of the Red Serpent's shed skin, emerge. They walk to their ruler and bow. The taller one is the high priest and he speaks, "Will my god dine on the female now or save her for later?"

The Serpent towers over the high priest, "This sacrifice has emerald eyes. She may have a strong will, so put her in a heated cage next to my pool's window, then slowly break her spirit with the black snakes. Vipurr asks for the position of high priest, as a reward for bringing me this sacrifice, but we already have a high priest, don't we?"

The high priest scowls at Vipurr, "Yes, and I oversee all that you own. Have you ever suffered a loss as long as I have been in charge of your Krakens?" The high priest puffs out his chest.

The captain transfers Shalee to the other priest and they slowly walk away.

Vipurr smiles, "Well, will you make up for the two subs that were lost and the closing of Mine 100?"

The high priest explodes, "That was your loss!"

Vipurr smirks, "Her mate killed one of the Krakens. I saw him fire the shot before I entered the submarine. We have not been able to communicate with Mine 100 since we left. Your Krakens guard all the mines, so it is your loss."

Shalee's ears perk up, as she violently wrenches her arm from the priest and turns to face the Red Serpent, "Yes, Matthew Wolverine, my husband, killed your Kraken and he will kill you, unless I am released! So release me now!"

The Red Serpent's skin glows crimson and his eyes flame, as he charges toward Shalee. The Serpent plows through the high priest and Vipurr. The crack of their heads hitting the floor startles Shalee. He stops only inches from her, then rises to tower over her. She stares up at the large fangs. The Serpent's mouth opens, then it unhinges its jaw. The gaping hole slowly descends upon her. She stands perfectly still, until the forked tongue fondles her legs. When she loses her lunch all over the Serpent's forked tongue, he flings her to his left, toward the pond. She sails in an arc and dives into the water. It is fresh water, so she quickly washes out her mouth then drinks several big gulps. This is her first water since she was captured. She

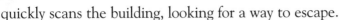

quickly scans the building, looking for a way to escape.

The Red Serpent thrashes into the water with its mouth wide open, to get rid of the horrible taste. The foulness gone, it dives, to come up between Shalee's legs. Her legs and hands slide over the silky skin and it feels surprisingly sensual. Her mind gets caught up in the sensation, until the tail flips her into the air and she comes down close to the shore. She lands in the water, but scrambles up onto the dock. The high priest and Vipurr awake and hold their heads. The lesser priest and the captain grab Shalee's arms and drag her until they reach her cell, then they throw her inside.

The cell has a window running the entire length of the right side, with the water from the Red Serpent's pool splashing against it. She walks to the left wall and spits on it. The spit sizzles and she knows that the heat comes from this wall. It must be a hundred degrees in the cell. There is a cot with one filthy blanket with small holes in it and a bucket in which to relieve herself in the corner. Shalee goes to the cell door, "Matthew Wolverine won't rest until you all die. Release me now!"

The high priest is outside the temple with a large round basket and a splitting headache. He grabs handfuls of the small black snakes, each about a foot in length, and places them in the basket. Once inside the basket, the snakes rise to attention, awaiting their orders. Two priests come up behind him. The high priest turns, then growls at the basket, "She has emerald eyes so, if you kill her, you will die, but I want her tortured night and day until she screams for mercy. You snakes do your worst! Priests, carry this basket into her cell and leave it."

Shalee examines the cell window, as the Red Serpent swims over to it and stares in. She grits her teeth. The fact that he put his slimy mouth all over her body has her boiling. Shalee is determined not to be terrified and she glares back at the Red Serpent. If she must die, then she will die fighting, because she is a Wolverine. Her cell door opens quickly and the priests enter and drop the basket by the door, then exit immediately. The snakes slowly slither out of the basket. Shalee's eyes bulge, then her mind snaps and grabs the filthy blanket. She shreds it in half to wrap a portion around each hand. She grabs the closest snake by the tail, smashes its head against the hot wall, and then flings the bleeding serpent into the clean window. The Red Serpent smashes against the window, trying to protect his followers, but it is unbreakable. Snake after bleeding snake smashes against the window, until it is coated in black blood. A small number of the remaining snakes gather by the door, utterly terrified of this green-eyed monster. The giant Serpent flails in his pool, then leaps out of the water, onto the deck, in front of the gold statue. He blares out, "Stop the massacre of my babies!" The high priest rushes for Shalee's cell door and flings it open. As he steps into the cell, the snakes exit in mass and he falls forward. Shalee throws down the blanket scraps from her hands, and uses her fingernails to go for the priest's eyes. His falling body drives her nails deep into his eyes. His scream echoes through the temple. Other priests rush in to drag this monster off the high priest.

Vipurr and the captain charge into the temple, then into Shalee's cell. The high priest wants her killed immediately, but Vipurr warns the other priests that only the Red Serpent has this right. The priests play it safe and carry her and the high priest to the base of the golden serpent idol. The Red Serpent glows with hatred and anger. Neither the priests nor Vipurr have ever seen him this mad. The black snakes from outside enter the temple to protect their god. They surround Shalee, as the Red Serpent spits out these words, "You have blinded my high priest. Just look at that red blood streaming down his cheeks. Your death will be slow and painful."

Shalee holds back nothing, " Worm, do your worst!"

Vipurr seizes the opportunity and steps in front of the prisoner, "Has the Red Serpent ever seen such fire in a sacrifice? Can you imagine this flame coursing through your body after the red tide? She has more spirit than O and you can still remember her sweet taste. I gave this offering to you. When has this high priest given you a green-eyed sacrifice with this much fiery courage? She even destroys your babies." At this point, Vipurr looks tearfully at the black snakes surrounding Shalee and the high priest. Vipurr extends his arms to the black snakes, "My brothers, the high priest abandoned our brothers to this monster. He placed them in her cell, which was a death sentence and, now, they lie here, dead. Look at his red blood and notice that it is not black. My blood is black like your blood, my brothers. He is not one of us. What should we do with one that threatens this prize sacrifice?" Vipurr folds his arms, then turns to stare at the high priest.

The high priest is in such pain that he cannot answer. The two priests supporting him release their holds and he falls on all fours. The Red Serpent is now calm and thinking. He studies Vipurr, then turns his attention to the bleeding high priest. The black snakes around the high priest are highly agitated, and one snake strikes his heel. The rest do the same, and cover him completely. The high priest screams, as the poison surges into his veins, and the Red Serpent scoops him up into his mouth, and slowly swallows. Many of the black snakes don't have time to slither off the high priest, so they wind up inside their god's stomach. He smiles, "My babies, we have a new high priest: Vipurr. What is your first order?"

Vipurr beams, "Take the emerald-eyed beauty to the palace, assign ten attendants to her, bathe her in our sweetest perfumes, then clothe her in silk, adorn her with our finest jewelry and, above all, treat her with respect. You priests untie her and convey the high priest's orders to the slave girls in the palace."

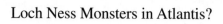

Chapter 4

Whales, Dolphins, and Tigers?

Eric opens his eyes to a new day and the first thing he does is look for Eli. The sub is gliding gently through the water, as Eric nears the captain. Eric tugs at Eli's shirt, "Captain, when do we dock in Atlantis? Soon?"

Eli doesn't look at Eric, "Now is the time for me to reveal one of Atlantis's secrets. Atlantis is at the center of the spiral of currents that surround the Sargasso Sea. Most derelict ships from the Caribbean find their way into our waters before they sink. These waters are the graveyards of the Caribbean." The sub spotted a derelict freighter sailing to the south center of the Sargasso Sea, and followed it. "Sperm whales gather over that graveyard. You can swim with dolphins."

Eric comes unglued, "Really, Eli? Swim with dolphins? I will wake my dad and sister." Eric rushes off, as Eli gives the order to surface.

Eric shouts, "Dolphins!" Matthew shakes his head to wake up. Raquelle rises quickly, "Did you say dolphins?"

Eric nods and tells them of a derelict freighter they are preparing to board. Eli already has the hatch open and is on the deck. He waves to the dolphins and whales in the distance, then he puts both hands over his head in a point-like position. The dolphins recognize the sign and come to the subs. Matthew, Raquelle and Eric rise to the deck and stand beside Eli. Whales surface off in the distance. Immediately, dolphins flank both sides of the subs. Suddenly, all the dolphins shoot ahead of the subs, their sonar pinging all the way. The whales sense the pings, and respond. Soon, the sea bubbles, as whales surface side-by-side with dolphins. Some dolphins go nose-to- nose with the whales. The whales slowly and gently push the dolphins backward. Other dolphins try to leap over the whales' backs. It is a great game until a few of the dolphins smash directly onto a whale's back, then the leaping abruptly ceases.

Whales come up to rub the sub. They want to make sure it is not a real Kraken. The bumps shake the sub and Raquelle falls into the water. Two dolphins glide up to her, so she grabs a fin in each hand. They pull her alongside the sub. It looks like fun, so Eric cannonballs into the water, then Eli cannonballs into the water but, instead of playing with the dolphins, he swims toward the freighter. Two dolphins come up beside Eric and he hitches a ride. A large sperm whale surfaces and spots Eli then heads, at top speed, directly for him and Matthew fears that the whale will pulverize him. More sailors come topside and stand beside Matthew. He points his wrist weapon in front of the whale, but one of the crew gently touches his wrist and shakes his head. He tells Matthew to just watch. Eli raises his hands straight over his head, as the large sperm whale dives. Then the water explodes, as he flies straight up in the air on the nose of the sperm whale. The captain does a swan dive, as the whale falls to his left just next to the sub. The whale's splash covers the deck of the sub, soaking Matthew. All but three sailors dive into the water, as more dolphins appear.

Matthew turns to a sailor, "Is this normal?"

The sailor smiles, "Aye, it is a festival when a derelict arrives among the whales. If there is corn or grain or any dead animal on board, we share it with them. Do you see those four whales in front of the ship? As I clasp my hands together over my head, they will stop the ship from moving."

Matthew watches the four whales push against the starboard side of the ship. It becomes still in the slow current of the Sargasso Sea. One sailor grabs an air rifle, with a grappling hook clipped to a light rope, then he and Matthew climb onto the back of a whale, which heads for the freighter. As they come beside the ship, the sailor fires the grappling hook at its deck. The hook finds a hold, then the sailor and Matthew scurry up the rope. Once on board, the sailor heads for the captain's cabin, while Matthew heads for the hold. The rope is left hanging over the side. Eric urges his dolphins toward the rope, and he climbs on board, with Raquelle close behind.

Matthew descends into the cargo hold. The smell of animal and bird feces overwhelms him. He fights the urge to turn back and proceeds down into the hold, until he finds the switch to open its top. He throws the switch and the top of the hold slowly opens. The daylight shows row after row of cages. Beautiful red, green, yellow, and blue parrots lie on the cage floor. Most are breathing, but a few are on their backs, feet pointing skyward. Matthew looks for keys to the cages and finds a set in the third cage door, which is open. Someone tried to free a few of these birds. Matthew's mind senses a faint call for help. Was it from Elizabeth? Matthew concentrates hard. A soft call for help enters his mind. Matthew mentally asks, "Where are you?"

The voice responds from a cage in the back. With keys in hand, Matthew races between the cages, until he comes to a large one with a mass of yellow and black fur, in a ball, by the cage door. Matthew cautiously opens the door. Out fall the giant front paws and monstrous head of a tiger. This is the largest tiger Matthew has ever seen. It must weigh over 1,000 pounds.

Matthew points his wrist weapon at the tiger. The tiger slowly opens its deep aquamarine eyes. One thought pierces Matthew's mind, "I starve. Please help." At that instant, Eric and Raquelle join Matthew. Both of the children nod their heads, "How can we feed him, Dad?" Matthew shakes his head, "You can hear him, too?" They both answer, "Aye."

Matthew shouts orders, "Raquelle, get a sack or bucket and bring it back here. Eric, take these keys and open the cages of any birds that are moving, then bring them here." The children scurry off and Matthew kneels beside the giant tiger and cradles his head. Aquamarine eyes speak to aquamarine eyes, "I am getting you food and here it comes." Eric has four parrots' necks pinned under each arm. Matthew gently releases the tiger's head, grabs a parrot, places it on the ground and, in one quick movement, removes his dagger and swiftly cuts the parrot's head off. Matthew picks up the parrot's body and drains the blood into the tiger's mouth. A black tongue reaches out to lick the parrot's body. Raquelle returns with four buckets and Matthew tosses the parrot's body and head inside a bucket, then he proceeds to guillotine the next parrot. Tears stream down Raquelle's face for the parrots, but she turns to get more buckets.

Eli appears beside Raquelle and he grabs the full buckets, takes them topside and throws the parrots over the starboard side. Dolphins move to the port side as the whales move in to feed. Eli throws the bodies of the parrots as far as he can from the ship. They look like jelly beans, and the whales line up for their shot at the treats. Most of the parrot parts don't even hit the water. As soon as Eli makes his throw, the whales become major league outfielders, who are trying to make an all-star catch. Two whales leap simultaneously from the water and collide. Like one shiny red jelly bean, a red parrot's body hits the water. A baby whale scoops it up and takes it to his mom. He is still on milk but he enjoys the game. The mother whale bolts down the red parrot. A giant flipper brings her baby close to her side and the baby wags his tail in excitement.

Raquelle comes topside and climbs down the rope. The

dolphins chatter, as she descends. She shouts, "Sick animals on board, so bring me many fish. I will lower a trap; you put the fish inside." The dolphins chatter back, then speed away. Eli is waiting for Raquelle at the top of the rope. "Eli, I need you to lower some type of trap to bring the fish that the dolphins deliver, topside." Raquelle does not wait for a response, but grabs the buckets and goes below the deck, to her father. Her tears have stopped because she focuses on saving the tiger.

Matthew has a pile of dead parrots, but the tiger is up on shaky paws. The tiger thinks, "I have nine mates. Will you feed them?"

Matthew smiles, "Of course. Can you walk to their cage?"

The tiger holds his head high and puts one unsteady paw in front of the other. Matthew quickly opens the next cage's door, but stands beside it until the tiger enters. He moves to the largest of the female tigers, then drapes his body over her paws. The aquamarine-eyed tiger looks at Matthew, "My name is George and I will sit on Sonya's paws, so she doesn't hurt you, while you feed her." Matthew nods, then quickly pours parrot blood down Sonya's throat. Her big tongue emerges and she opens her eyes and tries to seize the parrot- -and Matthew's hand. George growls and Sonya relaxes her body. Matthew loudly commands, "George, I don't want to lose a hand. Another outburst like that, and they die in this cage. Do you understand?'

George's shoulders sag and he thinks, "I owe you my life and this is my pride. You have my word that none of them will hurt you."

Raquelle, Eric and Eli enter the cage, carrying armloads of fish, which they drop beside George. Up like a shot, George starts wolfing down fish, while using his behind to push Matthew away from Sonya. George chews one fish until it is mush, then places it in Sonya's mouth. Sonya opens her mouth and lets the mush ooze inside, then slowly chews it. George chews another fish to mush and places it in another female tiger's mouth. Matthew watches from inside the cage, as Eric, Raquelle and Eli continue to bring in more fish.

The female tigers begin to revive, then they roll over on their paws and lay waiting for George to deliver more fish. Matthew grabs a fish then, with his dagger, slices down both sides of it. Matthew tries to offer the sliced fish to a female tiger, but she turns away. He gives the fish to George. After a few chews, it is mush; the female accepts it from George. Matthew smiles; in this pride's eyes, George is the hero of this day. So, Matthew continues to slice the fish for George.

After about fifty fish, he tries to offer George another. George moves his lower jaw back and forth. He stares at Matthew and thinks, "I'm chewed out. My mates can eat or starve, because the fish is here." He just lies down.

The pride rises, on shaky paws, and encircles Matthew. They sniff him and some give some low growls. George swiftly rises and shoves in between the females, then he makes an ever- widening circle around Matthew, driving the females back. He then maneuvers under Matthew's right hand, to stand by his side. The females form a pack and face George. His mind is strong and he blares out a telepathic message, "This human saved our lives and, under my War Cats Code of Conduct, I owe him ten lives. We must serve him until our debt is paid. Now, you females protect the children."

Raquelle can't wait for George's speech to finish before she runs up to the nearest tiger and throws her arms around its neck and squeezes, as hard as she can. For one instant, the tiger can't breathe, and it growls. Matthew's heart is in his mouth, as he quickly, but gently, grabs his daughter's shoulder, "Raquelle, release your death grip!" She releases her hold and strokes the tiger's head. Matthew swallows hard. Raquelle may be fifteen but, in some ways, she is so innocent. "These tigers are tired, so lets go topside."

Eli enters the cage, "No, we need to get your tigers hoisted over the side and into my sub, along with some of the birds you haven't killed because, in one hour, this ship dives with the whales. So, you tigers, do your business now, on this ship, because I don't want my sub smelling." George immediately lifts his leg and wets down the bars. As Raquelle, Eric, Eli and Matthew head topside, the tigers do their business.

The sub pulls alongside the freighter and the tigers are hauled up from the hold, then lowered to the sub's deck. George shows the female tigers how to go through the hatch butt-first, although he gets stuck and Matthew can hear the female tigers laughing at him. Eli promptly comes forward and lifts George's front paws straight up and he slides through the hatch. The females quickly follow George through. The tigers are herded into the front of the submarine. George gets in the very nose of the sub, then orders all lights extinguished.

The lights go out and Matthew speaks, "George, how did you turn off the lights?"

He turns his head over his right shoulder, "When our engineers design any combat vehicle, it must be War Cats friendly. Every Atlantian knows that. Why don't you?"

Eli hears the conversation and quickly enters the room, "Because he and his children are recent surface dwellers, so don't share any of our Atlantian secrets or those about your origin."

George shakes his head, "So I owe my life to a surface dweller and not to an Atlantian. What is your name, Surface Dweller, and what must I do to repay my debt?"

"My name is Matthew Wolverine; this is my daughter, Raquelle and my son, Eric. My wife, Shalee, is a captive in Abaddon. When she is released, your debt to me is paid in full--but not until she is released!"

George nods his head, then suggests that Matthew and his children rest in this chamber, so the tigers can become accustomed to their scent and they can become accustomed to the sweet smell of the tigers' aroma. George lays his right front paw over Sonya's neck, then immediately falls asleep. Raquelle snuggles up to a female tiger and goes to sleep. Matthew lays between two tigers and goes to sleep. Eric shakes his head and sits as far from the tigers as is possible, and he doesn't go to sleep.

After about two hours, Eric goes to see Eli. He tugs on his sleeve, "Are we close to Atlantis?"

Eli turns, "No, we dock, in a few minutes, at an old storage depot. If we approach Atlantis in these Abaddonian subs, they will sink us. Now, I need to talk to the storage depot."

Eli goes to the communications area of the submarine and tries different frequencies to contact the depot. Finally, he is successful, and a booming voice comes over the radio, "Back off, you sons of Kraken, before I make you shark bait!"

Eli clears his throat, stands at full stature, then speaks, "This is Eli, commander of the Atlantian fleet, requesting permission to dock at your depot."

A stuttering voice comes over the mike, "You, you are dead. I saw you drown in the 'Five Hundred Kraken Battle'."

Eli tilts his head, then bursts out in a fit of laughter. When he stops laughing, he speaks in a clear voice, "Michael, I didn't drown, but was captured, because there was a traitor in our ranks. I have been a slave all these years in the mines of Abaddon—a real fish guts of a place. A surface dweller and his children released us from Mine 100 and we captured these two subs. You were second in my command. Why are you the guardian of a remote depot? You should have taken my place as commander of the fleet. Give us permission to dock."

"How do you know my name? You can't be Eli. Destroy this depot, but I won't give you permission to dock."

Eli sighs, "Does your wife still stuff her pillows with Dodo feathers? How can you sleep on those pillows? After my family and I spent one night sleeping at your home, I sneezed for a week. You know, my wife kicked me out of our bed and I had to sleep on the couch, until the sneezing stopped. And your wife used too much seaweed sauce on our sea perch. I prefer Mexican lime juice on all my fish, but especially on sea perch."

"She did not use too much seaweed sauce. Eli, you don't know an excellent meal when you eat it. I am letting you dock, but our weapons will be trained on you, from the moment you surface and, if the first person out of your sub is not Eli, we will fire."

Eli orders both subs to enter the depot. After they surface, he opens the hatch and comes on deck to take a deep breath. "Sweet Atlantis air!" Twenty warriors have their weapons aimed at them, as Eli strolls down the plank, directly to Michael. "You've gained at least twenty pounds, but it looks good on you."

Michael just shakes his head, as he stares in disbelief at Eli, "You have lost forty pounds, but you are more muscular than I remember." Then Michael salutes Eli, "My commander!"

The rest of the crews slowly pour out of the subs. The twenty warriors lower their weapons. Matthew, Eric and Raquelle are the last to leave. Eli and Michael are swapping stories, as Matthew approaches. Eli turns to Matthew; "This is the man that freed all of us. His wife is a captive of Abaddon and she is O, re-incarnate."

Michael looks at Matthew and the other sailor's uniforms, "We need to get you into Atlantian uniforms and burn those!"

Matthew's response is instantaneous, "No, we may need these uniforms in future attacks on Abaddon, so we will save them."

Eli smirks and slaps Michael on the back, "He is a warrior. Now, get us new uniforms and some food." Michael and his men get Atlantian uniforms and the sub crews, Matthew, Raquelle and Eric change. Then, they head for the mess hall. The cook had already received word and had fresh fish baking. Fresh seaweed, cooked like spinach, fresh turtle soup, and oyster stew were already waiting. Matthew grabs what looks like a soft taco shell. He closes his eyes and takes a bite. The sweetness of maple sugar permeates his mouth. He motions the cook to his side, "How can you create the taste of maple sugar?"

The cook's eyes glaze over, as he speaks, "My great-grandfather was a master chef on naval patrol, when an abandoned Canadian freighter found its way into the Sargasso Sea. It carried tins of maple syrup. He opened a tin and tasted the contents. He loved the sweetness, so he determined to recreate that sweetness with our sea plants. It took him two years, but he did it. Most of what you are eating comes from Sargasso seaweed. Our seaweed provides most of our medicine, paint, cleaners, and food. Sargasso seaweed is God's gift to Atlantis, to make up for sinking us."

Eli quickly rose, "Enough! He and his children are not from Atlantis and our secrets must remain with us."

The second in Michael's command, Cruelblade, voices a stronger objection, "Surface dwellers have no place with us."

Matthew defused this tone in Eli but not in Cruelblade, "Speaking of God, does anyone have a Bible I can borrow?"

Michael orders a guard to retrieve a Bible for Matthew. He studies Matthew before he speaks, "The Bluegreen you carry on your subs will be confiscated by the Fiends, as you dock. The Fiends are a gang of terrorists that now extort wealth from all Atlantians. Their allies are the priests and the nobility."

Eli tilts his head, as his eyes narrow, "How could they take over from our naval guards?"

Michael spits as he speaks, "In the 'Five Hundred Kraken Battle', the entire naval guard was wiped out. We thought you dead and, when we returned, the Fiends had killed all the people living by the docks and taken their property. Our subs' firepower was depleted and most of us were badly wounded. The will to fight was not in us. We were betrayed, so we let the Fiends or Ghouls rule. I believe that the Fiends are the tools of the nobility and the priests. They extract half or more of all profit from every business and every person in Atlantis. The people are fed up with it. You could lead a revolt, Eli. Atlantians consider you a hero."

Eli shakes his head, "I just had my chains removed. My crew needs time to regain its strength. We only have two subs against the Atlantian fleet. The priests and the nobility are too strong."

Matthew clears his throat then points at Michael, "Did you say that the Fiends would steal my cargo?"

Michael nods his head, "Then they will take your children--at least the female--and sell her into slavery as a lady of the night."

Matthew grunts, "So I must defeat Atlantis, so I can use your ships to attack Abaddon and free my wife. Tell me, Michael, how loved is Eli? Some commanders are hated. Will the troops die for him?"

Michael responds from his gut, "Aye, they will kill and die for him. So what is your point?" Matthew notices that Cruelblade stiffens at the statement.

Just at that moment, George and his harem enter the mess hall. Michael's troops rise to fire at the cats, but Matthew and the children swiftly stand in their way. Eli orders them to stand down. The troops swallow hard, then they comply. Matthew orders George to sit behind him, as they discuss battle strategy. Instead, George puts both front paws on the table, rises to his full stature, then thinks, "I heard from the corridor, the situation, and I suggest that you contact the Atlantian fleet and inform them that many prisoners of war, who have escaped from Abaddon, will arrive in Atlantis in exactly one week, at your artificial sunrise and that they should have all Atlantian ships recalled to welcome them. Then contact your allies in Atlantis, to have all the families of the men and women captured by Abaddon over the years, waiting at the dock, as we arrive. Each family should carry a sword and a dagger for each captive, so that they can be armed, to make them feel safe after their slavery. Inform Atlantis that our captured subs are filled with Bluegreen; if the Fiends are the thieves you say they are, then they will be the first to board the subs to confiscate the cargo. Allow my tigers to exit the subs in loose, but unlocked, chains. We will remain docile on deck until Wolverine kills the leader of the Fiends. Then the captives' families will attack from the dock, as we and the naval forces attack from the sea. Show me a map of the buildings by the dock that house the Fiends' wives and children. We, War Cats, will destroy every remnant of your enemy." George studies the faces of the men at the table, as he shows his fangs and extends his claws.

Matthew reaches up to stroke George's head, as he speaks, "George came up with a great plan! Let me explain it to you. "

Eli grinds his teeth, then softly speaks, "Matthew, we all heard him. Mental telepathy is practiced by all Atlantians and it is now one of the secrets that has been revealed to you and your children. Well, this is a plan that will succeed but, if I die, it will be with a sword in my hand, fighting to free Atlantis. What do the rest of you say?"

Matthew notices that Cruelblade is standing with his arms crossed, but does not speak.

For two hours, the warriors discuss the pitfalls of the plan but, in the end, they can come up with no better plan. The Atlantian fleet will be contacted in six days. Michael will be vague on what prisoners had escaped and he will say that they will be delivered, in two captured subs, at artificial sunrise, the next day, to the docks in the lake of life. As many ships as possible should be there to meet them.

Then Atlantis will be contacted, just before the subs proceed, with Michael and his men on board, for the lake.

Eli asks if his son, Joshua, is still in charge of naval communications in Atlantis. Michael nods his head, "He is well liked by the nobility and the priests. After your death--er, capture--they left him in his post. He could have requested sea duty; but, then, who would have taken care of your wife? She knew you were alive. How? I don't know. She waits every day at the dock, until our artificial sunset, then she and Joshua walk home. He remains single. He is a good son."

Eli's eyes fill with tears, as Matthew puts his arm around his shoulder, "My friend, we will kill the Fiends and you will be reunited with your wife, then we will build up the Atlantian fleet to rescue my wife. Now we must lay out the details of our plans, so show me maps and pictures of Atlantis."

Eli and Michael both nod; whether they like it or not, this surface dweller is their ticket to freedom from the Fiends. Maps and photos of Atlantis fill the table. George studies every subtlety of each photo. His giant paws secure each photo on the table, as his head goes from side to side and his tail twitches. The female tigers crowd the table until, on one side, there are only tigers. Matthew pushes his way beside George and Sonya gives a low growl. George shoots her a stare that would freeze a blowtorch. Sonya lowers her head.

Matthew firms the details of the plan, "Do the Fiends only carry short swords?"

Michael responds, "Aye, they won't be expecting trouble from escaped slaves."

Matthew points to the buildings by the docks. "George, can you and your pride annihilate all the wives and children in these buildings?"

George surveys his pride, "Tell me where to dispose of the bodies and you will never see them again, after the attack." Eric and Raquelle shuffle their feet, then look at each other. George notices the movement and sharply thinks, "Do you, children, want the Fiends' wives and children to live, but your mother to die? I must know your desires, because I am sending my mates into possible death and I love them very much. These female tigers are the best of your planet and, if you want tigers to survive into the next century and subsequent centuries, I must father as many cubs, as possible, before I die. So, Wolverines, I need to know if you hold the wives and children of your enemy in higher regard than you do your wife and your mother. I need an answer now!" George stares directly at the children, but they only slightly shake their heads. Their sadness shows in their eyes.

Matthew's eyes narrow, as he bellows out a command, "George, you and your mates annihilate all the wives and children. I want my wife rescued, no matter what it takes. Now, Michael, where do George and his mates drag the bodies?"

Cruelblade looks disgusted and his contempt for the tigers shows, "George, why can't you just eat them after the kill?"

Matthew sees only a blur, as George leaps onto the table, then grabs Cruelblade's head. He puts one front paw behind Cruelblade's head and the other, with claws extended, at his throat, and a small stream of blood flows from each slightly imbedded claw. George looks deep into Cruelblade's eyes then, in a growling, guttural voice he speaks, "I have defended humans longer than you have been alive. I am not a Slither. I do not eat humans. We can be allies or enemies, but my enemies tend to die quickly." The tiger applies more pressure from the paw behind Cruelblade's head, and the flow of blood increases. Not a person moves, as this scene plays out.

For a moment, Cruelblade can only blink then, in a cracking voice, he speaks, "I am sorry for my comments. It was stupid of me. We are allies."

George relaxes and removes his paws from Cruelblade, then turns toward his mates. The female tigers are up on the table and prepared to defend George with their lives. He thinks, "Down, Ladies." Then he marches up to Matthew and Eli, "You need to get your acts together. I need to see more from you, Matthew, before you are a leader in my eyes."

Matthew is not easily surprised, but his eyes bore into George's eyes. He finally stammers, "You can talk out loud!"

George growls, then violently shakes his head. Finally, he thinks, "Only when I get mad. A Cat, speaking in combat, will cost someone his life. Since Patton the Liberator, we have used mental telepathy. I am sorry for the outburst. Besides, it hurts my vocal cords to talk. How you humans do it all the time, I will never understand."

Then George takes his pride into the kitchen to ask the cook for fresh fish. The cook leads them into a narrow, clear tube that descends five hundred feet, at an angle, into the water, into a large room, about one hundred feet by one hundred feet, with a platform in the room. The room is opaque to the sea surrounding it. A small pond of salt water fills half the room. The cook heads for a large panel with three buttons. The top button is green, the middle button is blue, and the bottom button is red. The cook presses the green button and the water in the pond gently vibrates. There is about a five-minute wait until the blue button lights, then the cook pushes the button. From a metal shaft in the wall close to the panel, pellets drop into the water. Before the pellets hit the water, fish are jumping up to grab them. The red light flashes and the cook presses it. On the farthest wall from the panel, a large translucent net, with unevenly spaced holes, the size of a man's head, begins to move toward the panel. It moves slowly, as fish escape through the holes. Then, it moves within ten feet of the panel and a gigantic net from under the water throws large fish onto the platform. The net remains upright to prevent the fish from escaping. Tigresses snatch the fish by their tails and drag them off into the shadows for a meal.

George is amazed, "How did you imagine this design?"

The cook breathes in deeply, as he smiles, "Over one thousand years ago, my ancestor designed this invention. Atlantis was expanding its outposts in the Sargasso Sea, but getting food to the outposts was a problem. So, the fish box was designed. We build a walking tunnel, five hundred feet long, into a room one hundred feet by one hundred feet or larger. There is a storage chamber, five feet high, the length of the room, at the top, which is filled with seaweed pellets mixed with eel sperm. The fish go nuts over these pellets. The green button starts an ultrasonic fish call. There is a tunnel that runs the length of the room, under the water, and the fish enter from either side but, once I push the blue button, a clear glass wall closes on the panel end and the translucent net falls over the other end."

George interrupts, "But why do you have holes, the size of a man's head, in the net?"

The cook gives a sly smile, "That is to give the smaller fish a chance to escape. We feed the fish five times a day. They don't know when I am taking fish for meals or when this is just a free meal for them. But the smaller fish don't care, because they get the free meal and keep coming back until they cannot fit through the holes. Then they are our meal. We always have fresh fish. Now, are you going to eat, because any uneaten fish goes back into the sea after a half hour."

George takes a bright green fish, an orange fish, and a silver fish. He saves the orange fish for dessert, and it is delicious.

Meanwhile, Matthew, Eli and Michael formalize their attack plan. For the next six days, Raquelle and Eric are taught the art of fighting with the short sword. Eli is a master of the short sword and Matthew, Raquelle and Eric become deadly after four days. George and his mates continue to eat, as the Abaddonian subs become battle ready. The sixth day arrives and Michael makes the call to the fleet, then the one to Atlantis. Joshua grills Michael to see if his father is among the captives. Michael affirms that he is and tells him to have all the relatives of the captives bring a sword, a short sword, and a dagger for the men, so they will feel safe in Atlantis. Then Michael tells Joshua that both Abaddonian subs are filled with Bluegreen, and he is not to let the Fiends know of the cargo. Joshua tells Michael that the Fiends monitor all lines of communication, so they now know of the Bluegreen. Michael sighs loudly, "Well, at least your father will return; but do you think the Fiends will kill him?" Michael cuts communications before Joshua can answer. He leaves the communications room, then Cruelblade slinks in and makes a transmission to Atlantis.

The crews board the subs, then Michael's team boards, then George tries to board, but the hatch seems to have shrunk. He can't understand how the hatch got smaller; after all, his pride had no trouble boarding the sub. Matthew, Raquelle and Eli try to push George into the sub, but he won't fit. The cook, from inside the sub, pushes George's rump through the hatch, as he comes on deck. The cook rushes to his kitchen and grabs a container of fish oil. When he returns, he rubs George's back, sides, and stomach with the oil. George backs into the hatch and puts two back paws on the ladder, but they slip. George slides, rump first, down the ladder and smacks into the floor. George growls under his breath, as he enters the nose of the sub. The pride comes to George. They lick his body. They love the fish oil, but George just enjoys all the attention.

Matthew advises the tigresses to leave some of the fish oil, so George can get out of the sub in Atlantis. The voyage is tense; George sits in the very nose of the sub and his tigresses crowd around him. He comforts his pride, "I have fought hundreds of battles and this will be an easy one. You have fed well for six days. Our strength has returned and we have the element of surprise. I watched the humans train with their swords. They are deadly--even the children. Remember to protect each other's flanks and, if another tigress is in trouble, help her."

Matthew holds his children close, as they listen to George. The sub slows in front of the naked gold statue of O. Eric's eyes bulge, "That's mom and she's naked!" The faces of Matthew, Raquelle and Eric flush to a bright crimson red. They stand there, motionless. Eli enters the cabin and rattles his sword, "We submerge under O's legs, then go into a tunnel that surfaces in the lake of life. So prepare for battle."

The sub proceeds between O's legs, then into a large tunnel where fresh water flows out. The Abaddonian subs enter the tunnel and, immediately, they are surrounded by Lake Guardians. Matthew walks over the tigresses, comes up beside George, and stares at the Lake Guardians. Matthew notices a large Plesiosaurus, which stares directly into the sub, and smiles. It is Elizabeth, and she waves a flipper at Matthew. He thinks, "Elizabeth, I need your help. Shalee has been captured by Abaddon and will be sacrificed at the next Red Tide. The Fiends will seize this cargo, so they need to be eliminated just after we surface. I need the help of the Lake Guardians. Will you attack with us?"

Elizabeth orders the sub to stop, as she confers with the other lake guardians. She tells them, "Matthew Wolverine is a man to be trusted and Shalee is a woman of honor. She has been captured by Abaddon. We know the Fiends and their families; they must be eliminated today. Are you with me?" Lake Guardian flippers begin to violently wave. They hate the Fiends and, today, their hatred will have its way. Elizabeth goes to the sub and tells Matthew to move ahead. When the first body hits the water, the Lake Guardians attack.

Eli proceeds to surface, as the crew arms. The two subs rise. The first hatch opens and Eli climbs to the deck, then Cruelblade follows, with a long chain with collars attached, and climbs on deck. As the tigers climb the ladder, Cruelblade closes the latch on each collar, then he slyly inserts a pin into the latch. This is done on the first eight tigers; then Sonya climbs the ladder. She studies the tiger closest to her and sees the pin in the latch. As Cruelblade closes the latch and starts to insert the pin, Sonya steps on his foot with all her might. Cruelblade jerks with pain and the pin drops. Sonya covers the pin with her paw and slides it along the deck as she sits down. Cruelblade quickly closes the latch around George's neck, as he leaves the hatch, and puts in the pin. The collar is very loose around George's neck because he is so big. It, also, quickly becomes soaked with the fish oil on George's body.

Matthew, Raquelle and Eric quickly exit the sub. The crews of both subs now stand on their decks.

The crowd on shore parts to let a massive man, wearing a Viking helmet with horns, ascend the gangplank. The rest of the Fiends and their families push through the crowd until they line the dock, prepared to board the subs. Short swords are drawn by even their wives and children. The massive man stops in front of Matthew, then shouts, "The Fiends claim this cargo!" At that instant, Cruelblade steps behind Eric and places a knife to his throat. Raquelle stiffens, but Matthew just glances over at him. The huge man smirks, "Your children will be my slaves. I especially like young girls."

Matthew grips the hilt of his short sword, "I don't negotiate with terrorists!" Matthew draws his sword to engage the gigantic man in combat. Cruelblade pulls the blade a bit tighter against Eric's neck. The fighting is fast and furious. The crews on deck draw their swords but, both the Fiends on the dock and the crews, wait for the outcome of this combat.

With all eyes riveted on Matthew and the Fiends' leader, Sonya raises her left front paw to unlock the latch and with her other front paw catches the collar. She quietly places it on the deck. On silent paws, she slinks, then rises straight up on her back paws, behind Cruelblade. Just before her front paws gently touch Cruelblade's shoulders, Sonya seductively bores into Cruelblade's mind, "Cruelblade, let me tell you a story. My family was killed by three Siberian poachers. I tracked them down, one by one, until each was alone, then I slowly crushed their necks. Their blood-chilling screams are forever etched into the minds of the settlers and the other animals in my valley. I found that I really delight in the slow kill." Sonya, ever so slightly, licks the back of Cruelblade's neck. At that instant, in one move, Eric raises his right foot, and steps with all his might, on Cruelblade's right foot as his hands push Cruelblade's arm above his head. Sonya immediately seizes the back of Cruelblade's neck, with fangs on either side of his backbone and slowly applies pressure. A blood-curdling scream rises to the very height of the dome, then echoes back.

Matthew's opponent stops fighting, to stare in terror, as Cruelblade wiggles like a rabbit in the mouth of this vicious tigress. Matthew notices that goose bumps erupt all over the other man's arms. The waters around the subs move and Lake Guardians pop to the surface. Elizabeth sees that the gang's terrified leader has turned his back to her, and her mouth comes down over his head and jerks him into the water. She swiftly drags him down, then out, past the legs of the statue of O, spits out the thrashing body, then heads back for the subs.

The Fiends and their families try to rush the subs. Eli and his crew block the gangplank. The crowd behind the Fiends surges forward to push them into the water and, as soon as they hit the surface, the Lake Guardians appear, to grab their victims by their heads, so that they are unable to breath. Their squirming bodies are dragged down, then out, past the statue of O. As each Lake Guardian spits out the live bodies, their victims struggle for air. The dinosaurs' thoughts blare out, in all directions, only one word, "FEAST." Sharks appear, like magic, and swarm into a feeding frenzy.

George strains at his collar, then he roars. His roar drowns out Cruelblade's screams and he, for a moment, stops his squirming and shivers in fear. With his mouth wide open, George's roar pierces every ear in the dome. In a sparkling white marble building, the priests and royalty cover their ears but, from the distant corner of the dome, a cotton-haired man starts running, flat out, for the docks. George pulls on the collar until he slips out of it. He looks in the water, but all the Fiends, along with their families, are gone. Then he walks toward Sonya, but her stare pierces him, as her mind blares out, "My kill! Stay away!" She paws the air, as George approaches. Cruelblade continues to scream, as George places his right front paw, with claws extended, on the dying man's throat, then shifts all his weight to his front paw. Cruelblade dies instantly. Sonya gives a low, vicious growl, as George removes his front paw, then she flings the body into the water. Raquelle unleashes the other tigers. George sees that the enemy is vanquished, raises his head and releases a reverberating boom, which fills the dome. This is the first victory roar of a War Cat to ever fill this dome. All the humans and all the other cats cover their ears.

The cotton-haired man, his hands over his ears, approaches George. He bows from the waist, "I am known as the Acquirer of Dreams, and a War Cat's credit is as good as Atlantian blue diamonds with me. Do you desire any food or comfort?" He holds his bow until George responds.

George walks over, to stand beside Matthew, then turns to look at the Acquirer of Dreams, "I owe this man ten lives. When his wife is released from Abaddon, then I am released. You will deal with him."

The Acquirer of Dreams realizes that Matthew is a surface dweller and promptly rises, "I deal with only Atlantians and War Cats. I don't deal with surface dwellers." He turns and walks to the palace of the priests. The priests and the ruling class are agitated. They confer together. Arms wave in the air and scowls cover each of their faces.

The crews from the Atlantian fleet disembark and wait for

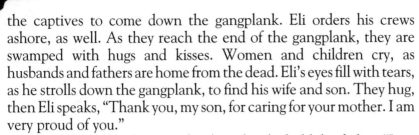

the captives to come down the gangplank. Eli orders his crews ashore, as well. As they reach the end of the gangplank, they are swamped with hugs and kisses. Women and children cry, as husbands and fathers are home from the dead. Eli's eyes fill with tears, as he strolls down the gangplank, to find his wife and son. They hug, then Eli speaks, "Thank you, my son, for caring for your mother. I am very proud of you."

Joshua's face becomes bright red, as he holds his father, "I am your son and I never lost hope that you would return. But how did you escape?"

Eli holds his wife tightly, as he turns toward the sub, "The Wolverines rescued us."

Joshua starts shouting at the top of his lungs, "Wolverines, we love you!"

The other crewmen join in, then the whole crowd is shouting, "Wolverines, we love you!"

Matthew, Raquelle and Eric, with broad Texas smiles, wave. George comes to Matthew's left side and nudges him. Then he raises his right paw and waves, as he thinks, "It was my plan. Yes, it was my plan."

Matthew laughs, as he strokes George with his left hand, "Yes, George, your plan was great, but we also need to thank the Lake Guardians." At that moment, Elizabeth and the other Lake Guardians surface. Matthew turns to face a sea of dinosaurs and starts to clap. Raquelle and Eric turn and do the same. Soon, the whole crowd is applauding the Lake Guardians. The royalty, the priests, and the Acquirer of Dreams, spit in unison, then turn to go into the palace.

Joshua runs up the gangplank and offers to show Matthew the property and wealth that are now his since the deaths of the Fiends. Matthew marvels that it is the same in all cultures, "To the victor go the spoils."

Eric pets Sonya, then whispers in her ear, "Thank you, Sonya. I thought I was dead until you entered Cruelblade's mind. You gave me time to escape and I will not forget it. I will get you the freshest fish to eat. Only, I wish you had killed him slowly and made him really suffer. I didn't like that man." Sonya turns to lick Eric's face and a bond of mutual admiration forms between them.

Joshua leads Matthew, his children, and the cats to a group of white marble buildings beside the lake of life. The luster of the marble is a hands-breadth thick. Raquelle tries to put her hand into the marble. Even with dust on the stone, it shines in the artificial sun light. Matthew marvels at the grandeur of the buildings. They remind him of classic Roman and Greek architecture. The first building that they enter has a huge square opening in the ceiling over a large pool in the center of the building.

Chapter 5

Blue Diamonds from Where?

Joshua explains, "When Atlantis was first settled, we built our buildings to allow the sun and rain to enter. One end of the pool has a constant flow of water from the lake of birth into the pool and the other end sends water back into the lake of birth. So no going to the bathroom in the pool!" Joshua looks directly at the cats. Sonya shakes her head, as she blurts out, "Then where do we go?"

George steps forward, "Joshua, could you put sand in one corner of each room?"

Joshua shakes his head, "We are at the bottom of the sea and sand is expensive to haul into Atlantis, but we have sea water converters that extract the salt so we can use the water for farming. I could have salt piles in each room of this building."

George nods his head, "Have men start hauling at once. We need those salt piles in place before we eat our next meal. Also, have one salt pile in every other building within the next day."

Joshua orders some men to start hauling the salt and the men leave. They, then, continue the tour. A back room reveals two large metal doors with handles and a dial-type combination lock. It is a huge vault. Matthew steps forward to try the handles and the doors open. He shakes his head in disbelief. "The Fiends were that arrogant, that they didn't even lock their vaults!"

The room contains trays of blue diamonds, rubies, emeralds, Spanish doubloons, Spanish silver ingots, Aztec gold bars, bags of silver pieces of eight and black pearls. Raquelle grabs two handfuls of black pearls and gazes into them. Eric runs his fingers through the rubies, as his father studies a few Spanish doubloons.

George and Sonya push their way to the blue diamonds. He leans his head against Sonya, so only she can hear his thoughts, "In the vaults of a Swiss bank sit four times this amount of blue diamonds, in my name. Other War Cats are buying land in Argentina so, after we free Wolverine's wife, we travel to Argentina." Sonya snuggles George, as she thinks of how a Siberian tiger can come to roam the hills of Argentina on her own land.

Matthew exhales, "This much wealth could build subs that would free my wife. How did the Fiends accumulate so much wealth?"

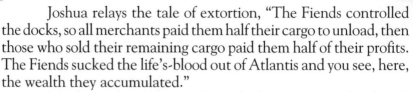

Joshua relays the tale of extortion, "The Fiends controlled the docks, so all merchants paid them half their cargo to unload, then those who sold their remaining cargo paid them half of their profits. The Fiends sucked the life's-blood out of Atlantis and you see, here, the wealth they accumulated."

Matthew's face tightens, "I saw this happen in Scotland, with dragons, in 999 A.D. That is where I rescued my wife, Shalee. Now, there are no more dragons in Scotland."

George whirls around so fast that the tray of blue diamonds spills and scatters on the floor. "Are you over 1,000 years old?"

Matthew chuckles, "No, George, I traveled back in time through a stone cross. Maybe it was a portal. Maybe it was something else. My wife and children have questions about the event, but I know what happened and it changed the future. The fact that I am talking with you through mental telepathy is astonishing, but everyone in the room hears you, so they believe. Atlantis, we thought, was a myth, but here we are. So, do you think I am crazy?"

George studies Matthew for a few moments, then shakes his head. A portal in time is just too much for George to believe, so he turns to Joshua, "Is the salt pile ready? I've really got to go!"

Joshua leads George and his pride to the salt pile, then quickly turns his back and the pile immediately turns yellow. When Joshua turns back around, Sonya loudly demands, "Larger salt piles!"

Joshua orders the salt pile to be changed and replaced with triple the amount. He returns to the vault, as Raquelle and Eric put the last blue diamond they could find into the tray.

Matthew surveys the vault doors, "A locksmith needs to change the combination, so post a guard until he completes the work."

Joshua posts a guard and sends for a locksmith as Matthew, Raquelle and Eric explore the rest of the house. The kitchen has a clear glass table in the center and clear glass cabinets that house clear glass pots, pans, and dishes.

Chapter 6

Pampered

Two priests escort Shalee out of the temple. A sea of wiggling black snakes, at first, blocks their path, but the surviving snakes, who were in Shalee's cell before, are between them and Shalee. Fear of this green-eyed monster causes them to slither quickly over the other snakes to escape. The other snakes sense the smell of fear and terror spreads among them, so that, miraculously, a five-foot corridor instantly appears. One large black snake charges from the crowd to attack Shalee. Before the priests can stop her, she grabs the snake, as it tries to strike, whirls it over her head until her hand slides down to the tip of its tail, then smashes its head into the ground and hurls its dead body, with all her strength, into the sea. The black snake's body hits the salt water, then foams away into nothingness. The two priests shoo the snakes back, and a ten-foot corridor is opened before them.

The trio approaches a colossal, domed black marble building. On each side of the glass doors is a glittering harp of gold and a sparkling gold chair. Both priests sit down and start to play the harps. The music is so melancholy, that Shalee's eyes start to tear. Just then, the glass doors open. Ten beautiful, voluptuous young girls, clothed in dark blue, black and white porpoise-skin bathing suits, appear, heads bowed.

One priest steps forward, "The new high priest, Vipurr, orders that this sacrifice be bathed in our sweetest perfume, Oil of Dolphin, dine only on our best food, wear jewelry to enhance the beauty of her green eyes, and dress in silk with snake skin underneath. Your goal is for her to enter the seventh level of sensual pleasure. Each time she tries to escape, I will kill one of you. Protect your lives well." Then the priests turn to return to the temple.

The girls, all at once, start questioning their prisoner about what happened to the old high priest. Shalee, tired of being threatened with death, physically drained, her hold on her temper disintegrated, explodes, "Vipurr captured me and brought me here and the Red Worm swallowed your old high priest in one gulp. May he burn in hell for eternity! Since scum rises to the surface, your Red Worm made Vipurr, high priest. Now, do you have any food inside?"

The girls gasp at Shalee's bluntness. Her patience wears even thinner, "Well, do you have any food or do I starve out here?"

The girls nod, in unison, and escort Shalee past the glass doors. Inside the room, is a long table, set with large bowls of steaming soup and chowder. She rushes forward, grabs a bowl and fills it with soup, then wolfs it down. A tall redhead takes a large spoon, scrapes the bottom of the large bowl and deposits some meat into Shalee's bowl. She smiles. "Eat the dolphin's meat; it is sweet, chewy, and life giving."

Shalee stops eating and looks up, "This is dolphin soup?"

The redhead nods, "Yes, the dolphins are Atlantis's allies, so they are the Red Serpent's enemies. His troops catch them in huge nets, skin them, and give us the meat to cook. All of our bathing suits are made from dolphin skins. The white is the underbody, with golden stripes on the sides. My top is made of one golden stripe fastened in the back. The black and dark blue are from the upper bodies of dolphins. My swimsuit bottom is all black and feels smooth as snakeskin against my skin. Do you like the soup?"

Shalee is glad that Raquelle is not here. She would never understand anyone eating dolphin. Shalee and Matthew are one in this very important respect--they will do whatever it takes to survive. Shalee bites the dolphin meat and it melts in her mouth. A bowl of sea turtle chowder is placed in front of her and is empty before the second hand on a watch can complete one circle. Shalee is full and she pushes the bowls away.

The redhead beckons her to a black marble whirlpool, which is built into the floor, "Volcanic waters will cleanse all your pores and relax your fatigued muscles, so remove all body coverings, to allow the waters to cleanse your body. Shalee removes her bathing suit and steps into the water. It is very hot and she hesitates. The redhead moves to a control panel and releases some cooler fresh water into the whirlpool and Shalee sits down. Five of the girls smooth her long black hair and lather it with a slick oil, which they then massage through her hair. The redhead turns up the temperature of the water and Shalee's muscles totally relax and she falls into a deep, deep sleep. Now, the other four girls apply the oil to her face, shoulders, arms, chest and back. Then they lay her down, as the five working on her hair rinse it with warm water, until the water runs clear. They lift her out of the water and apply the oil to her legs, feet and buttocks. The redhead inspects Shalee's body, to make sure that every inch of it is oiled, then she orders the girls to put her back into the whirlpool for twenty minutes.

One of the girls, a brunette, questions the redhead, and asks why so much dolphin oil, from the foreheads of ten dead dolphins, should be wasted on this sacrifice. She fears that the Red Serpent may not be able to resist the scent of the oil and will feast on this sacrifice immediately.

At that moment, the Red Serpent slithers in and the girls freeze. "Place the sacrifice in my mouth." The Red Serpent's mouth opens wide and each girl swallows hard. The girls lift Shalee and place her on the forked tongue. The Red Serpent rolls his tongue all over Shalee's body. Then he spits her out. "Dress her in my shed skin and put her to bed."

The Red Serpent slithers to the whirlpool and drinks deeply. The taste of dolphin oil and woman saturates his mouth and he smiles. He will remember this sacrifice for ten thousand years. Vipurr honors his god. It is good to be a god. Then the Red Serpent, satisfied, with a full belly, turns to slide out of the black building, as the redhead's lowered eyes close tight and her brow knits. If thoughts could kill, the Red Serpent would be stone cold dead now. But, for the time being, she had to work with this worm, and this sacrifice may be her ticket back to Atlantis.

The redhead orders the other girls to wrap Shalee in a cocoon of snakeskin and put her to bed. She dreams that she is caught in a red spider's web. Her hands press against it. They tingle, as they slide down the satin-smooth surface. The sensation is erotic. Her mind snaps to the danger; this is a trap, so she desperately claws for freedom. The harder she claws, the more the spider web constricts her. This web is like a snake constricting her body. Now, she can't breathe. She slashes at the web, until her hands puncture a small hole. She digs, ferociously, through the hole. Shalee awakens to find herself covered in shreds of red snake skin. She leaps out of her bed, and this horrible dream, and screams for Matthew. In rush the redhead and her nine cohorts. Shalee's shoulders sink, as she realizes that this is not a nightmare.

The redhead sighs deeply. "Shalee, we are all prisoners here and we are trying to stay out of the Red Serpent's belly. The priests could kill us at any time, so we try not to cause any trouble."

Shalee's voice gets loud, as she spits out her words, "I do not capitulate to that worm! If I wind up in his belly, then Matthew Wolverine will take his revenge on the Red Serpent. He slaughtered dragons over 1,000 years ago, to win me, and this worm is not a dragon." At that moment, Shalee wills, with all her might, to believe that Matthew had gone back in time a thousand years and destroyed the dragons of Scotland.

The redhead becomes very grave. "No, the Red Serpent is not a dragon. He is the illegitimate father of all dragons. Many eons ago, a female pterodactyl, from Scotland lost her bearings in a storm at sea and flew for many days, finally landing on Atlantis. She landed on the beach, drained of her strength, and immediately fell into a deep sleep, hoping to regain her strength. The Red Serpent had just eaten twenty Dodo birds, so his appetite was sated. He slithered up and coiled around the pterodactyl, bruising her wings, before she awoke. The Red Serpent mated with her then, just as he finished, she pecked him in the eye. He released his grip and she flew, awkwardly, to the tallest mountain of Atlantis. She built her nest on that high mountain, lay ten eggs and sat on them until they hatched. What hatched was a cross between the Red Serpent and the pterodactyl, which you know as a fire-breathing dragon. Neither the Red Serpent nor the pterodactyl breathed fire, but these babies did and the pterodactyl loved them as only a mother could. Daily, she flew the skies over the sea surrounding Atlantis. Fresh fish, turtles, and Dodo birds filled the nest, as her dragons grew and learned to fly.

The Red Serpent contemplated the flying reptiles overhead, and envy mixed with hatred grew until he couldn't take it. There was a stream flowing from the mountaintop to the ocean. After many days, he worked his way up the mountain, to the nest, then he waited for them to come to roost for the night. The pterodactyl sat in the middle of the nest, and her children tried to lean against her, before they went to sleep. The Serpent was able to kill three of the dragons and eat them, before a fourth dragon awoke to give the alarm. The mother attacked the snake and they locked in mortal combat. Her beak encircled the Red Serpent's head. The dragons blew fire on him, so he quickly coiled around the pterodactyl and rolled down the hill into that deep mountain stream. The Red Serpent kept the coils on his prey until she drowned. The dragons poured fire on the barrier of the water, but to no avail. The last scene they saw was that of the Red Serpent slowly devouring their mother, under the water, so they abandoned Atlantis and flew to Scotland. The dragons, in Scotland, came from Atlantis."

Shalee doesn't say a word for a few minutes. "Well, Matthew Wolverine, with the help of the other Scottish clans, the Irish clans, and many Vikings warriors, destroyed the dragons of Scotland. The Red Serpent can also be destroyed."

The redhead's mouth flies open, as her eyes widen, "You are married to the butcher of the Scottish dragons?"

Shalee's eyes flare, as she leaps upon the redhead. The girl rains solid blows down on her attacker's head and shoulders. Shalee squeezes the redhead's neck, until her knuckles turn white. The other nine women drag her off the redhead and pin her to the ground. The redhead staggers, coughing, to her feet, "You are quite a fighter, but I am not your enemy. I used the terms that the priests' god taught them, and which they passed on to us. At the battle of Hadrian's wall, one dragon escaped with a Viking battle-ax in his side and flew to Atlantis. The Red Serpent found him, bleeding, on the north beach and removed the ax. He asked the dragon how he had been injured. The dragon told how Matthew Wolverine had appeared, one day, and started killing all the dragons in Scotland and how he feared that he was the last Scottish dragon alive. Then he asked if the Red Serpent was the original father of all dragons. He smiled, nodded, then coiled around the dragon on the pretext of keeping him warm. The dragon went to sleep, then the Red Serpent squeezed the life out of him. There is no mercy, love, or caring in the heart of the Red Serpent and I hate him, more than you ever will.

The other priests considered Matthew Wolverine a butcher and I only related their opinions. For that, I am sorry. My name is Nicole; they are Amber, Heather, Colleen, Tara, Brooke, Danielle, Kimberly, Darcy and Alexis. We are all captives from Atlantis and can be sacrificed or killed by the priests at any time. The Red Serpent is our enemy and escape is our nightly dream. Working together, we can all escape." Nicole extends her right hand to Shalee, as the other women release their holds on her.

Shalee rises slowly, while studying Nicole. Flaming red hair crowned a beautiful, athletic body. A Viking war ax would fit into either of Nicole's hands and be very much at home. Shalee turns her gaze to the other women and they are all very voluptuous, except Alexis. Her hair is stringy and her black eyes have a haunting stare. She looks underfed. Shalee takes Nicole's hand and receives a firm, strong handshake. She looks around, "Before I can plan any escape, I need to see as much as possible. What is this city called?"

"Abaddon, which is the city of destruction. I am not sure how far we can go outside of our dome. The black snakes guard us and threaten to strike us, when we try to leave. Their poison takes two weeks to kill and it is an ever-increasing, painful death."

Shalee tells Nicole to wrap her hands and arms in the skin of the Red Serpent, but to leave it loose enough so that she can move her fingers. This is done and Shalee leads the women to the glass doors.

Black snakes slither past the doors, and Shalee quickly opens one of them and grabs a snake by its tail, then smacks its head on the floor, instantly killing it, then opens the door wide and hurls the lifeless body as far as she can. The other snakes see the lifeless body sail through the air and scatter. Nicole shakes her head, "There isn't even a snake in sight. They are hiding from you."

"Right; now show me as much of the city as you can, before we are discovered."

The group of eleven moves toward the docks. Two long black subs, in the shape of giant Krakens, are tied to the docks. Shalee looks up at the bubble dome, which surrounds the temple, the black dome and the docks. When she sees the subs, she stops dead in her tracks. "Are those giant squids alive?"

Nicole shakes her head, "No; those are not squids. They are Abaddon's subs, but they do look like Krakens because our navy hunts with the Kraken packs. The Red Serpent controls the seas around Atlantis and the northern Atlantic with his Krakens. They do his hunting and bring him slaves to work in his mines. Some join with him and become priests, while others are methodically drained of their blood, which is replaced by the Serpent's poison. The black snakes are victims who have more than 90% poison in their bodies. As they turn into snakes, they blindly serve the Red Serpent. When they bite, they inject a slow-acting poison, which takes about two weeks to work. The victims' screams increase daily, as the poison works its way to the brain."

Shalee interrupts to question Nicole, "What about this glass dome? Are there more of these or just the one?"

"Hundreds of glass domes make up Abaddon. The Red Serpent knew that Atlantis would sink, so he had the domes built over the city. The fact that O's father built domes over the east side of the island caught him completely off guard. He expected Atlantis to sink into the sea because he made O a goddess. Then his Krakens would bring him the bodies from Atlantis to feast on. The Red Serpent did capture O but, as he plunged deeper into the lake of life, one of the remaining Lake Guardians attacked and the Serpent swallowed her, so he could open his mouth to fight. He killed the Lake Guardian and returned to Abaddon on the currents of the lake of life. The lake provides fresh water to both Atlantis and Abaddon. The fresh water that the Red Serpent swims in, in his temple, originates from the lake of life, which is also called the lake of birth."

As they walk from the dock, toward the next dome, Shalee asks, "Why is this water called the lake of life?"

"When O first arrived on Atlantis, she noticed that the dolphins gave birth in the shallow waters. Sometimes the mother became so frustrated with the pain or the birth process that, after the baby was born, she would beach herself to die in the hot sun and the baby, wanting to be with its mother, would beach itself and they would both die. O felt compassion for them so, when she saw a dolphin giving birth, she entered the water and held the dolphin's head, to comfort her during the birth process. The first things a baby Atlantian dolphin saw were its mother and O. Other Atlantian women began to help, with the dolphins' births, so the bond between the Atlantian dolphins and humans became stronger. The eels also gave birth in the lake beside the dolphins. So it became commonplace to be holding the head of a dolphin, while baby eels swam around your legs. As a joke, the men started calling it the lake of birth. The Lake Guardians saw the humans help with the dolphin births and the eel births and, because they are such big babies, they wanted O to help with their births, so she did. The Lake Guardians have always been the protectors of the lake. The dolphins and eels trust them and the Atlantians grew to trust them, too. The Lake Guardians talk by mental telepathy, which they taught O, and she taught the rest of Atlantis.

All was great, until the Red Serpent arrived in Atlantis. He started killing the eels, the dolphins, and even the babies of the Lake Guardians and, when they told O, she called them liars. Then the Red Serpent ordered the Krakens to attack the Lake Guardians in the salt water of the seas around Atlantis, as they ventured out to feed. They had had enough. Most of them, one night, abandoned the lake of birth and headed northeastward to search for cod. At that time, the North Sea was packed with uncountable schools of codfish. They needed a home and they found Loch Ness, Scotland. Huge caverns, about 800 feet below the surface of the loch, were ideal. They hunted in the North Sea and slept in the caverns of Loch Ness."

Just then, Nicole reaches a massive glass door. She unlocks it and the eleven females enter. A large sweaty man, with only pants on, sits in the center of the room. With intense heat, he is melting gold and pouring it into molds. Dried seaweed baskets filled with emeralds, rubies and blue diamonds lay scattered throughout the room. He makes the pour, wipes his forehead with a filthy cloth, and looks up, "Nicole! So you are still alive. Well, come look at my great creations, which will wind up in the Red Serpent's belly but, then, they will eventually come out without the sacrifice."

Nicole picks up a necklace with three separate rows of stones. The top row is blood-red ruby, the second is shamrock-green emeralds and the third is sky-blue diamonds. Each row intersects a strand of heavy gold chain with a clasp in the shape of a serpent's head fastening over a dolphin's head, at the back of the neck. Nicole fastens the necklace on Shalee, then stands back to appraise it. She shakes her head. "Too much color. I want a necklace of light blue diamonds set in silver on the top, two rows of thumb-nail sized emeralds set in gold in the middle and I want the bottom third to offset her green eyes. How soon can you have it made?"

The large sweaty man shakes his head, "I want you ladies to wash me in your black marble pool, slowly and seductively feed me two baskets of sweet grapes and give me a full body massage in your black-domed sanctuary, before I start any necklace for you. Don't try to threaten me with the priests of the Red Serpent. I am filthy, hungry and ready to die. Nicole, it will only take eight of you beautiful girls to attend me so you, green eyes and stringy hair take a tour of this cesspool we call Abaddon."

Chapter 7

Unicorns and Saber Tooth Tigers?

With the Fiends vanquished, the next two weeks consist of learning what vessels they once owned that have now become Matthew's property. The religious order and the nobility try to take the Fiends' submarines but the navy sides with the Wolverines. Matthew starts equipping the submarines for war, but wants the navy to help in a joint attack on Abaddon to free Shalee. The nobility stands, as one, to openly oppose such actions. The navy is supposed to protect Atlantis from enemy attacks. Matthew will have to attack with the subs he has--and no more. Eli is sympathetic and will command the submarine attack. The freed slaves and their relatives, that have combat training, will be Eli's navy. Matthew will take over, when the subs land inside Abaddon. The priests remain strangely quiet concerning this attack.

Matthew, Raquelle and Eric rise at dawn, to go to the docks to outfit the subs. George stations four of his mates at the house, around the clock. Then George and the rest of his pride travel through each dome in Atlantis, to inspect it and see its function. There are over a hundred domes, but the one that impresses him the most is the Dodo birds' dome. He enters this dome and the Dodo birds march right up to him and inspect him. They have no fear of man or animal. He marvels at how these birds have survived. After the birds look George and his pride over one time, they fluff their rumps at the tigers, then go back to eating. Clearly, they are not impressed with tigers and George makes a mental note that his whole pride will eat Dodo birds at least twice a week.

Eli's wife drops off dinner at Matthew's house. The wives of the freed slaves rotate this duty. The four female tigers, on duty, accept receiving gifts daily. The merchants also bring bags of money; the tigers sniff the bags and, since you can't eat money, they stack them in a room beside the vault.

The domes of the library, museum, schools, theater, and government offices are viewed in one day. The dome of the submarine factory and the manufacturing of parts intrigues George.

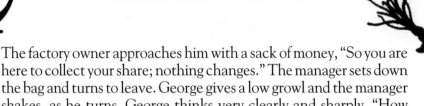

The factory owner approaches him with a sack of money, "So you are here to collect your share; nothing changes." The manager sets down the bag and turns to leave. George gives a low growl and the manager shakes, as he turns. George thinks very clearly and sharply, "How could I know this is the correct amount? You will explain your operation from top to bottom. This may take the whole day, so tell your assistant not to disturb us."

The rest of the day, George learns that it takes three months to produce a finished sub. The navy is the chief buyer. The owner has had to shut down eighty percent of his factory and lay off two-thirds of his work force, because of the Fiends. These men have gone into being servants to the nobles, just so they can feed their families. As they walk the factory floor, George notices the shabby clothing and the depressed, haggard faces of the workers. They go to the next dome and the workers' houses are shabby, rat infested places. A large rat, bold as brass, strolls out of a house. Sonya nails him to the ground. She hates rats, so she orders the other females to search all the homes and kill any rat that might be moving, then bring the body to the street. George and the owner continue their walk as if nothing had happened. They return to the bag of money, which is still in the hallway, and George picks it up in his mouth. Then he tilts his head, "How much would you sell the factory for?" The owner shrugs his shoulders. "Transform the weight of that sack of gold coins into blue diamonds and it is yours. But there is as much chance of that happening as of Wolverine defeating the Abaddonian navy and its Krakens." The owner gives a hardy laugh, as he walks away. Atlantis feels secure behind its navy, but not secure enough to conquer Abaddon.

George returns to Sonya and is greeted by a pile of dead rats that blocks the street. There are hundreds of them. Sonya and the other females trudge up to George, "We need ten fish each and a good bath tonight, so let's go home." The workmen are returning home and cursing the pile of dead rats, because they can't get to their homes and they know they have to dispose of them before they eat tonight.

At Matthew's home, George and his mates bathe and eat their fill of fresh fish. After an hour, Matthew, Raquelle and Eric drag themselves home. They look as bad as the factory workers. The meal that Eli's wife has prepared is cold, but they eat it anyway. The tiger suggests to Matthew that he wait on the attack and think about buying the submarine factory and building new subs. Matthew won't hear of waiting to rescue his wife. George suggests that attacking too soon could cost Matthew his fleet. Matthew counters with, if Eli loses the fleet, then George can buy the factory because he and Eli will be dead. George accepts the offer and asks Eric to come with him. A very tired Eric slowly rises and follows George to the vault, then opens it. George takes the bag of gold and finds a scale with two buckets and sets the gold coins in one bucket. Then he tells Eric to get an empty bag and fill that bag with blue diamonds, until it equals the weight of the gold coins. He takes a deep breath, snatches an empty bag and starts shoveling in blue diamonds. The bags finally match in weight, and Eric asks if he can go to bed. George nods, as he grabs the bag of blue diamonds, and they lock the vault.

After two weeks, the subs are ready and they can launch their attack on Abaddon the next morning. Matthew calls Raquelle into Eric's room and prepares to read them a bedtime story. Raquelle interrupts, "Dad, don't you think we're a bit old for bedtime stories."

Matthew shakes his head, "I hope you never get too old for bedtime stories. I get to spend time with you before you go to sleep and I want you to imagine and have sweet dreams."

Eric chirps in, "Can we go tomorrow and help fight to free Mom?"

Matthew's shoulders droop, "No, I want you two to be safe but, if this attack fails, then you can go for the next one." Matthew feels sure that this attack will succeed.

The next morning, a fatigued Matthew boards the sub and goes to fight the Krakens, as an animated Raquelle and Eric wave from the dock. As the sub dives, Eric turns to Raquelle, "I want to explore some of the Trader's domes. I heard he has some rare animals."

Raquelle sighs, "I just want to go with my father, to fight the Krakens and rescue mom, but we're stuck in Atlantis. So how will you get into the Trader's domes?"

Eric smiles broadly, "George and I played hide and seek a few days ago--one of the few days Dad let me stay home—and, while I was hiding, I saw a repairman come into our dome through a sealed door in the floor. I jumped out from hiding and scared him. I asked him why he was in our dome and he told me, to repair the cables that give us light. He showed me a map of Atlantis and there are tunnels under all the domes for the light cables. I looked at the Trader's dome and saw a way inside. I'll show you."

Eric and Raquelle walk to a park with a large waterfall. Eric strolls right into the waterfall. Raquelle stops and stares, open-mouthed. For a moment, she cannot believe what just happened.

Then Eric emerges from the waterfall, soaked, and takes Raquelle by the hand and leads her through the waterfall. The cold water brings his sister to life, "Are you nuts? That water is cold!" A warm flow of air quickly dries them.

Eric ignores his sister and pushes onto a seal. He turns the seal, then opens it. It is dark just beyond the seal, but he pushes ahead, arms extended. He feels dirt, so he pushes hard. The dirt is a trap door through which Eric and Raquelle pass. Lush green grass, about a foot high, covers the ground. There are apple trees with ripe pink, red, and yellow apples overloading the trees. Raquelle pushes ahead of Eric, to get to an apple tree, and takes an apple. She wraps her lips around it and takes a big bite. The sweetness of chocolate brownies fills her mouth. Raquelle closes her eyes and is transported back to their Texas home and Saturdays, when her mom made delicious mouth-watering chocolate brownies. Eric takes a bite, and his mouth waters with the sweetness. Raquelle and Eric each pick six apples; then they both sit down with their backs against the tree. They each have their eyes closed, as they dream of home.

After they have eaten their sixth apple each, Raquelle feels a sharp prick in her right arm, which causes her to jump to her feet. A lustrous white horse with a golden spiral horn protruding from the middle of his forehead and a golden mane and tail meets her eyes and she stammers, "Wha-, what are you?"

The beast crosses its front hooves and thinks loudly, "I am a unicorn and you are stealing my food supplies. The Trader only allots us so many fruit trees. After a hard day of running and frolicking, these apples are our treats. So, you have taken twelve of our treats. Were they delicious?"

Eric tries to explain, "We didn't know these were your treats. We could give you fish to eat."

The unicorn snorts, "We don't eat fish, or Kraken or any type of sea animal. We eat delicious fruits. Do you have any delicious fruits?"

Raquelle and Eric think hard, then Raquelle finds the answer, "Yes; do you like sweet red grapes?"

The unicorn nods, "Deliver to me, in a short time, a basket of grapes from each of you, and I will take you for an exhilarating, but dangerous ride."

Eric and Raquelle sprint to the tunnel, like jackrabbits racing for their home. They hit the front door, pass the four tigresses who are on guard, and go directly to the vault. Raquelle opens the vault and they go in. Eric, in his rush, knocks over the trays of blue diamonds. Raquelle flips up the trays, "We don't have time to pick up all the diamonds, so give me those bags of silver, and help me put the diamonds into the bags. We will put them on the trays later."

Eric grabs the bags of silver pieces of eight and shoves in handfuls of blue diamonds. Most of the blue diamonds are picked up, and Raquelle grabs five gold coins. Then they lock the vault and head for the market. The farmers trade their produce in the market dome every morning. Raquelle questions each farmer on the sweetness of his grapes and she tastes one grape from each of them. Some are sour, but she finds a very sweet grape. Eric is eating a bunch of grapes from that farmer, as Raquelle negotiates with him. "Two gold coins for two baskets of these sweet grapes."

The farmer counters, "My children will starve; these are the sweetest grapes in all of Atlantis and two baskets go for six gold coins."

"You children will not starve, and one gold coin is a fair profit but, if you want me to buy another farmer's sweet grapes, then turn down my offer." Raquelle turns toward the other farmers.

The farmer panics, "Yes, one gold coin is acceptable."

Raquelle smiles, because she knows her father would be proud of her negotiating skills. She hands the farmer one gold coin. She looks at the other twelve baskets and tells the farmer that, if he will take the rest of the baskets to the dock and feed them to Elizabeth, she will give him four gold coins. The farmer shakes her hand, takes the gold coins and rushes to the dock. Then she and Eric race back to the unicorn. The animal is eating grass with his mate and six offspring. Breathing hard, Raquelle and Eric set the baskets in front of the unicorns. They gather around the baskets and chew on some grapes. "Umm" and "ah" escape from their lips, as they consume both baskets full.

The unicorn parents think, "That was exquisite. Now would you like a dangerous ride?"

Both Raquelle and Eric nod their heads and mount the unicorns. They race for the wall of glass, with their heads down and leap at the wall. Eric and Raquelle tuck their heads in behind the unicorns' necks, sure they are going to die. The unicorns' golden horns open a hole in the wall and they sail through and land on a barren, rocky patch of ground. This dome has some green grass, but it also has areas of dry, stony ground and dirt mounds, with caves, and one lone tree. The unicorns race to the cave entrances, quickly turn, then race away. Saber-toothed tigers launch from the caves, sprinting as fast as they can, to catch the unicorns. They slow down, just a bit, and one tiger leaps into the air. Raquelle's hair is flying straight out and one of the tiger's claws passes through her hair. The loose hairs remain in the claw, and she shivers, as the tiger's paw brushes the rump of the unicorn. The unicorn turns quickly, but the tiger has turned and races for the lone tree. Raquelle looks back, expecting to see the saber-toothed tiger's claw marks, but the unicorn's rump is blood-free. As the cat is about to reach the tree, the unicorn's horn lightly touches the tip of the saber-toothed tiger's tail, then the unicorn whirls around. Raquelle grabs the mane with both hands, but still her legs fly straight out and she almost falls off.

Eric gives a Texas war cry, as he and his unicorn chase down a saber-toothed tiger. This tiger does make it to the tree. The unicorn stares intently at the huge cat and thinks, "Yes, he is heavy and you need to take him. Boy, get down and ride on the tiger for a while."

Eric bounces off the unicorn's back and onto the tiger, "Come on, tigers! We can catch them!" The unicorn whirls around and races, flat out, for the barren area. Raquelle's unicorn turns its head, "You need to ride the saber-toothed tiger, for a while, so switch." She reluctantly dismounts, and the unicorn dashes for the barren area. She just stands there, staring at the tiger until it thinks, "Get on my back; I am losing this game because of you." Raquelle hesitantly gets on the tiger's back and it makes a mad dash to catch the unicorn, but the unicorn reaches the barren area first. Then the unicorns race for the lone tree, but the saber-toothed tigers catch them before they reach their goal. All the animals are huffing and puffing, so they lay by the tree to rest.

Eric looks directly into his tiger's eyes, and the tiger asks what is on his mind. "Can I touch your big teeth?" Eric asks.

A twinkle grows in the saber-toothed tiger's eyes, "Grab them both."

Eric grabs the two giant teeth and the tiger moves on top of him. Eric's arms are extended, as he clutches the two massive teeth. The tiger snarls and places his right front paw on Eric's chest.

Raquelle's mouth goes dry and she fears they may be eaten.

The tiger glares at Eric with a menacing look, "Got ya!" It starts to laugh and the other tiger and the unicorns join in the laughter. Their stomachs jiggle like jelly and some roll over on their backs. The fruits of this tree are long, black, sticky swirls. One of the unicorns plucks a fruit from the tree and begins to chew. Eric grabs two and gives one to his tiger. Eric and the tiger merrily chew, as Raquelle asks, "The unicorn and the saber-toothed tiger are only legends in my country. How have you survived and why aren't you two fighting?"

The unicorn sighs, "The bubbles were first built by the people after they moved to the island, and we moved right inside. The saber-toothed tigers did the same, but the people were afraid of them, so they built us our own bubbles. They put us both in the bubbles, assuming that we would kill each other. The tigers had the dome with all the fruit trees and we had this one, with the lone fruit tree. What saved us was the fact that, when we drink, our horn goes into the water. The scent from our horns must be like an aphrodisiac to fish, because they swim right up to it and some even impale themselves on our horns. We have to flip the fish off to the sides to go on drinking. The tigers saw all the fish we caught and offered to feed us from the fruit trees in their bubble, in exchange for the fish. We, unicorns, had only one taste of that delicious fruit and we agreed. About a hundred years ago, our trees began to die. Then the Trader showed up and offered us more fruit trees, if we would leave with him after we had five foals. We agreed, because we had no choice."

One of the tigers roars, "The Trader offered us adventure and combat with the Slithers. There is really nothing to hunt around here, so we accepted. He trains us in combat for a year, then we ship out. I will ship out in two months. How did you get here?"

Eric starts to speak, but Raquelle cuts him off, "Our mother was captured by Abaddon and the Red Serpent will eat her, as a sacrifice, unless my father saves her. He is out fighting the Krakens, so he can enter Abaddon. We're stuck here."

The saber-toothed tigers nod their heads, "Krakens are tough. I fought one over there, by that lake. He tried to use his tentacles to drag me into the water and drown me. I snatched his tentacle and we started a tug of war. Then I roared for help. My companions and the unicorns came to aid me. The other tigers seized the remaining tentacles and pulled the Kraken toward our cave. Yes, we were able to pull him right out of the water. Then, a strange thing happened. As the unicorns thrust their golden horns into its mantle, it exploded! I mean, pieces of Kraken even stuck to the ceiling of this dome! The horn reacted violently to the ammonia in the Kraken's body and KA-BOOM! The Trader was furious because he had to clean up our domes. Do you how hard it is to clean the tops of these domes? They spent weeks getting that ammonia smell out of this dome. We lived with the unicorns until our dome was smell-free."

Eric gets up, walks to the lake and takes a drink. "This is fresh water. How can a Kraken live in fresh water? Is that a true story?"

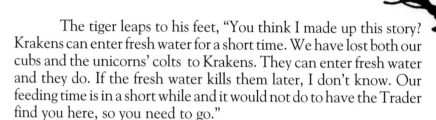

The tiger leaps to his feet, "You think I made up this story? Krakens can enter fresh water for a short time. We have lost both our cubs and the unicorns' colts to Krakens. They can enter fresh water and they do. If the fresh water kills them later, I don't know. Our feeding time is in a short while and it would not do to have the Trader find you here, so you need to go."

Eric and Raquelle give the unicorns and the saber-toothed tigers big hugs, then they leave. As they pass through the waterfall, Raquelle eyes twinkle, "We're all wet anyway, so let's go for a ride on Elizabeth." That is a great idea, so Eric and Raquelle race to the docks and dive into the water. Elizabeth and two of her offspring pop up, "Those grapes were delicious. We ate each grape, individually, until my children started spitting them at each other and they fell into the water. Then, fish came to eat the grapes that fell into the water and we had fresh fish with our grapes. What a great meal! Thank you! So, do you want to go for a ride?"

Eric climbs on Elizabeth's back and Raquelle climbs on one of her children. Giant flippers propel these enormous bodies through the water at breakneck speeds. Eric and Raquelle hang onto the long necks, but they cannot get their arms around them. Elizabeth is leading her child by four body-lengths, but Eric feels her strokes slowing. The youngster thinks, "I'm going to pass you, Mom!" With a burst of speed, the young dinosaur overtakes his mom and, for a moment, turns to look at her. From under the water comes a needlenose, pointed, small, one-man sub and it pierces the young one in the neck. Raquelle falls into the water, as Elizabeth grabs the sub and lifts it out of the water, by its needlenose point. The hood of the sub opens and a nobleman's son speaks, in a loud clear voice, "Put me down immediately or my father will hunt you down and kill you."

Elizabeth slams the small submarine down, and holds it under the water, until the young man releases his harness and floats to the surface. Then, she releases the sub and it slowly sinks. Elizabeth looks at her child, and at the cut in his neck. The gash looks deep, but the bleeding has stopped. Elizabeth bends down to lick the wound with her enormous tongue. Her tongue tells her that the wound is not that deep, and that her youngster will heal quickly. Then she turns her attention to the nobleman's son.

He is cursing all the Lake Guardians and their ancestors. He threatens that his father will have her hunted down and killed, for destroying his sub. Elizabeth wiggles her body to slide Eric off her back and into the water. Then she goes under the water and gently secures the other boy's feet. She rises out of the water, with the boy hanging from her mouth. As matriarch of her clan, she speaks with absolute authority; "Lake Guardians have ruled the lake of life since before humans came to our island. We allow you to live here but, when one of you shows us this kind of disrespect, then that one needs to be taken to the bottom of the lake of life, as quickly as possible, and into our caves for a breath of air. The air is very compressed and, when I quickly return you to the surface, you will explode. It is a painful death but, perhaps, you will drown on the way to the cave. So, now, you can either apologize to my child and bring him one basket of sweet grapes, each day, for a month, to help him heal or you can keep silent and I will show you the interiors of our caves."

The boy just dangles there for a moment, but Elizabeth can feel his body begin to shake, "I am sorry for hitting you with my sub and I will have one basket of sweet grapes delivered to you, on the dock, each morning, for one month."

Elizabeth drops the boy into the water, then she goes under, to come up, again, with Eric on her back; afterward, Raquelle climbs onto her back. Elizabeth looks at her other child, "You help this boy get to shore, but not on your back. Follow him, as he swims to shore. Just make sure he does not drown." Eric and Raquelle are delivered to shore.

They go back to their home. George is worried, and is pacing the floor, so he jumps on them, as soon as they enter the house. "Where were you?"

Raquelle gives a sideways glance, and waits for Eric to explain. He squares his shoulders and straightens his back, "Well, George, we went exploring. Since you won't tell us anything about the Trader and where he's from, we explored two of his bubbles. We met some unicorns!"

George jumps five feet into the air and, when he lands, he is foaming at the mouth, "You pea-brained little humans. The Trader could be dealing with the Slithers. Let me tell you how a Slither enjoys its food. First, they subdue you on the ground, then they start snipping off your fingers. They love fingers and toes, and the screams of humans are music to their ears, as they feast. Slithers take four hours to enjoy a whole human and most of them are alive for over three hours of incredible pain."

Sonya interrupts, "George, you are frightening the children."

George whirls around to face Sonya, "Shut up, Sonya." This is the first time he has ever snapped at Sonya and her head jerks backward. George's snarling face turns again to the children, "I came to this planet to retire, mate, and raise a thousand cubs. I owe you and your father ten lives. If you die under my protection, the Trader can send for the Light and they will come and take me away to a trial by the War Cats, and certain death."

Raquelle shakes her head, "George, we don't have any idea what you are talking about. Who is the Light?"

George roars loudly, "I will make this real simple for you. Our lives are intertwined, so I want to know every move you make. Do you understand?"

Eric puts his hands on his hips and makes a sour face, "We are not children and you can't watch us all the time, so we will have time away from you." Raquelle looks directly at George, and nods her head.

"Get to your rooms now!" Eric and Raquelle tromp off to their rooms.

George turns to Sonya. "A little sympathy would be appreciated."

"Go to your other mates. You growled at me." Sonya turns her back on him.

Chapter 8

Betrayed

A group of subs dives into the lake of life, then heads through the giant hole into the Atlantic Ocean, and sails west. A school of dolphins surrounds the sub; Eli concentrates very hard, to warn the dolphins that these subs are headed to attack Abaddon and the Krakens that protect the city. The school of dolphins heads off to round up whales for the coming battle. Sperm whales have the largest brain of any animal that has ever lived, so the whales are the aggressors in battles with giant squids. Whales love squid for lunch. The Kraken, or giant squid, fight valiantly because they are fighting for their lives. After an hour, a group of one hundred sperm whales follows the fleet of subs, flanked by the dolphins.

Eli concentrates on the maps, as Matthew approaches, "Eli, can we capture a Kraken and tow it back to Atlantis?"

Eli looks up from the maps, "Why would we want to do that?"

"I want to study it and have my children examine the body."

Eli goes to a shelf and removes a book on Krakens, "We have time before the battle, but I will make this brief. A Kraken has ten legs. Two are long tentacles and they are always positioned between the third and fourth arms. The eight arms are thicker than the tentacles, and they have a double row of suckers that decrease in size toward the ends. The suckers are made up of rings of chitinous teeth, which look like little white spikes and, when they latch onto you, they bite into your skin. The squid's mouth is a buccal cavity. This is like a giant parrot's beak, except that it is dark brown or black. The tentacles and arms bring food up for the beak to gouge out chunks of flesh, then the tongue-like projectile, a chitinous ribbon of backward-pointing teeth, shreds all skin, flesh, scales, or muscles into mush, to be digested. Squid's blood is hemocyanin, which means 'blue blood', and oxygenated squid's blood is almost colorless, with a bluish cast. The oxygen content of the water in which squids live is very important to cephalopods. If the oxygen content is low, the squids quickly lose their strength, become droopy, and die."

Matthew pounces on the last statement, "So, if we can reduce the amount of oxygen in the water, they will die?"

Eli nods his head, "Yes, Matthew, but how would you reduce the oxygen in the water? We have known this for years, but we haven't been able to find a way to reduce the oxygen level and kill the Krakens."

"Look, I need a small live Kraken to experiment on, so we can learn how to kill it. Have the dolphins bring two small Krakens back to the lake of life and deposit them by our dock."

"OK, Matthew, you try to contact the dolphins through our sub's hull and get them to bring you back two small Krakens."

Matthew goes to the front of the sub and concentrates hard. After a few moments, two dolphins are right outside the nose of the sub. Matthew explains that he wants two small squid captured and taken back to his dock.

Simultaneous answers explode inside Matthews's head. "Are you nuts? Do you know how tough even the small Krakens are? One wrong move and we are dolphin steaks. We will not take a live Kraken back. Besides, the trip is too long."

Matthew does some back-peddling to win the dolphins' cooperation, "Yes, you are right. A live Kraken would be too much trouble. But how about two small dead ones, taken back to my dock, in exchange for their weight in fresh fruits?"

Both dolphins flip their tails, and circle around the front of the sub and smile, "I love grapes, some purple berries, and some of those juicy, deep yellow fruits. Yes, a lot of those juicy, deep yellow fruits."

Matthew claps his hands. "This will all be done, when you bring the Krakens to my dock."

The dolphins bob their heads, then swim back to the main convoy of whales.

Matthew returns to Eli, as he prepares for the sea attack. Matthew feels useless because he is only an observer. Eli is the commander of this assault. He takes the intercom and coordinates the other subs' attacks, "When we see the Tears of Lucifer, the Krakens will attack. Keep in tight formation and wait for my signal to fire."

No light escapes from any of Eli's subs into the pitch-blackness. Matthew moves to the nose of the sub. He squints, as faint red glows appear in the distance. Eli orders the subs to cut their speed in half and to be on the alert for Krakens and enemy subs. Sonar reveals nothing in the water. Eli hovers over the sonar screen. They cautiously approach the two streams of magma, a half mile apart, flowing out of the side of the mountain. Matthew can vaguely make out a sinister face in the side of the mountain and it does look like he is crying bitter droplets of fire. This face holds Shalee, and Matthew's heart has a sharp pain pierce it. Suddenly, out of the magma, a firestorm of laser blasts flashes, that hits all of Eli's subs and causes the formation to crumble. They dive to escape the laser blasts, but from five hundred fathoms down, a barrage of mantles swiftly rises to meet them. Like a huge wrecking ball, the Krakens ram the subs and the mass of tentacles, arms, and mantles that floats to the surface attests to the fact that the Krakens held nothing back. Tentacles wrap every sub, and many whales become entangled with multiple squids. The dolphins are confused, but only for a moment; then they turn and slam into the squids' eyes. With the force of a cannonball, some of the dolphins break through the squids' eyes, so that their whole faces are embedded in the jelly of what once was the squids' eyes and they become stuck. Free whales bite the mantles of the dead squids in two, releasing the dolphins and the other whales. The fight becomes squids' tentacles versus dolphins' noses and whales' teeth.

Eli shouts into the intercom, "Break off the attack and return to Atlantis!"

All the subs are covered with Krakens and none of them can break free. The weight of the squids forces them down into the abyss. They use their jet propulsion to speed the descent. As they go beyond two hundred fathoms, Matthew grabs the intercom. "All subs, change your outer surface to clear and shine your whitest light, on my mark. Eli, on four, you switch on our whitest light. One, two, three, four--now!" The pitch darkness becomes as bright as a supernova, and the brilliant white light causes the Krakens to scatter and head deeper into the abyss.

The Krakens release the whales and the fleet is now free, as they turn to head back to Atlantis. More laser blasts from Abaddon's submarines hit the top half of Atlantis's fleet with deadly accuracy and, why not, because the Atlantian fleet is lit up like Las Vegas. Before Eli can order the lights to be turned off, half the Atlantian subs explode. This explosion blinds the Abaddonian subs, as the rest of the Atlantian fleet escapes. Eli shrieks into the intercom, "LIGHTS OFF AND FULL SPEED AHEAD!"

The concussion of that blast catches some small Krakens in its wake. They are stunned and just float in the water. One dolphin grabs a small Kraken in its teeth and heads for Atlantis. Another dolphin does the same and the pair heads for home.

The shattered fleet races for Atlantis. Eli is trying to communicate with the part of the Atlantian fleet that guards

Atlantis, but he can't raise them. Eli wrings his hands. "Raise the Atlantian fleet." The communications officer shrugs his shoulders and keeps trying.

Matthew takes on a bulldog face, "What just happened to us, Eli?"

"We just got screwed and didn't even get a kiss! They knew we were coming and we walked directly into their trap. The Abaddonian subs hid behind the flow of molten lava, so our sonar could not detect them. All their Kraken massed five hundred fathoms down in the abyss, waiting for the first laser fire from their submarines, then they rose to ram us. I can't contact the Atlantian fleet and, with our damaged subs, the Abaddonian fleet has a good chance of catching and destroying all of us. Any suggestions, Wolverine?"

Matthew turns and goes to the nose of the sub. Not only will Shalee not be rescued today, but his children may be fatherless. A massive sperm whale swims in front of Matthew's sub and, as he sees the giant tail go up and down, Matthew has an idea. He concentrates in the direction of the whales and, after a few moments, the pods of whales make a ninety-degree turn and head straight up toward the surface. Eli's fleet is losing speed because of the laser damage to their hulls. The Abaddonian fleet is closing fast and laser blasts are almost reaching the rear subs. The Krakens have stayed in the abyss because the fleet's captains want to enjoy this kill all by themselves. The Abaddonian captains pass under the rising whales, so they can fire on the Atlantian subs and they are almost within range.

Suddenly, the last trailing Abaddonian sub starts into a steep dive. It tries to rise, but continues its steep descent. Then the next submarine forward starts a steep dive. The whales have rested their massive bodies on the subs and are forcing them deeper. Soon, all of Abaddon's submarines are headed into a steep dive. The whales are piggybacking each other, to increase the weight on the enemy fleet, and doubling their tail speed, to hasten the dive.

The sonar operator on Eli's sub gasps, "Captain, the enemy subs have all taken a steep dive. I don't understand why, but they are breaking off the attack."

Then Matthew enters the cabin, "How deep can the Abaddonian subs dive before they implode?"

Eli looks puzzled, "Three hundred fathoms, maybe three hundred fifty fathoms, but no more."

"Stop your fleet and wait for the implosions."

Eli stops the fleet, but only under protest, and they wait for over two minutes. Every member of the crew is sweating profusely, but Matthew remains cool. From far, far below comes a resonating shock wave of compressed air. Sperm whales are racing for the surface inside this shock wave, and they break through, gasping for air. Eli surfaces all his subs, and whales spontaneously surround them, all the whales thinking the same thing at the same time. Matthew opens the hatch and walks on deck, to the largest of the sperm whales. It leans against the sub and Matthew strokes its skin, "Thank you for my life and for the lives of all these crew members. Did you lose any of your fellows in your descent?"

The whale's mouth turns into a smile, "Not a one; this was a good plan. You look sad. I am sorry we could not rescue your mate, but we live to fight another day, so you and your offspring have hope."

Whales have the largest brains of all animals and, as the sperm whale submerges, Matthew begins to understand just how much of their brains the whales actually use. They know compassion and empathy. He shakes his head and wonders why any man would hunt these giants of the deep. Then he goes below, as Eli submerges slowly, taking the fleet back to Atlantis for repairs.

Chapter 9

Repairs

The dolphins are the first to enter the giant hole, which leads to the lake of life. Lake Guardians greet the dolphins and learn of Matthew's defeat. Two dolphins struggle, as they swim; each drags a small Kraken in its mouth. Elizabeth challenges the dolphins on allowing Krakens to enter the lake of life. The dolphins are so tired, that their thoughts are confused. One dolphin drops its squid, and it slowly rises to the surface. "Eli's fleet was defeated and Abaddon's subs pursued them, as we raced ahead. We don't know if they were destroyed. Krakens for Wolverine-- exchanging for sweet grapes."

Elizabeth turns to the Lake Guardian on her right, "Help these dolphins. The rest of you follow me to rescue Matthew Wolverine." Elizabeth and about twenty other dinosaurs speed out of the tunnel.

The dolphin is so tired, it releases its grip on the squid. "Drop this Kraken on Wolverine's dock because we go to the nearest cave to rest." The dolphins don't even look to see if the Lake Guardian reacts, they just swim to the nearest cave and settle into the mud. It snatches the Kraken, then the sour taste of ammonia fills its mouth. The Lake Guardian swims, very quickly, to Matthew's dock and flips the squid up into the air. It seems to fly, then it hits the dock and rolls. Raquelle and Eric almost jump out of their skins, as this flying creature's tentacles brush their legs, as it comes to a stop on the dock. They rush down the dock looking for weapons with which to kill the Kraken. One of the Lake Guardians pops its head above the water and watches the children scurry for weapons. They wait for their father. The lake guardian quietly sinks below the water and heads for the giant hole. The matriarch of his family can tell them the bad news.

Eric convinces Raquelle to just let the squid die on the dock. They sit at the end of the dock and wait for their father. Soon a crowd of relatives of the submarine crews forms. A half-hour passes, before a battered sub emerges. The hatch opens and the crew rushes out. The relatives dart to the crewmen, hugging and kissing them and thanking God that they are alive. The majority of the crowds wait for the other submarines. A second sub docks and this crew disembarks more slowly, because they are wounded from laser blasts. They turn to see if any other subs appear. Raquelle reaches for Eric's hand; they wait as the minutes drag by. Then, with difficulty, a third sub struggles to surface, but cannot rise to the dock. Elizabeth and twelve other Lake Guardians push on the bottom of the sub to raise it to the dock.

The hatch quickly opens and out rushes the crew, then Eli and then Matthew. Just as Matthew leaps for the dock, the submarine slowly sinks. The Lake Guardians move from under the sub and it starts its descent to the bottom of the lake of life. Matthew turns to watch it sink. After it is gone, he looks at Elizabeth, "Are there any more subs coming back?" Elizabeth just shakes her head, "When we found you, we didn't go any farther back. I didn't think your sub was going to make it to the dock. Matthew, your fleet is gone."

Raquelle and Eric come down the dock and flank their father. At the other end of the dock, George appears and sees only two subs docked, so he heads back home to retrieve the blue diamonds. He goes straight to the submarine factory and hunts down the owner, "You were right about Matthew Wolverine defeating the Abaddonian fleet. Here is the bag of blue diamonds for your factory." He places the bag at the owner's feet. The man gives a hearty laugh, "I was just kidding about selling the factory. Why, with the defeat of Eli's fleet, submarine orders will double."

George inspects his front claws. Extending the claws and extending his pads to full size, he swipes the air, before he thinks, "Atlantis has a dome especially for combat. It is there that disputes are settled with the sword. I, of course, will use my claws, but you will use the sword. We start fighting at sunrise. It might take me an hour, or so, to disarm you, but the rest of the day, you will die a slow, agonizing death. So, by artificial sunset, you will be dead. I can go now to reserve the combat dome for us tomorrow or you can honor your offer and live a good life. Don't let me influence you but, when you are dead, who inherits the factory? I want to be able to set up the combat dome for them, the next day, so that I can slowly kill them, until your final heir honors your offer."

The owner swallows hard, as he appraises the black and yellow killing machine in front of him. He had made the offer in jest but, under Atlantian law, this War Cat has the right to challenge him for ownership. He had also made the mistake of bragging to his factory workers about the offer and they hated him for it, so they would testify for the War Cat. He is not going to die for the priests or the royalty. The owner calls his assistant and the man draws up the papers, selling the factory to the War Cat for a bag of blue diamonds.

George puts his paw print on the document, then the owner signs it,

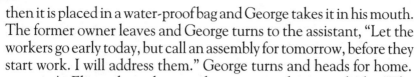

then it is placed in a water-proof bag and George takes it in his mouth. The former owner leaves and George turns to the assistant, "Let the workers go early today, but call an assembly for tomorrow, before they start work. I will address them." George turns and heads for home.

As Eli speaks to the crowd, one more submarine docks, "The other subs were lost in battle. You saw your relatives one last time before they died, thanks to the Wolverines. I am sorry for your losses." The crowd breaks up, and the tears are flowing freely.

"We tried, Matthew, but we were betrayed. We cannot fight Abaddon with only three subs. If you can get another fleet, I will lead the attack, but only with a fleet that has a chance of winning."

Matthew watches Eli leave with his wife and the other families that lost relatives today. His shoulders slump and Raquelle and Eric feel all of their father's weight leaning on them, as they help him back to their home. Matthew showers, then goes to bed.

George enters the home all excited, "Sonya, I purchased the submarine factory and I need your help!"

Sonya is surprised, "Why would you want to purchase and run a submarine factory?"

"Matthew suffered a humiliating defeat today. He needs another fleet of subs, so he can attack Abaddon and save his mate. This factory will build that fleet. Your expertise is needed to remove all the rats from the workers' homes. I know it is a hard job, but you can lead my other mates and have it done within two weeks."

Sonya smiles at George; killing rats is always a pleasurable experience and she will have two weeks of it. Sonya snuggles close to George, as they lie down to rest; they can hear Raquelle and Eric crying, softly, in the distance, as Matthew tosses and turns in his bed. Defeat is never easy, but they come in every war, and must be accepted. George closes his eyes and dreams of final victory.

The next morning, George is up before artificial sunrise. He eats quickly, then leaves for the factory. No one is there, and George has to wait an hour before a guard comes to let him in. He quickly reinspects the factory before his assistant arrives. Sonya and his other mates arrive at the same time. George has a makeshift stage erected and he and his mates ascend the steps. The workers drag themselves into the factory and turn to listen to their new boss. He stands upright, and roars. The rafters of the warehouse shake, then George thinks, "I am in charge of this factory now. The first area of business is your rat-infested homes. My mates, for the next two weeks, will kill all the rats they can catch in your homes and pile them in the street. It is your job to dispose of the rats at night. Your hovels will be torn down and new homes will be built, one at a time. You will pay for the new home out of your weekly wages, for the next twenty years, but you will have clean, rat-free homes to come home to, after your hard day's work. Next, you will shower every morning, and put on the green uniforms, which I will furnish for you. The uniforms are your responsibility. If you show up for work with a dirty uniform on, you will be sent home without pay. Two uniforms will be issued to each worker. There is a tailor at the end of the stage; get measured for your uniforms. Third, there will be a second shift. You will work on your homes after your shift. The lights in your dome will have a different sunrise and sunset. Lastly, this factory will be so clean, that I will be able to eat my fish off the floor tomorrow. If I find dirt in my fish, then you will have the choice of eating a meal off the floor or quitting. I will have workers that keep themselves clean and have pride in their work. Dismissed."

Sonya leads the pride to the workers' homes and they start killing rats. Before noon, the street is filled with rats. Sonya, with two large dead rats in her mouth, starts to climb the rat pile. The dead rats are slick; when these rats die, their bodies secrete an oil that covers them and makes them a challenge to climb on. As Sonya reaches the top of the pile, her right rear paw slips and down she rolls. She hits the ground hard and stares at the rat pile. "Ladies, we leave until tomorrow morning. Now, go home and get some sleep." Sonya returns home, exhausted, and finds Matthew still in bed. The children have gone to ride on Elizabeth, so she goes into a deep sleep. George arrives home long after sunset and bumps into her, as he lies down. She growls, gets up, and walks outside.

That night, Sonya ditches George and heads for the temple. The two black cats, which guard the temple, had extra fish tonight, and are sound asleep. Sonya slinks past them, and enters the temple. A staircase leads to an upper balcony. She quietly ascends the staircase, and peers down into the main sanctuary. It is empty, so she heads deeper into the temple. At the end of the next room, is a large hole in the wall. Sonya cautiously approaches and peers inside. The sound of the sea greets her ears and she sees a dim light at the end of the tunnel, as she enters. It is a tight squeeze and the tunnel is long and slopes down but, finally, Sonya comes to a ninety-degree turn. She lets all the air out of her lungs and stretches as flat as her body can, to make the turn. She comes out on a ledge, half the length of her body. The sound of water splashing against the shore assails Sonya's ears. She looks over the ledge, as two black-hooded priests emerge from a cave onto the beach. This chamber has artificial sun. The priests carry what looks like a statue of a huge black cat stretched straight out. They drop the statue near the water, and one priest reaches down to open it. The inside is hollow. Just then, Sonya begins to slip off the ledge. She looks up to see a figurehead, in the shape of a squid's head, embedded in the wall above her. She reaches up with both front paws and pulls herself up onto the top of the squid.

Now, with full view of the priests and hidden by the sculpture, Sonya sits down to watch what happens. A cotton-haired man walks out of another cave entrance and up to the priests. He hands the first priest something small and Sonya squints to see it. The priest holds two objects up to the light. They are blue diamonds. He motions toward the cave entrance and two other priests come out, each carrying a screaming naked baby. Each priest extends the child he holds and Sonya and Cotton-hair can both see that they are females. He nods and the babies are placed in the hollow sculpture. The white-haired man waves the priests off. After they disappear into the cave, Cotton-hair moves to the statue, closes the lid, and locks it. Then he moves to a small boulder on the beach and moves the rock. The water bubbles in the small pond, as four small Kraken surface. They stare at the statue of the black cat. Cotton-hair pushes the statue into the water, toward them. The babies inside the statue freeze with fear, as the cat drifts toward the squids. The man laughs, with a high-pitched sound, as one baby shifts her weight and the cat sculpture moves slightly in the water. One Kraken swiftly enfolds the statue in his tentacle, then submerges. The other three squids scan the waters and, seeing no other cats, return to the water.

The older man moves the small boulder back into place, then retreats into the cave, where he turns the artificial sun down to twilight, then leaves.

Sonya considers what just happened, as she waits a full five minutes before she stirs. She drapes herself lengthwise over the squid, then extends her paws toward the ledge. With her back legs braced against the sculpture, she lightly scratches the right wall of the tunnel exit. Then she slides down to the ledge to view the scratch's height. It is the height of the rump of a black cat. Sonya purrs, as she studies how to get to the beach. She turns and runs along the ledge, as it circles downward toward the beach, but it stops at three times her body length above the sand. She reckons that she can make the jump back up to the ledge, so she leaps down to the ground. She scans the water for Krakens, but the surface of the water is like glass. Sonya goes to the small boulder and moves it and, just as quickly, moves it back. Violent bubbles rush to the surface, and they carry in them, the strong smell of ammonia. She curiously goes to the water; the tip of a Kraken's tentacle floats to the beach. The tigress muses that the Krakens wait there, to be summoned. With her curiosity satisfied, she leaps back onto the ledge, then heads for home.

George is still asleep in the hallway leading to Matthew's bedroom. Sonya slinks within a body's length of him and starts to purr softly. He quickly opens his eyes, "Feeling a bit frisky, are we?" She increases her purring. George rises, moves over to Sonya and begins to rub her face. The rubbing becomes more intense and they both rise up on their hind legs.

Just then, Eric steps out of his bedroom and bumps into Sonya and George, knocking them over. Eric, still half asleep, blurts out, "What are you doing, George?"

George stammers, "Well, we were stretching our legs. Why are you up? Are you sick?"

Eric shakes his head, then Sonya blasts out, "We weren't stretching our legs, we were trying to make little tigers. Now, go to the bathroom and get back to bed!"

Eric shakes his head to wake up, then goes to the bathroom and back to bed, but he listens. As George and Sonya continue playing, Eric snickers. Sonya storms out of the house, with George close behind.

From the shadows, four figures watch the tigers move away from the house until they are out of sight. With the animals out of sight, four priests come out, each carrying a large wicker basket. They go to the door of the Wolverine house and dump the contents through the tiger entrance in the front door. Black snakes slither out of the baskets, and into the Wolverine house. A black carpet moves over the floor toward the Wolverine's bedrooms. The black snakes enter the first room, where George's other eight mates are sleeping. As the river of black snakes tries to back out of the room, black snakes slither over black snakes, and tempers flair. The hissing and striking of the snakes moving over the pack, wakes the tigers. Before they fully awaken, the river of black snakes enters Raquelle's bedroom and she awakens and jumps out of her bed. She lands in a sea of the creatures, and three of them strike her legs. Raquelle screams, "Snakes!" then jumps back onto the bed, but the three serpents have buried their fangs in her legs.

Raquelle pulls the first snake's fangs out of her leg, and throws it in the air; it lands on the salt pile in the corner of her room. The sounds of the snake sizzling and its death hiss fill the room. She snatches the other two serpents' fangs out of her legs and throws them on the salt pile. The river of black snakes heads for Eric's room.

84

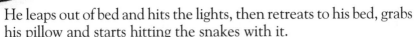

He leaps out of bed and hits the lights, then retreats to his bed, grabs his pillow and starts hitting the snakes with it.

Raquelle shouts, "Salt kills them! Throw salt on the snakes!" She leaps from her bed, to the salt pile, and launches handfuls of salt onto the black sea. The snakes retreat into the hallway.

Matthew grabs his sword, as he rises from his bed. He pulls on his boots and heads for the hallway.

Eric sees many snakes arch up to full height, then slither onto his bed. He makes a leap for the salt pile, but falls short. Two of the snakes rush to strike his heel, and sink their fangs in deep. He turns, with two handfuls of salt, and coats the snakes. They remove their fangs and try to retreat, as the salt burns through their skin. They don't make it to the door before the salt burns them to cinders. Eric throws handfuls of salt as far as he can, into the hallway. The hisses of dying snakes fill the house.

Matthew meets the snakes' head on; his arm is like an electric fan, severing snakes' heads from their bodies, but the black river keeps coming. One snake uses Matthew's sword stroke to become airborne and lands on his shoulder. This snake quickly strikes at the base of Matthew's neck. Its fangs sink deep below the skin and quickly inject poison. Matthew's left hand rises to wrench the snake off his shoulder but only the snake's body comes away. Its head and fangs remain embedded in Matthew's neck.

The tigers scoop pawfuls of snakes onto their litter piles. The snakes strike at each tiger and some strikes hit their marks and inject poison into the cats. The black river dwindles to a trickle, until, at last, all snakes are covered with salt.

Matthew reaches up to pull the snake's head from his shoulder and notices that the poison sacs are still attached to the head. The sacs are empty. He knows he got the full dose of venom infused into his body. He just drops the serpent's head on the floor.

Eric crawls from his room, "Dad, my foot is on fire." Matthew picks up his son and places him back in his bed. He looks at Eric's heel. It is scarlet. He wipes his sword on the sheets and cuts an "x" in his son's heel. Eric screams, as Matthew sucks out some of the poison.

Raquelle crawls from the salt pile, as one of the tigers enters her room. The tiger puts its tail in her face and she grabs hold. It pulls Raquelle into Eric's room and to Matthew. She releases the tiger's tail, "Dad, three snakes bit my legs. Help me!"

Matthew rises from the bed, but fire rushes to his brain. He grabs his head, clenches his teeth, then everything goes black, as he falls on top of the tiger's back. She sags, but bears his weight, as the other tigresses enter the room. They discuss what to do and it is decided to wait for George to return. Raquelle is helped back to her bedroom and Matthew is carried to, then dumped on his bed.

After an hour, the humans and the cats are moaning with aching pain. George and Sonya cautiously enter their home and see the black-coated floors. George goes up to one of the tigresses, who is grimacing with pain, "What happened?"

"Poisonous snakes attacked us and we were all bitten. The girl was bitten three times. The Wolverines fought hard, but Matthew was bitten in the neck and his son in the heel. As we fought the snakes, we found that salt dissolved their bodies. All the bodies should be cinders by now. Can you counteract the poison, George?"

George tells Sonya to go get Eli, and she races out the tiger door. He goes to Matthew's room and, with a giant paw, pushes Matthew over on his side. The fang marks on his neck are scarlet red. George gently places his paw on the fang marks and they are hot. He turns and goes to Eric's room. He removes the blankets and sheets from Eric and inspects his heel. The heel is a deep purple and George knows that Matthew has sucked out most of the poison. Eric will be sick, but he will survive. Raquelle is a different matter; her leg is inflamed. He counts the fang marks. Because of his combat experience, George knows that three wounds from a viper spell death within two weeks, unless there is a blood transfusion.

Eli storms into the house, "George, how could you let this happen?"

George's shoulders fall, as he thinks, "I was derelict in my duty. Now, can you get the Trader and his cats out of their compound for about an hour?"

"It is the middle of the night. How can I get him out of his compound?"

George turns to Sonya, "I can get him out of his compound, but you must send a message on his large transmitter. You fit your paws into what look like large gloves. Your head slips into a round gold band and you think your message. Your message must be thought word-for-word, 'A Slither's Nightmare requests the repayment of three life-debts by his leader, with three pints of the leader's own blood, but it must be delivered only by a Centurion. I command, as a War Cat, who has been awarded Five Bloody Paws, that all War Cats that receive this message relay it to our leader. My leader's blood must be delivered to Atlantis, on the planet Earth, with the speed of light. May God grant you death in battle with a

Slither's flesh on each fang! Until our final victory, A Slither's Nightmare."

Sonya concentrates on every word George says, then she thinks it back to him. He nods, "Sonya, I will go to the Trader's compound. When I leave with him and his cats, you sneak into the compound. Find the transmitter, then broadcast my message for one hour. Eli, you go with her, to time the transmission."

Eli shakes his fist violently. "No, I will stay and comfort the Wolverine family."

George growls. "They are dead, unless they get blood from my leader. So, go with Sonya and do some good."

George goes out the tiger door and races to the Trader's compound and scratches on the door. He hears growls from the other side of the door, as the lights come on. The Trader opens the door slowly and stares at him. The man holds an equalizer. The laser blasts from this weapon can cut through a battleship, lengthwise, in less than a minute, and George knows he faces death. Two small black cats run between the Trader's legs and attack George. He falls backward and George leaps straight up, then does a one hundred eighty-degree turn, and lands on the two cats. He has one paw on each of their throats. George makes his offer, as the Trader rises, " What does the blood of a War Cat sell for today?"

The Trader curses, as he rises, "One blue diamond per pint."

George shifts his weight to his front paws and the black cats' air shuts off. The cats claw wildly at his paws and, just as quickly, he releases them. The cats rise, choking and spitting, but they stagger back inside, to stand behind the Trader, who now has the equalizer pointed at George. The tiger sighs, then turns to walk toward the docks. After he has taken ten steps, he turns his head, "The blood of a War Cat, who has been awarded Five Bloody Paws is worth far more than that, but we can talk as we walk."

The Trader's head snaps toward George, as he half-heartedly pulls the door, but the War Cat picks up his pace, and is around a building, as the Trader races after him, his cats on his heels.

Sonya and Eli sneak to the door and push it open. It had not locked. They search the compound, but can't find the transmitter. Eli stares at a wall of books. He reaches for a book titled, "The Red Serpent and the Fall of Atlantis". The bookcase slides open, and there is the transmitter. Sonya pounces on the machine, puts her paws in the gloves and the band around her head, and starts broadcasting. After almost an hour, Sonya is tired and there has been no response from out there. Sonya wonders where "out there" is. Eli

puts his hand on her shoulder. "We must leave, now."

Sonya tries to pull her paws out of the transmitter's gloves, but they hold fast. She panics and pulls as hard as she can, trying to withdraw her paws. One glove bends slightly, as they release her paws. Eli tries to bend it back into shape, but it remains crooked. They leave, and she heads to the Wolverine house and Eli heads for his home.

It takes the Trader over an hour, before he asks George the question that he wants to ask, "How would you like to go back into service for five years, guarding the daughter of a leader?"

George shivers all over, "No way! Good night." He races to the Wolverine house.

Chapter 10

Madness

The next morning, Eli goes to Matthew's room, to comfort him. As he stands beside the bed, Matthew's left hand flies up to Eli's throat and Matthew lifts him off the ground. He is screaming at the top of his lungs, "Die, serpent, die!" Eli fights to free himself, then he races from the room. George stands at the door and is bowled over by the fleeing man.

George and Sonya stare at Matthew, who is violently tearing at the air around his bed. George's thoughts run deep, "Sonya, they need a human to care for them day and night. I hate human slavery. I have fought my entire military career for human freedom, but if your message didn't get through, then they are headed for one long, excruciating, painful death. We can purchase a slave girl to comfort them in their last days, then set her free when they die."

Sonya lowers her head, "What about your other mates. Will they die?"

George takes a deep breath, " If the Trader takes eight pints of blood from me, then injects one pint into each of them, they will live--but I will not survive that much blood loss."

Sonya jumps to her paws, "That is unacceptable. I need you! The future generations of tigers on earth need you. How much blood can you give safely?"

"Three pints, but I need a week of total rest to restore my strength. Half a pint of blood to each of six mates gives them a ninety-percent chance of surviving. Two will have to die, and you must choose the two."

Sonya nods her head and goes to the safe and opens it; then she picks up two bags of coins and George does the same. He shuts the safe and makes sure it is locked. After they walk out the door, George looks back, "We leave them unguarded, but our enemies would not give them such a merciful death as to kill them now." George's and Sonya's tails shoot straight up and they walk to the Trader's shelter.

A black-robed priest answers the door, "Your business?"

George pushes his way inside, "We are here to bid on a slave girl. Now, where are they bidding?"

The priest touches one of Sonya's bags and feels the coins. "This way."

George and Sonya enter a large hall, with the nobility seated on the left and the priests seated on the right. One of the priest's black cats creeps up to Sonya's bags and sniffs them. Sonya's right paw moves in a blur and smashes the cat's head into the floor. Her claws dig into the unconscious cat's back and she flings him into the pack of yowling black cats at the priests' feet.

The Trader appears out of nowhere, "We are here to buy and sell, not to fight. Now, bring the five girls out for all to behold."

Two shirtless muscular priests escort five cream-skinned blondes onto the stage. Sonya jumps on the stage and inspects each girl for disease and cleanness. George performs the same procedure, but they all smell good to George. Sonya meticulously examines each girl's feet and hands for fungus and human waste under the nails. Then she licks the palm of the last girl. The girl stiffens, and Sonya tastes fear in her sweat. The tigress asks the girl her name.

In a soft voice, the girl breathes, "Desiraa." Desiraa's eyes call to her father in the front row for protection, but he shakes his head.

The Trader comes on stage and orders George and Sonya off, so the bidding can start. George glares at him, "When my mate and I are through inspecting your merchandise, we will leave. You forget your place, Trader. You are only a merchant, while I am a War Cat, who has won our highest honor--Five Bloody Paws and, if you give me another order, your face will be on the ground in front of you. Go over and count the money in my bags."

The Trader's face tightens, but he proceeds to George's bags and opens them. He grabs a fist full of Spanish silver pieces of eight and sneers--worthless silver. Then his eyes narrow, as he raises his hand close to his face. Among the pieces of eight are sprinkled blue diamonds. The Trader quickly shoves his hand into the bag and releases the contents, opens the bag wide and closely inspects the contents. About a fourth of the bag is blue diamonds. The Trader calls over a priest and tells him to get four cords to tie the bags. Each bag is one-fourth full of blue diamonds. The Trader shakes his head; the Ghouls were smart to put their wealth among silver. Who would even stoop down to pick up a bag of silver? The priest returns and the Trader ties the cords double tight. That stupid War Cat doesn't know the value of his bags.

George finishes his inspection and sits in the middle of the aisle, as Sonya retrieves the four money sacks and sets them beside him.

The Trader glares sharply at George. "War Cat, I am sorry to

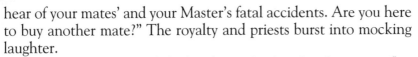

hear of your mates' and your Master's fatal accidents. Are you here to buy another mate?" The royalty and priests burst into mocking laughter.

George waits until the laughter subsides, then he rises to flex his muscles and answer the Trader, "I am new at slave trading, but I had heard that what I do with my property is my business. So, Seller of Humans, what is the truth?"

The Trader swallows hard; one swipe from either of George's paws could cleave a man in two. The Trader stiffens his back and booms out his words, "All sales are final. You buy the property and do what is good in your eyes. Now, let us start the bidding."

Desiraa's eyes open wide, as they scream to her father to stop this madness. She is a good daughter and she wants her family to have a better life, but not this way. Her father sits rigid, staring lovingly at the four bags by George. Desiraa feels her mouth go dry, then she watches the tigers closely to see if he or his mate would bid on either of the first four females. The average bid for a female is twenty-five gold coins. Each of the first four girls is beautiful, in her own right, and the royals and the priests bid over one hundred gold coins for each. George and Sonya are as still as the Sphinx, as the priests and royalty fight over the first four girls. Bags of gold coins amass at the Trader's feet. The fourth girl is won by the royalty, for one hundred fifty gold coins, and is escorted from the stage. The Trader distributes a bag of money to each girl's father after each sale. The priests working for the Trader find this unusual because he usually has them count the money, then pay the fathers.

The Trader scratches the back of his hand, counts the bags at his feet, then weighs the number of guards present against the strength of a War Cat. He leaves the stage and walks to the back of the room. He would give four-to-one odds on the War Cat winning. Joshua enters the room from the side and the Trader turns to face him. He carries a large red eel skin bag bulging with gold coins, "For Desiraa, so start the bidding."

The Trader wets his lips and leaps onto the stage, "Look at her skin. Why, it is as soft as dolphin skin and she is as strong and quick as a Mako shark. She has been trained to give all known pleasures to a man, but she could also be trained to give pleasure to a beast, because she is smart. Start the bidding at ten gold coins? A priest in the front row raises his hand, and the race is on. The Trader looks to the royalty and a young nobleman raises the bid to twenty gold coins. George stands and thinks fifty gold coins. Joshua loudly shouts, "One hundred gold coins!" Desiraa's eyes flash for her

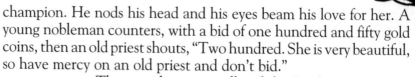

champion. He nods his head and his eyes beam his love for her. A young nobleman counters, with a bid of one hundred and fifty gold coins, then an old priest shouts, "Two hundred. She is very beautiful, so have mercy on an old priest and don't bid."

The room becomes still and the Trader sees his blue diamonds flying away, so he blurts out, "George, you have at least three hundred gold coins. Is that your bid?"

George nods his head, as the blood drains from Desiraa's face. Joshua recounts his gold coins, in his head, but still only comes up with 297 gold coins.

The Trader quickly counts, "Going, going…"

A gray-bearded nobleman booms out, "Four hundred gold coins for this wench, as a birthday present for my son and, perhaps, to me after he is done with her."

The royalty section cheers the bid, as they point and laugh at George and Sonya. The Trader's rules are clear: the gold coins must be inside the room, once the bidding starts.

The Trader will not be cheated out of his blue diamonds. "Priests, count the gold coins available for that bid in front of me."

The royalty section and the priests boo the Trader, but his priest brings the bag forward and starts to count. The count records only 275 gold coins. This nobleman had bought another girl and forgotten to deduct that purchase. The other noblemen quickly loan the grey-bearded man coins and they are passed up to the front. The count reaches 398 gold coins but that is all the gold from the royals' section.

George looks at Sonya, "I miscalculated, but we need that woman. Are you sure she is healthy?"

Sonya nods her head, then George rises, "Trader, how much is five years of guarding by a War Cat worth?"

The Trader stares hard at George and rubs his chin, "You would serve anyone I sell you to for five years?"

"Only for five years, and then I am free to return to Atlantis."

The priests rise in unison, "No, we will accept only money to bid on this prize and the money must be in this room." The nobles side with the priests and the Trader sees future profits slipping away.

"The money must be in the room. Those are the rules, but I stipulate that George has three hundred gold coins in his bags. So, are there any other bids?"

The nobleman's son and his father jump up and rush the stage to grab Desiraa. She looks at her father, at Joshua, then at the lust in the noblemens' eyes and her head sinks.

Joshua strides up to George and Sonya and lays his bag beside Sonya; then he shouts, "The War Cat bids five hundred ninety-seven gold coins, and I suggest that the Trader take that bid. This War Cat is unfamiliar with slave trading and might just start killing priests, if they cheat him out of this woman, by lending money to this nobleman--and I would help him. So, Trader, avoid violence and accept the bid."

"Going, going, gone" The Trader grabs two of the bags of gold coins from around his feet and thrusts the bags into Desiraa's father's arms. "You are paid. Run out of here." The father clutches the bags, as he races up the aisle to the door, then outside to his home.

Desiraa's heart sinks, as her father flees. Her head drops, so her blonde hair conceals her face. Then her eyes fill with tears, as the flow begins. The tips of her blonde hair catch the droplets and soon are soaked.

George leaps onto the stage and releases a roar that shakes the chairs. One old priest falls over another, trying to escape, as pandemonium follows. Royals, priests, and guards scurry out the doors. Then there are only Desiraa, Joshua, the Trader, George, and Sonya.

"This gold and your bags are mine for this girl. Now, take her."

George cautiously approaches Desiraa. His ears pick up her soft crying. He rises on his hind legs and places his front paws on her shoulders. Desiraa screams, "No! I won't mate with you! Kill me, if you must!"

Joshua moves to pull his sword. Sonya's paw lights on his hand, forcing him to the floor, as she throws her body weight on top of him. As she falls on him, her other front paw, claws out, covers his throat.

Desiraa is now sobbing uncontrollably. George's thoughts blast into Desiraa's mind, "Snap out of it! I want you to care for my sick friends, day and night. That is why I bought you."

Desiraa lunges at George and grabs him in a bear hug. "Thank you, thank you, thank you!"

George gently pats her on the back, with one front paw, "Desiraa, we need to leave. My friends are violently sick from the poison of black snakes. Sonya, release Joshua; we need to get back home now!"

Sonya releases Joshua and he flies to Desiraa, to hold her. She clings to him, as they leave to go to Matthew's home. When they arrive, George smells intruders by the front of the house. He enters alone, with fur bristled. He starts at the front of the house and examines each room. When he reaches Raquelle's room, the scent is strong. She is awake, but tied with ropes, and she calls to George. "They came into the room, but I couldn't even get out of bed. Then I lapsed back into convulsions. The convulsions led to blackness and, when I awoke, they were gone. Did they hurt Eric or my father?"

"I will check and report back to you." Eric is tied with rope and is repeating one word over and over, "Water". George turns and rushes to Matthew's room. He has broken one bond and grabbed his sword, which he swings over his head. George jets under Matthew's arm and seizes his wrist in his mouth. He forces Matthew's arm to the ground, then puts his rump on the sword and breaks Matthew's grip on the sword. He slides the sword to the door, then releases Matthew's wrist and proceeds to scout the rest of the house. The vault door is wide open, so they had the combination. George enters cautiously. About half the bags of gold are missing; all the gold bars and all the blue diamonds are gone. They left in a hurry. George takes a deep sniff. The scent of the incense used by priests fills the room. They stole Matthew's wealth. So much for retirement on this beautiful planet. George heads outside to confer with Sonya, Joshua, and Desiraa.

"The priests ransacked the vault and stole much of the gold and all the blue diamonds. Desiraa, you and Joshua go inside and tie Matthew's loose arm. Then Joshua, run to Eli to see how many men will follow you to attack the priests. Sonya and I will attack the temple."

George and Sonya walk toward the temple at a slow pace. Sonya questions George about attacking so soon, "Shouldn't we wait for Eli's men?"

George's face becomes hard as flint about the coming battle. "No. There are traitors among us, and I don't know whom to trust. Eli will either come with his men or he won't. We take the priests by surprise by attacking now." As they near the temple, Sonya races ahead and loudly thinks, "I will take out the black cats, while you kill the priests."

The two black cats, on guard in the front of the temple, roar loudly, as Sonya bounds up the stairs and smacks the first cat against the wall. It hits, rump first, breaking both back legs and its spine. Howling in pain, it lays where it landed. As she runs toward the temple, the second cat leaps at her and her left front paw slides between its outstretched paws and her claws rip into its throat, driving it back to the door. She hits the door with such force that the cat is just a bloody mess on her left paw, as the doors fly open. Cats from all over the temple converge in the front of the sanctuary. Sonya flings the remains of the cat off her left paw and into the herd of cats. She quickly ascends the staircase and heads into the hole in the wall. She squeezes into the hole and inches her way in deeper. The hole seems to be smaller or, maybe, Sonya has just been eating too much fish. She reaches the ninety-degree angle and gets stuck. She exhales completely, but still, she is stuck. What a way to die. Those cats will claw her back legs and butt, taking chunks of fur and flesh, until she slowly bleeds to death. With a violent roar, Sonya exhales all the air in her lungs and pulls herself, with her front claws, onto the tunnel's floor. Her front claws dig into the stone and catch. Inch by inch, her midriff comes forward, but her fur doesn't. Sonya can smell her blood and feel the cutting away of her fur, but still, she pulls and makes the turn. She crawls out of the hole and onto the ledge. Her middle section is furless and blood seeps out, so she rolls on the ledge, to deposit her blood, then she pulls herself onto the figurehead of the squid and waits for the first cat to come out.

A snarling black cat materializes from the tunnel and sniffs the blood. Sonya moves a front paw behind his rump and throws him off the ledge. The cat squeals all the way down, until it goes under the water.

The cat swims in the water, trying to climb the wall, to get at Sonya. As the other cats pour out of the tunnel, she flings them into the air, and into the pond below. Her claws are extended and, after the first few cats, she discovers that, by reaching lower, she can rip the tendons in their back legs, clear up to the butt, as she hurls them into space. Now, they hit the water and sink. Their back legs are too badly damaged to keep them afloat. Only the first few cats that she threw into the water still claw at the wall, as they swim. The last black cat emerges from the tunnel, but Sonya's left front paw aches, so she waits a full minute before phase two of her plan commences.

When she is sure all the black cats are in the water, she leaps onto the ledge and races for the beach. She jumps down to the beach and swiftly moves the rock. The pond bubbles, as the black cats try to swim to the beach. Up from the deep, pop four Krakens; the black cats splash and claw at the water, trying to reach the beach. The Krakens are confused by all the moving boxes, but only for a moment, then their tentacles ensnare the black cats and they return to the water. Then four more squids appear, and drag more cats to their deaths. Other Krakens enter the trapdoor to see dead cats on the lake bottom. They grab the dead cats in their tentacles and turn to go back to the Red Serpent. Soon the pond is calm; Sonya turns to sprint into the tunnel to help George with his battle.

George is in the main sanctuary, fighting over one hundred priests. They have swords and spears. George sends some of the spears from the priests' hands back into the advancing crowd. He is sustaining minor cuts from the swords and is being forced out the front door, as Sonya ascends from the lower level. The priests are facing George, and have their backs toward Sonya. Her eyes twinkle, as she launches herself, with all claws extended, into the backs of the priests. Like dominoes, a wave of priests falls forward, shoving swords and spears into the backs of the priests in front of them. George just catches a glimpse of Sonya, so he leaps backward; then they pounce on the pile of fallen priests and slash away. George transforms into a War Cat in battle and the heat of fresh enemy blood seizes his mind. His claws sling arms, legs, and heads into the air. George glares in Sonya's direction and his eyes are bathed in hatred and are blood-red. She leaps backward and lands beside five priests, who are trying to escape. Sonya rips through their flesh to get safely away from George. She turns about in front of the tunnel's entrance. He is still launching body parts, as Eli and the other sailors enter the temple.

Eli's men attack the fallen priests and the battle is over in a few minutes. To their knowledge, no priest has escaped. Sonya ascends the pile, "Eli, your men need to dispose of the bodies-- through this tunnel and into a pond at the end. When the last body is placed in the pond, remove all your men to the tunnel and go onto the beach and push the rock forward, then hurry back into the tunnel to watch."

Eli orders the men to transport the bodies, as George and Sonya head back to Matthew's house. The first of Eli's men throw the body parts into the water, and a Kraken surfaces to snare the body parts and start eating. The man jumps back, just as other men fill the beach with bodies. They throw them into the water, as more squids rise to feast. The Krakens do not attack the men on the beach, but patiently wait for more bodies to be deposited into the water. Sonya forgot to close the stone, so the creatures remain, until the last body is dumped into the pond. Then the Krakens submerge and Eli pulls the rock back into place, closing their doorway.

Chapter 11

Shalee's Nightmare

The next day, Nicole and Shalee slip out the door and into an alleyway. They approach an airlock and pass through to a large deck, where they hide behind some boxes. The Krakens throw dead black cats onto the deck. From a large glass tunnel, out slithers the Red Serpent to feed on the black cats. The cats keep piling up and the Red Serpent keeps eating. Vipurr and another priest approach the Red Serpent, "Why are there so many black cats, instead of babies? What do you think the priests of Atlantis desire from us?"

The Serpent swallows a large black cat, then he stops eating, "We supplied the black snakes to kill Matthew Wolverine, his children, and the tigers. They will all be in excruciating pain, for two weeks, before they leave this planet. What is more precious to a priest than his familiar--a black cat? These Atlantian priests give their god a delicious sacrifice. The Atlantians are so stupid; their priests have worked for me for centuries, but the royalty and the navy stopped me from taking over Atlantis. Now that the Ghouls are dead, so is the power of the royalty, and Atlantis will be mine. Vipurr, you will rule over the priests of Atlantis, until I eat them one by one."

Nicole struggles to restrain Shalee, but in vain, as she marches toward Vipurr and the Red Serpent. "You are mistaken, if you think I believe that black snakes could bite my husband and my children."

Vipurr is nervously looking for guards to subdue Shalee, as the Red Serpent dances with joy. The Red Serpent's speech is coated with honey, "Yes, my children have bitten your family and they die an agonizing death. This gives me such joy. So you have no hope, but now you have free access to all Abaddon until the red tide. Vipurr, make sure that this sacrifice and all the maids have free access to all of Abaddon, because she has no hope—no reason to leave. Priest, go to the other priests, and inform them of our supreme triumph over Atlantis and tell them to give the sacrifices free admission to all of Abaddon." Then the Red Serpent rises as high as it can off the ground. The bulges from the numerous black cats he had eaten stretch his skin. "Vipurr, have the other priests, and all of our people, come to my temple to worship me. Victory is sweet and I need to be told how wonderful I am."

Nicole pulls Shalee's arm, and a stunned Shalee turns to

leave. At just that instant, a Kraken hurls a skull onto the dock and it rolls into the Red Serpent's bulging stomach. "Where did you get this skull?"

Krakens are slow thinkers and it takes it a few moments to remember where it got the skull. "From the pond in the Atlantian Temple. We ate the rest of the bodies, but saved this skull for you."

Nicole guides Shalee out the door and she is determined to explore Abaddon. Shalee is in shock, at the news of her family. Nicole needs to snap her back into escape mode. "Could you help your family if you were there?"

Shalee's whole body shakes. "You have a plan?"

"No, but we have freedom to explore all of Abaddon. Will you waste this opportunity?"

She comes to her senses, and they explore the next dome. After Nicole shuts the hatch, the dome is dark, and it takes a few moments for their eyes to adjust to the darkness. A railroad track runs to a gaping hole in the wall. Nicole hears movement coming from the other end of the track and, soon, they see a large metal cart, filled with rocks, coming toward them. A muscular man wearing only a loin cloth, and with sweat pouring down his filthy face, stares dumbly at the women, but only for a moment. "This is the best dream I have ever had--but you are wearing clothes. The women in my dreams don't wear clothes."

Shalee steps forward, "This is not a dream. We are from the temple."

Before she can finish her sentence, the man is on his knees and he grabs Shalee's feet, "Please, don't take me to the Red Serpent. I don't want to turn into one of his little snakes. I mine the blue diamonds from the meteors. See, this cart is full of them."

Shalee reaches into the cart, and pulls out a rock, the size of a giant chicken's egg. Nicole does the same. The rock is smooth, but it is too dark to see any more. "So, you mine blue diamonds from a meteor? Explain."

The man looks up and wonders if this is a test, "As you know, many eons ago, a shower of blue meteors struck Abaddon. The creatures that lived inside them bored five miles deep into our coal field. They metamorphosed our coal by absorbing it and excreting small blue diamonds, the size of your fingernail, in the middle of their white excretion. These are like birds' eggs, but with a blue diamond in the center. Crack what you have in your hand and remove the blue diamonds."

Nicole strikes her rock on the side of the metal cart and it turns to dust, but in the middle is a smooth gem. Shalee does the same.

"See, I told you they contain the blue diamonds. We are having a hard time finding them now because, as you know, the Red Serpent ate all the blue creatures as they surfaced to absorb sunlight over a one thousand-year period. That is why he lives forever. Once a year, he must expel all his old tissue in the red tide, which kills many fish in the sea; then, afterward, he must obtain fresh blood. That is why he needs the sacrifices every day for one month."

Nicole goes to the hatch and slightly opens it, to see her blue diamond. The blue hue of the diamond envelops her whole body. The man shields his eyes from the light but, eventually, he can look at Shalee and Nicole, and he gasps. "You have green eyes. Your chemistry mixes with the blue creatures' to give the Red Serpent even more power. You can't be one with the Red Serpent, can you?"

"No, I am supposed to be the next sacrifice, after the red tide. So, I want the Red Serpent to die, as soon as possible. Will you help us?"

The man's eyes twinkle, "I hate the Red Serpent and, if I help you, I want to be released from this mine into sunlight. I want to die in the sun, as a whole man."

Shalee clasps his hand, "You have my word; your help will be justly rewarded. Only, how can you help us?"

"I, Jon, will rally the other miners to your cause. On the day of battle, you can count on the other miners and me to fight for you. Just let me know when you need us to fight. Now, go, before they discover you here."

Nicole opens the hatch and they exit into the sunlight. They proceed to the next dome and open the hatch. Inside, is a swamp filled with shimmering black snakes; hoardes of the snakes slither over each other in the dismal swamp. Their hisses sound like, "Please, let us out." Nicole quickly closes the hatch, "These are men and women in the final stage of conversion to black snakes. The Red Serpent keeps them in this swamp, for six months after conversion, to win their loyalty. They would do anything to escape from here and I would do anything to never wind up here."

Shalee needs some answers, "You say that these are men and women. For all these eons that the Red Serpent is supposed to have lived, I don't notice a large population. Where are all the people?"

Nicole bites her upper lip. "The Red Serpent drains blood daily from our population, but it also needs calcium from new bones. Very young bones are best. So, the other nine women and myself

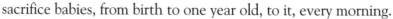

sacrifice babies, from birth to one year old, to it, every morning.

Abaddon's population is now too small to feed the Red Serpent so he has the Trader, and the priests of Atlantis send him fresh babies. We all share the guilt."

Shalee just looks at Nicole for a long while. This much vile information causes revulsion, and Shalee feels her stomach sour. Shalee and Nicole walk slowly to the next hatch and cautiously open it. Inside, are scowling men, cursing, as they manufacture the Kraken submarines for the Abaddonian navy. The word has spread throughout Abaddon, that these women have free access, so the men continue with their work and their cursing. Shalee approaches the partially completed sub and runs her hand along the tentacles. A large man curses especially loud, to shock them. Shalee spies a round metal bar about a foot long and picks it up. Then she faces the large man. "Can you still curse with a shattered arm?" Her eyes narrow, as she plants her left foot and turns her left shoulder to the man. She imagines the bar sailing through the man's arm and, as he raises his left arm, she swings. The metal rod catches the man's left arm, just below the wrist, and shatters it. Shalee pushes the bar to the left, then steps with her right foot, planting it, as she arcs the bar down toward the man's left kneecap. The kneecap cracks, and the man falls to the ground, squealing in pain.

The other men approach the women and Shalee holds the iron bar like a pistol, pointed toward the men. "Harm us, and you will be in the Red Serpent's belly before the sun sets. If we hear any cursing, when we enter this factory tomorrow, I will break that man's arm. Now, get out of our way." Shalee drops the iron bar with a resounding clatter, as she walks tall, toward the hatch. The men move out of her way, though Nicole's fear freezes her to the ground. Shalee reaches the hatch, looks back for Nicole and forcefully shouts, "Move!" Nicole springs, like a rabbit, for the hatch, and blows by Shalee, who then steps through the hatch, locks it, and collapses on it.

Nicole turns on Shalee with wide eyes. "We could have been killed! Do you have a death wish?"

Shalee takes a slow deep breath, to collect her thoughts, "A coward dies a thousand deaths, but a brave woman, only one. The workers of Abaddon will push us as far as we let them. I put the fear of God into those men and we will not hear any cursing, as we enter the factory, in the future."

Nicole stammers, "B-but they could have killed us both!"

Shalee tilts her head, "I was raised in the oil fields. You take a chance every time you drill. I know what it is like to go without food. I am scheduled for sacrifice at the red tide so, if I die now, at least I won't wind up in the Red Serpent's belly but, you can bet your life, that each of our murderers would suffer a painful death for killing us. I am a Wolverine and we take risks."

Shalee notices that Nicole's eyes changed with her fear. They, then, turn to walk back to the palace. Inside the palace, Shalee assembles the ten women. Each one is assigned a specific job--to collect information on the number of Abaddon's subs docked at the harbor, where the food is stored on the subs, how many men guard the subs, and when they change watch for those guarding the subs. "Do any of you know how to guide a submarine?"

The women just shake their heads. "Then, we must enlist the help of some of the sailors. Are they all loyal to the Red Serpent?"

A tall blonde steps forward, "I sneak out at night, after the others have gone to sleep, to see a sailor. We were planning an escape. He can guide the sub, but he needs three more sailors to operate the sub to ensure our escape."

Shalee wonders if this is just pillow talk, or if the sailor will really help in their escape.

Nicole inserts a barb. "If the Red Serpent tells the truth, and your family has been bitten by the black snakes, then they will die. Who, from Atlantis, will help us?"

The women all look at Shalee. "I don't believe the Red Serpent. My husband will rescue me, but we need to make plans to flee this palace, as soon as possible. We will sail to Atlantis." The meeting breaks up and the women proceed outside to collect information.

About an hour later, Vipurr enters the palace with a small disk in his hand; he is surrounded by five guards. Shalee braces herself, as she watches Vipurr install the disk into a wall slot, and the wall begins to show a movie. At first, it is just images of lava falling, then the picture moves to blackness. Laser blasts leap onto the screen and Shalee flinches. Vipurr puffs out his chest, "Abaddon's subs repulsed your husband's invasion fleet, and he was killed. See all the Atlantian subs we destroyed."

Shalee sees the invading subs becoming damaged and retreating. She studies the video of the Krakens jetting from the depths and ramming the Atlantian subs. The Atlantian fleet appears mortally damaged, as they flee. The Abaddonian fleet chases the Atlantian subs, then the picture abruptly shakes, as it turns toward

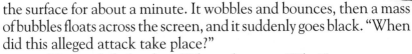

the surface for about a minute. It wobbles and bounces, then a mass of bubbles floats across the screen, and it suddenly goes black. "When did this alleged attack take place?"

Vipurr shifts his feet. "Three days ago. Why?"

"If you are going to be chief among liars, then get your stories straight with the Red Worm. If you killed my husband three days ago, then the Worm lies about black snakes biting my family. So, why should I believe that my husband is dead or was bitten and suffers from poisoning? This film shows your fleet being defeated."

Vipurr's face flushes bright red, as he raises his hand to strike Shalee. Her right fist drills into his solar plexus. Vipurr is paralyzed for fifteen seconds, and his men quickly subdue Shalee. The men hold her arms back, but she spits out her words, "Go ahead and hit me, you coward. You might get lucky and kill me."

Vipurr's body shakes, but he holds his temper and orders the other women to go to the temple to feed their god.

Chapter 12

Is there really a 150 foot Mega

Mouth Shark?

George and Eli search the temple for Matthew's wealth, as Eli's men strip the temple of all artifacts and set them outside the church doors. A room under the main sanctuary possesses a reinforced steel hatch and Eli sends for a master locksmith, and welders, as a final option, to open the hatch. After three hours, the locksmith finds the right combination and the hatch opens. Piles of blue diamonds fill the room, and Matthew's treasure sits in one corner.

George scratches behind his right ear and thinks. "Do Atlantians have a mine that produces these blue diamonds?"

"No, George, the blue diamonds come from the Red Serpent's mines in Abaddon."

Eli picks up a list by the door and starts to read it. His face contorts in revulsion. He puts his hand on George's shoulder, then goes outside to throw up. George wonders about Eli's actions, and follows him outside. "What did you read?"

It takes Eli a moment to steady himself, as he plops to the ground. His men and Sonya appear by the hatch. Eli is now shaking, as he raises his head, "All the "still-born" babies, that the priests delivered, in the past, were alive. The priests were selling our children to the Red Serpent for his food." It takes a moment for Eli's words to sink into the crowds' brains; then they are filled with rage and hatred. The men storm out of the temple and begin smashing all the temple's artifacts. This draws the rest of the Atlantian population to the front of the temple and, when it is announced what the priests had done, even the royals lend a hand in smashing the artifacts. The metal is then sent to the submarine factory, to be boiled down into bars.

George stands at the temple's entrance and, in loud clear thoughts, proclaims, "This temple is now my property by right of combat. It will remain open day and night and any people that wish to pray are welcome. God has not deserted us, but these priests had sold their souls to the Red Serpent. May their spirits burn in a supernova for eternity! Now, I go in to pray for my master, his family, and my mates that were poisoned by the priests and the Red Serpent. The priests have been dealt with today and, eventually, we will kill the Red Serpent. Your prayers would be appreciated." With that, George and Sonya turn to enter the main sanctuary, where they lay prostrate on the ground, praying.

Eli tells the crowd that he will help George in prayer. Most of the crowds enter the sanctuary, but not one of the royal class moves. When the crowd has dispersed into the sanctuary, the royals walk back to their palaces, hatching a plan for total control of Atlantis, when the Wolverines die.

The screaming back at the Wolverine home permeates the air in that bubble. Desiraa and Joshua have cautiously bound each tiger's paws together, but still they roll on the floor, clawing at the air and roaring at the tops of their lungs, in pain. Matthew, Raquelle and Eric scream at the tops of their lungs, as if competing with the tigers. The house is in bedlam and Joshua urges Desiraa to leave. She shakes her head. "I have been bought by the tiger, to care for his loved ones, who are sick and I will comfort them until they die. Now, let us get fresh water from the lake of life and we will sponge cold water on their heads." Joshua and Desiraa find some buckets to use to retrieve the water. At the water's edge, Elizabeth appears and questions Desiraa. The story of the black snakes and the poisoning of the Wolverines' and the female tigers is related. Elizabeth realizes that she can do nothing, so she submerges to tell the other Lake Guardians of Matthew's fate.

With a heavy heart, Desiraa fills her bucket. "I thought that this warrior and his family would be able to save us from the Red Serpent. But the evil in Atlantis is just too powerful."

Joshua smiles. "George must have defeated the priests, or we would be dead by now. So, there is hope." Joshua squeezes Desiraa around the waist, then picks up his buckets, and they head for home.

Vipurr receives a message from the Trader, informing him that most of the priests of Atlantis have been killed and that the War Cat is in charge of the sanctuary. The Wolverines and eight female tigers are sick from poison and they suffer greatly in a slow death. But no more babies can be delivered from Atlantis, because the Atlantians know what happened to their children. The Trader is making his escape plans but, if they attack now, they can win Atlantis and he will be able to stay.

Vipurr hurries to the Red Serpent, with the news of the priests. The Red Serpent is still stuffed from gorging on black cats but, in two weeks, he will be starved for babies. "Vipurr, how many submarines do we have ready for an attack?"

"About fifty, but the Atlantian fleet could easily defeat this force. You do have over a thousand Krakens that could launch a sneak attack. If they could get through the hole, to the lake of life, then defeat the Lake Guardians, our subs can surface and take the Atlantians while they sleep."

The Red Serpent ponders this plan, "My Krakens going into fresh water, for a whole night, might kill them."

"Yes, but we would win Atlantis and raise new Krakens."

The Red Serpent's tongue extends to lick Vipurr then he slyly smiles, "Of all the high priests that I have had, you are the best, because you think as I do. Prepare the Krakens and the subs for the attack."

Shalee has been watching the temple and, as Vipurr leaves, she follows him. From a distance, she can see him go to the dock, open a metal box, press something, then wait. Out of the water, rises the mantle of a huge Kraken. The eyes are as big as basketballs, and it stares at Vipurr. He becomes nervous, then he thinks and speaks aloud to control the Kraken and to reinforce his courage. "The Red Serpent wants you to gather all Krakens, then wait just outside the streams of lava, for the subs. You will enter Atlantis under the statue of O, and stop to send in your most stealthy fighters to eliminate the Guardians of the lake, who are on night duty. When they return, all your warriors enter the lake of life to help our subs unload troops onto the dock. You will remain in the lake of life until Atlantis is in our possession. Do you understand?"

The Kraken's large eyes just stare at Vipurr, for a full minute, then it thinks, "I gather my people, we wait for the subs, go under O's legs and wait."

Vipurr hates dealing with Krakens; they are so stupid. "Yes, wait, but send in your most treacherous members to kill the Lake Guardians, then protect our subs, as they dock, and wait for Atlantis to be taken. Do you understand?"

The giant Kraken's mantle wavered from side to side, as if he was processing this latest information. "Gather Krakens, wait for subs, go under O's legs, wait, but send in Krakens to kill guards, protect subs through lake of life, then wait. Yes, I have the plan."

"Very smart, Kraken, now go to gather all the others and wait for the subs."

The colossal squid shivers, as it thinks of dolphins, "Kraken treat of dolphins before we go?"

The high priest breathes heavily, "Yes, take your Krakens to the dolphin pens, wait for them to be released, then gorge yourselves. Now go!"

Shalee listens and watches Vipurr converse with the Kraken, and she knows that she has to do something. Another pair of eyes watches her. They see her move behind the priest, as he goes to the dolphin cages. The keeper of the cages listens to Vipurr's instructions. When they are finished, Vipurr rushes away to inform the submarine commanders of the coming attack. Shalee watches the jailer, as he goes to a control panel and pushes a large red button once, then leaves to open the gates for the Kraken. She reaches the panel and presses the red button ten more times. She can see the water turn pink and the dolphins swim very slowly. This must be a knockout potion, so the Krakens can easily catch the dolphins. Shalee hears the giant gates opening, but the dolphins are now surfacing, bellies up. The water is now bright red, as the Krakens hurry into the small enclosure. Tentacles rise out of the water as they grab the dolphins. They also land on the deck and Shalee is knocked to the floor. She rises and tries to escape, but there is water everywhere on the deck, and she goes down again. Tentacles are splashing and flopping everywhere. She starts to crawl to the exit, but still, she slips on the wet floor and plunges into the water. A huge tentacle flips her out of the water, and drops her on the dock, as it makes an arc, then grabs three dolphins. Slowly, it slides back into the water. Dolphins are now flying through the air and hitting the walls. The squids are throwing the dolphins into the air. This red potion has a weird side effect on the Kraken. Shalee finally makes it to the exit, and leaves for the palace, soaking wet.

In the dead of night, a ship lightly touches the water, and slowly sinks into the Sargasso seaweed. The pilot thinks aloud, "It is always the Centurion that has to carry out the leader's special projects. Well, at least I get to meet the legendary Slither's Nightmare. That is one War Cat I would not want to meet in a dark alley. Oh, let me check the charts for holo-screen projection in this ocean. The ship has to be cloaked and I like that Mega-mouth shark. Vicious, bad looking, bite your tail off in a heartbeat. Boy, I made a good choice. Well, it will be the biggest Mega-mouth shark this world has ever seen." With that, he switches on the dial and his ship appears to transform into a one hundred fifty-foot Mega-mouth shark. The Centurion sets the ship on "hover", but the radar is useless in all this seaweed. So he gets up to check the three pouches of his leader's blood. "That War Cat must be precious in the leader's eyes for him to immediately give three pints of his own blood, and put his life at risk, as soon as he received the message. What a death wish."

The Centurion shakes his head at the risk of draining three pints of blood, at one time, from any human. The leader had to order the doctors, under threat of death, to take the blood, so they did, but immediately afterward, they had him in bed, and were filling him with fluids. If the leader dies, it's back to the front lines for this Centurion and, with less than two years to retirement, that is the last thing he wants or needs. If that happens, I will kill the doctors before I go, because seasoned warriors are expected to lead the charges. Slithers like to eat, as they do battle so, if you go down in battle, you go down into a Slither's belly. He shakes at such a repulsive thought.

The Centurion violently shakes his head to banish these thoughts. "Concentrate on getting to Atlantis, drop off the blood to A Slither's Nightmare, and pick up the War Cats for transport back to the training camp. Then go back to serving at the leader's headquarters.

He seats himself, then guides the ship deeper into the Sargasso seaweed. He has a small light at the front of the ship and the glow of the hologram has small fish scattering at the sight of the Mega-mouth shark, but some just freeze, as his ship slides past. A laugh bubbles from the Centurion's belly, until it floats to his mouth, "Yeah, you little fish, you'd better get out of the way because I am the toughest shark this ocean has ever seen!" Then he just starts belly laughing. The ship begins to slow and becomes sluggish, and develops a slight vibration. His first thought is mechanical trouble, but all the instruments show normal. Next thought--he is stuck in seaweed. So he turns the hull transparent. Huge red tentacles encircle his ship, as vicious black "parrot" beaks scrape up and down on his hull, trying desperately to break into the ship for a Centurion snack.

This ship was built for space battles and to deflect laser blasts, not to fight underwater. The scraping increases, as the ship vibrates violently; he can see the muscles of each tentacle tighten as the suckers become larger circles. Some of the suckers are now the size of his head and they are growing. Whatever these things are, they are the Slithers of this world. The "parrot" beaks are now opening and a tongue the size of his arm starts to scrape the ship. This tongue looks like a spiral of giant fangs, all pointing in the wrong direction, licking his ship. The Centurion switches to manual, then seizes the stick so hard, his hands ache, but he forces the nose slightly up, as he fires the front laser cannons. The Kraken covering his front disintegrates into bite-size pieces, but the blast was too close and the explosion knocks the front laser cannons off- line. The squids relax their grips for an instant, but that is all it takes for the Centurion to break free. He heads deeper into the blackness and away from the seaweed, as he shuts the front light off. He spies a fleet of ships gliding through the water, so he heads for them. Maybe they are friendly. The hologram projection fades, so they see his ship approaching, and start to fire. His ship veers right, as he tries to escape. This is all the time the Krakens need to reattach themselves to it.

The Centurion feels the monsters pulling on his ship. He goes directly to ram the enemy fleet and they fire on his ship, hitting the Krakens but, as one squid falls off, another one takes its place. The giant squids are actually shielding his ship, as he enters into the middle of the fleet. The subs turn inward to fire at him, but they hit their own ships, as they shoot. The Centurion is actually running into the enemy's ships, trying to dislodge the Krakens, but they just tighten their grips on the ship. It is like having a huge ammonia-filled balloon encircling his ship. In the laser blasts, many squids die, but others quickly take their places. The Centurion keeps plowing into Abaddon's subs, killing Krakens, but others always take their places.

He sighs deeply; he has to get away from these creatures. Three enemy subs' simultaneous laser blasts clear his ship of Krakens and he speeds, at full power, hopefully toward Atlantis. The front lights of his ship beam out into the darkness, as the hologram, again, makes his ship appear to be a Mega-mouth shark. Instantly, there appears the image of a naked golden woman, beckoning him, with open arms, to her bosom. He wonders if he is hallucinating. He thrusts the stick forward, but feels he will crash right into her belly. The top of his ship scrapes the statue and emits a loud, high-pitched squeal inside the ship. The centurion's back is covered with goose bumps, until the tail of his ship clears the statue. He quickly jerks the stick up, and blazes through the opening and zooms past two Lake Guardians. They almost have heart attacks at the sight of such a huge shark. The centurion fires the rear laser cannons, as two Krakens enter the opening, and the squids explode all over the stunned dinosaurs. The Lake Guardians quickly go for reinforcements, as the Centurion's ship rises to a dock--any dock--so he can get out and fight these creatures. He is praying that this is Atlantis, and not Abaddon.

As his ship breaks the surface, he sees a white marble dock straight ahead. He stops his ship, opens the hatch, grabs his short sword and buckles it around his waist, then exits his ship. As the Centurion steps out of the water, crazed Krakens attack his ship. Scarlet tentacles and legs quickly encircle the shark.

The centurion draws his short sword and a blazing gold liquid instantly outlines its blade. He is seven feet tall, and has a barrel chest and arms to match. He swings his sword over his head, then down into the tentacle, but the gold liquid severs it without actually ever touching it. One of the squids snaps his tentacle at this pest and the Centurion slices the tentacle down the middle. Ammonia covers him, as he hacks off another of the Kraken's legs. Soon, there are tentacles and legs covering the dock and floating in the water. One of the creatures, with only two remaining legs, pulls itself up onto the dock and lashes out at the Centurion. He moves to the side, as he slices the Kraken's mantle in two.

The other two squids continue to violently attack the Mega-mouth shark. The centurion smacks his belt buckle and a banshee-shriek fills the dome. George, Sonya, and the others have been praying for hours, in the temple, but they stream out toward the dock. George is in the lead, and he pounces on one of the legs, which encircles the centurion's ship. It removes the leg and quickly pins George to the dock. The Centurion immediately severs the leg, then shouts at the tiger, "You're not helping!"

George tries to claw a leg, but is again pinned to the dock. The soldier whirls around, cuts the leg and orders George to withdraw. Sonya holds herself back from this giant shark, but the Atlantians ferociously attack the Krakens with their swords, and cut off the legs, until there are none left, surrounding the Mega-mouth shark. Two huge, legless mantles lay across the ship. Hatred pours from the squids' eyes, as the Centurion pushes them over the side, into the water, where they float. Five of the Lake Guardians surface. Four of them drag the mantles under the water, under the statue of O, to the waiting whales, which gobble up this delicious treat. Abaddon's damaged subs limp back home, as squid entrails clutter the opening to Atlantis.

Elizabeth addresses the Centurion and the crowd, "Kraken body parts fill the opening to Atlantis. Whales will feast on them until no scrap remains. The Krakens fought to the death; this is very unusual. They just kept attacking and attacking. Their subs were damaged, but not by us. They retreated almost immediately, and we expected the Krakens to also retreat, but they just kept attacking. Maybe the Red Serpent put them on drugs. That Mega-mouth shark almost gave my guards a heart attack. Is that really a shark?"

The Centurion enters the ship and disengages the hologram. Then he exits, with a sour expression on his face, and looks directly at George, "You are not the Slither's Nightmare."

The Centurion only has time to see a blur of orange and black fur, as George's fangs seize his neck and the tiger's weight drives the man to the dock. George's hind legs, claws extended, slightly dig into the Centurion's stomach, ready to give a swift downward thrust. George's thoughts are menacing, "Would you like to reproduce after retirement, or not?"

The Centurion's arms are pinned to his chest, "Is this how you repay a life debt? Then go ahead and kill me."

"I outrank you and, in our military, after being given such disrespect, I do have the right to kill you or, at least, render you incapable of reproducing such disrespect." George lets the words sink in for a few moments.

He releases his grip and backs away. "I give you your life and ability to reproduce, so both life debts are paid in full. Now, did you bring the leader's blood?"

The Centurion quickly stands and lays his hand upon his short sword. He studies George and Sonya for a full minute, then turns and goes inside the ship and brings out the chest containing the blood. He opens the lid and George inspects the blood. He turns and the man picks up the chest and follows George and Sonya into Matthew's house. The Trader has appeared--and the Royals--but they keep quiet and keep their distance from this Centurion. They had not participated in the battle.

Desiraa and Joshua greet the trio, but the Centurion ignores them, and they quietly fade into the background. The female cats are whimpering, as are Raquelle, Eric and Matthew. The Centurion doesn't stop at Raquelle's room, but proceeds to Matthew's room. "Do you want him healed with the blood?"

George nods, and the centurion rips off Matthew's shirt; then he speaks to the bag of blood, "I am Alpha Centurion, son of Dar Centurion, grandson of Garth Centurion. Taste my blood to verify." With that, the Centurion places the bag of blood on his chest, over his heart. The bag moves, and a small head, with a long pin for a mouth, appears. The head rears back, then plunges into his heart and withdraws a sample of blood, which it tastes. The blood is confirmed

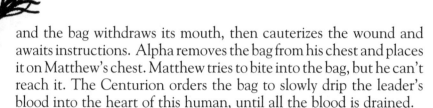

and the bag withdraws its mouth, then cauterizes the wound and awaits instructions. Alpha removes the bag from his chest and places it on Matthew's chest. Matthew tries to bite into the bag, but he can't reach it. The Centurion orders the bag to slowly drip the leader's blood into the heart of this human, until all the blood is drained.

He moves to Eric's room and performs the same procedure. Then they go into Raquelle's room. The Centurion stops by her bed, but does not open the chest. "She is a female, so she cannot have the blood of a warrior leader. I am hungry, so bring me some food."

George thinks nothing, so Sonya thinks, "Why aren't you giving her blood?"

Alpha ignores Sonya and repeats to George, "She is a female, so she cannot receive a warrior's blood. Haven't you explained that to your mate, or is she too stupid to comprehend?"

Sonya roars and prepares to charge him. George steps in front of her, as she rises and stands on her back paws. George also rises, as Sonya spits her words at him and covers his face with her foam, as she speaks, "I want to mutilate him; I am so sick of hearing about your life debts and your mysterious past. I could be with your other mates, across the hall, dying an excruciating death. This son of a hyena is not going to help us. The two male humans have their lives, but eight of your mates will die. So life debts are cancelled."

George and Sonya are dancing a jerky tango. The Centurion has removed his sword and stands ready to kill Sonya, when she attacks. George turns his back to Sonya and her front paws reach over his shoulders. Her head is by his left ear and she is spitting, in rage, at the Centurion. George braces his hind paws and, for the moment, the pair stops moving. He rapid-fires thoughts at the Centurion, "You mentioned your father, Dar, the Centurion. In the Battle of Syt, the Slithers were over-running the humans and the 1st War Cat Division was committed to the fight. We fought three straight days and took on twelve Slither divisions. We had 92% casualties, but the day went to the War Cats and I received my name, Slither's Nightmare. I saved an old Centurion named Dar; he lost his left hand, but kept his life and we became friends. He retired after that battle. Was he your father?"

Sonya is pushing hard and George starts to move toward the warrior. George sees his head nod and thinks, "Pay my life debt now."

Without a word, the Centurion moves his sword from above his head to the front of his body, with the point only inches from his stomach. Both hands are placed on the hilt and the soldier gravely speaks, "Thank you for saving my father and thank you for letting me be born and serve my solar system for ninety-eight years. May your line continue forever, but my father's line ends with me. Now, I pay his debt in full."

"Stop! I order you to stop."

After almost a hundred years of training, the Centurion's muscles lock, as his sword quivers in his hands.

George shakes Sonya off his back. "I don't want your death. Your father was my first life debt and he was a good man. Don't let his line die here. Give the blood to the female and live."

The Centurion shakes his head. George needs an out, so he snatches at his first thought, "Then sell me a blood pouch and take my blood to save my mates. Please let my line continue."

The warrior lowers his sword, but Sonya quickly moves in front of George's face, "If you give all that blood, you will die."

"Yes, but if that were you across the hall, then I would gladly give my life for yours. I love all my mates with that same love. Please, don't stop me, Sonya."

Her eyes start to tear and she uses her right paw to rub her face. The tears start flowing freely, as she begins to see the depth of this War Cat's love for his mates and she moves to the corner to grieve.

The Centurion holsters his sword and opens the chest. He strokes the pouch like a cat, and speaks gently to it. "I am giving you to a legendary War Cat and you are to drain his blood and give it to his mates, which are dying. This will kill him, but you are to override your central order."

Eyes form in the pouch and it thinks, "I am overflowing with the toxin. If you do not drain me, then the blood I take in is poisoned and I will die and his mates will die."

The Centurion removes a small vial from his belt and places it at the rear of the pouch. The vial is slowly filled with a gummy tar substance. George questions this procedure.

Alpha explains, "The pouch produces a poisonous toxin in its body, which it stores and releases into the blood, if captured by the enemy. Once a month, the pouch must be relieved of this toxin or it will die. It is so deadly that only one drop could kill you or me in three seconds. I store the toxin on my ship."

George goes into the next room and lies down. The pouch is placed on his chest, but it must extend its mouth way beyond its normal length to get to George's heart. It complains to the Centurion that his chest is just too large. A pint of blood is withdrawn and the pouch is placed on the first tigress. She violently twists in her pain, until the Centurion's massive hands put a stop to her movement and the pouch empties the blood into her heart.

As the next pouch is being filled, Matthew and Eric stagger into the room, with the help of Desiraa and Joshua. Sonya's sobs filter into the room and Matthew looks at George, "Thank you, George, for the blood transfusions for Eric, Raquelle and myself. Why is Sonya crying?"

The Centurion does not look up, but removes the pouch and places it on the next tigress, "The female tiger cries because the Slither's Nightmare will be dead in an hour, but his mates will revive. Only the males were given my leader's blood. I cannot give a warrior's blood to a female, at this time. I am sorry for the future loss of your daughter. Now, please leave, so I can save these female tigers' lives."

Joshua tries to guide Matthew out of the room, but he fights him. "I cannot let you kill George. Desiraa, bring my sword." Desiraa quickly retrieves Matthew's sword. He whispers into her ear, 'If I die, give my blood to my daughter; it may help.'

Matthew grabs the sword with both hands and falls straight to the floor. He continues to crawl toward the Centurion, who is ignoring him. When he gets close enough, he finds that he cannot lift the sword, so he slides it across the floor and gently hits the man's foot. He flips Matt over on his back with his foot. "What do you want?"

"I am not going to let you kill my friend. Find another way or, no matter where you go on this planet, I will hunt you down and kill you!" After all this exertion, Matthew passes out.

George's eyes are becoming glassy and his thoughts are slurred, "Good Friend, this human. He would be a great, brilliant, light. Heal many. Honor, honor, trust. "Then George passes out.

The pouch is filled with George's blood, and its eyes appear, "May twenty Slithers eat you alive in your next battle, Centurion. You are lower than my excrement. I won't help you kill this gallant War Cat. I tasted this human's blood and it is as pure as the lights. I return this blood back into this chivalrous War Cat." With that, the pouch swiftly empties the blood back into George's heart.

A red-eyed Sonya is now in the doorway and all eyes are filled with tears, as they stare at the Centurion. He fidgets for a moment, just staring at the pouch, whose eyes show total disgust. Then he turns and goes to his ship and returns with a hypodermic needle and five gray vials, the contents of which he injects into the remaining sick tigers. With a very sour expression, he leaves the building and goes back to his ship to sulk.

Chapter 13

Kraken's attack Mega Mouth

Shark?

Shalee makes it back to the palace, still soaking wet. Nicole meets her at the front door and quickly removes her clothes and places her into the whirlpool. After she is warmed, the ten women lay her on a table and massage her whole body with Oil of Dolphin. Shalee's flesh drinks in the Dolphin Oil and every wrinkle quickly fades away from her body. She is naked, on the table, and she runs her hands over her smooth face and down her chest, circling her firm breasts several times, then down over her stomach and down her legs to her feet. Shalee moans, "I want my husband so bad. Matthew would take six hours exploring every inch of my body. He would take me to paradise for hours. I need him so bad." She clenches her fists and squeezes her eyes shut.

Nicole twists her face, as she looks at the other women, "You mean he is better than the whirlpool, the oil of Dolphin? He could provide six hours of love making? You can't be serious!"

Shalee opens her eyes, "Yes, he is better than the whirlpool and the Oil of Dolphin and, yes, he can control his passion to give me six hours of pleasure. Afterwards, he is totally exhausted because he gives a hundred percent."

Amber's eyes light up, "Tell us how you met him."

Shalee grabs a white dolphin bathing suit and dresses quickly. "Well, I grew up in the oil patch. My dad was an alcoholic oil rigger. He would leave for months at a time, then come home with tons of money and lay all the cash on our coffee table, kiss me and play with me outside for an hour, kiss my mother and make love to her for an hour, then grab the money that was left on the coffee table, and merrily go on a drinking spree for three weeks. The first few years of their marriage, mom and I almost starved to death. She learned to deposit eighty percent of the money she took from the coffee table, in a bank in Houston, which my dad knew nothing--and really didn't care--about. When his money ran out, he got another job and was gone for months. He never asked if we had food or shelter, or even how we lived, while he was gone. He just didn't care. I swore I would never live like that. When I was fourteen, my dad got into a knife fight in a low-life bar and we buried what was left of him the next day.

My mom took it hard, and we sat down for a heart-to-heart talk the day after the funeral. Seems she had been to the doctor's and she had an inoperable brain tumor. It was slow growing, and she might live ten years or only one year. She found out the day my dad got into his fatal knife fight. So, she told me we didn't have any time for teenage rebellion garbage or feeling sorry for ourselves. She started attending church and prayed to God, and I found people that cared about my mom and me. She had all her savings invested in Wolverine Never-Hit-a-Dry-Hole Oil, because they have paid ten percent dividends forever and the Wolverines are honorable people. I was thinking this company was a con and we were in deep, above your eyeballs, doo-doo. I learned to read financial statements at age fourteen and went on to get a degree in advertising from the University of Texas. During my summers in college, I worked my tail off at an internship at Wolverine Never-Hit-a-Dry-Hole Oil in the advertising department. I had to fight the wolves off with clubs.

I had just graduated and started working full time at Wolverine Oil, when the president and his wife were visiting oil prospects in Iraq, and rebels ambushed and killed the whole party. The State Department, as they are so great at doing, did nothing. Matthew became president, but he was a bitter Vietnam veteran, and this just added fuel to his attempts at self-destruction. He picked a fight with O'Hara Oil. He was taking both companies down the tubes with lightning speed--and my stock along with it. I tried to get mom to sell, but she was too far-gone. I was working in the advertising department, when my mom died, on a Thursday. I had the funeral early Monday morning and came directly to work, dressed all in black. I hit the elevator at the same time as Matthew, and he made a snide remark about the lady in black. I told him that I had just buried my mother and that he was bankrupting the company. Even I could do a better job than he was doing. His temper exploded; he left the elevator and told his secretary to inform all departments that this 'Miss-Know-It-All' would make peace with O'Hara Oil today, and then supervise implementing that peace. So, he sent me to O'Hara Oil.

I went directly to O'Hara Oil and requested to see their president, Tim O'Hara . A gray-haired executive secretary put me off with, 'Do you have an appointment, Miss?' I told her I was representing Matthew Wolverine and that I was here to clear this mess up today and that, if I failed, her company would be in bankruptcy in a month. Did she think they would be beating down her door, to hire a fifty-five-year-old secretary from a bankrupt oil company? She ushered me right in to Tim O'Hara.

A man with bushy white hair, with the grace of the most refined southern gentleman, stood to greet me, 'Miss?'

'Miss Shalee Shark--and I just buried my mother today--and Matthew Wolverine is taking his company and yours into bankruptcy, causing me to lose my inheritance, so I am here to stop that and I need your help. Will you help me save your company?'

Mr. O'Hara studied me, while he stroked his chin, 'I can fight off Matthew Wolverine, and my company will prosper.' With that, Mr. O'Hara folded his arms in front of him.

I gritted my teeth, 'You have drilling rights to west Texas land and areas in the Gulf of Mexico, but they are about to expire, unless you drill and hit oil. Your company is cash poor. Mr. Wolverine has the money to fund all those wells, and we would split the profits with you, right down the middle, for the life of the wells.'

'I'm going to pass on your offer, Miss Shark. Now, leave my office.'

I planted both my feet and spit out these words, 'You served in the 101st Airborne Unit in the Second World War, and you came home to a hero's welcome, with parades and people patting you on the back. You saved our way of life and the nation was grateful. Matthew Wolverine fought in Vietnam, just as heroically, and came back to being called names like "baby- killer" and to being spit upon. He is hurting, and he just lost his parents to Iraqi rebels. He is a true Wolverine and, even in death, he will hemorrhage your company, as he takes his company down the tubes, and then your creditors and your competition will move in for the kill. I think O'Hara and W. Oil will make one unbeatable partnership--with you as controlling partner?'

Mr. O'Hara turned to look at a map of Texas and the Gulf and, slowly, he agreed. I implemented the partnership and Matthew and I were married in six months. He doesn't remember anything after returning from Vietnam, including his parent's deaths, until our Scottish vacation. He feels he went back a thousand years in time, and rescued me from dragons, and I am his beauty forever."

Nicole spoke sharply, "Is he crazy?"

"Marriage is not made between two perfect people, but between two imperfect people, who try really hard to make a good marriage. I made him promise not to drink because of my alcoholic father and he made me promise not to swear and I struggle with that daily. He would gladly die for me and he loves me with all his heart. If he believes he went back a thousand years and rescued a beautiful Scottish lassie and that I came forward in time and married him and he believes that I am the most beautiful woman in the world, then I live very comfortably with those ideas."

"Now, we need to escape from Abaddon very soon. Nicole, you take the other girls you trust to report to the Red Worm that I sabotaged the Krakens. Then we will know if my action stopped the attack. Now, go."

Nicole chooses Darcy and Alexis to go with her to the Red Serpent's temple. After the trio leaves, Shalee talks quietly to the other seven women. The noise of subs docking and men cursing draws the women to the docks to see severely damaged subs returning. The crews crawl out of the subs, black and blue, and some have bleeding cuts.

Heather helps a sailor she knows from his sub and asks him what happened. He tells her, "A one hundred-fifty foot Mega-mouth shark attacked us. The Krakens kept attacking, trying to cover and crush the shark, but it just ran into our subs and, as we fired on it, we hit our own subs. The Krakens ceaselessly attacked the shark, with a vengeance. It was like they hated that shark with every fiber of their bodies. As one died, another took its place, until the shark fled under the legs of O, and into the lake of life. The Krakens pursued that monster into the lake of life, as we withdrew. All ten remaining subs limped back to Abaddon. It was not our fault and I don't want to wind up in the belly of the Red Serpent." The sailor squeezes Heather tight and whispers that they must escape. Shalee hears the whisper, grabs the sailor by the arm, and lifts him up. She and Heather take him into the palace, strip off his shirt and place him in the whirlpool. As the sailor steps out of the whirlpool, Shalee grabs a handful of Oil of Dolphin to cover his wounds. Heather quickly seizes Shalee's hand, "Spread that on him and you sentence him to the Red Serpent's belly, as soon as he enters the temple." Heather grabs two vials of green sludge and pours one on the wounds and hands the other to Shalee. She sticks it in her bathing suit, then she puts on another covering, over her bathing suit. It smells like the stinkiest feet you can imagine. As Shalee races for the front door, Heather tells the sailor to report directly to the Red Serpent with this smell and without fear.

The sailor kisses Heather and leaves, as Shalee comes back into the palace, holding her nose. Heather starts to laugh, "That is one sailor that will not be eaten tonight. I love him and want him alive to help us escape. Once, the Red Serpent ate a sacrafice with that ointment, and he threw up for a week."

Ten priests come through the front door and violently lift Shalee straight up over their heads and carry her to the Red Serpent's temple. Heather and the other women follow. The sailors line up, as the Red Serpent's skin glows scarlet red with anger. "My plan was perfect and you failed me! How could you fail me?"

A badly wounded captain steps forward, "This one hundred fifty-foot Mega-mouth shark appeared and the Krakens went berserk. Agitation with total malice. Their attacks covered the shark so completely, we couldn't get a shot through them to kill it. Then, covered with Krakens, it plowed into our convoy. The subs' captains got scared, then started firing and we killed squid after squid, but they just kept covering the shark. So shots went wild and our ships were hit. The shark kept maneuvering right in among us and ramming our subs. Sub after sub went down, but the Krakens refused to back off. The shark went under the statue of O, with every squid in sight following, out to tear that shark into little pieces, right on its tail. Only ten of us made it back to Abaddon. It was not our fault. Berserk Krakens cost you the victory." With that, the captain bowed very low.

Shalee is carried in front of the Red Serpent and dumped on the floor. She quickly rises. "Attack didn't go too well? Are you going to accept responsibility for your failure?"

The Red Serpent rises, half his height, towering over the people, as he regains control of his temper, "This sacrifice sabotaged our conquest of Atlantis. A fitting punishment is for her to spend one week in my mouth but, if I forget she is there, I may swallow her." With that the Red Serpent scoops Shalee into his mouth and places her on the right side of his tongue. She is shocked and shaking, but she has room to stand. The Red Serpent drains his head of all pigment and the people can clearly see Shalee quivering, and they cheer the Red Serpent. They realize that he cannot eat them with a sacrifice in his cheek. The Red Serpent sniffs the sailor with the stinky ointment and motions to Vipurr to throw him out. Two priests grab the sailor and toss him out of the temple.

Chapter 14

Life Changing Decision

The Centurion walks slowly, until he boards his ship, then he walks to the nose of the ship and sits down, cross-legged. He stares at the white marble buildings, which glisten, even in the dim light. The Atlantians had built paradise and this is a good planet to retire to. Then, his thoughts turned to the War Cat. His father raised him on the news of every battle won by A Slither's Nightmare and those that they had to advance to the rear. His father never missed an opportunity to tell a stranger that he was a personal friend of A Slither's Nightmare. Tonight he had almost snuffed the life out of that legend.

Words popped into his brain, "That would have been a great waste."

He turned to face a massive head on a long neck, "My name is Elizabeth, and I am the matriarch of the Lake Guardians. Please tell me what happened to the Wolverines and the tigers."

The eyes of this Lake Guardian show compassion, even in this dim light. Alpha's muscles relax, and he relates the events of the day. Elizabeth listens to every thought and the tone of the Centurion's voice. The loneliness of space travel has him talking aloud, just to hear a human voice. She does not judge him, but weighs his every thought and feels his conflict.

"I have served ninety eight years in the military and, in less than two years, I retire. Only then, can I marry and raise my family. If I give the leader's blood to a female, he can revoke my retirement and turn me out. That is our law. I will not give up my retirement and my future family." The Centurion hardens his face and looks at Elizabeth.

Her thoughts turn more practical, "Your ship is badly damaged and it will take a while to repair. Don't repair it too quickly. Stay here a while. Weigh your options, as the repairs proceed. How long does Raquelle have until the poison kills her?"

"My repairs, if done slowly, at half days, will take only a week, and that is all the time she has left. The poison will increase her pain, so her end will be one constant scream of agony, which you will hear, even in the lake of life, on her last day."

Elizabeth moves close, and puts her head only inches from

the Centurion and he reaches out and strokes the top of her head. Her skin is elastic and smooth. She gently places her head in his lap. "Tomorrow, after you do some repairs, swim in the lake of life and ride on my back." He smiles and tells Elizabeth he looks forward to the ride.

The artificial sunrise illuminates the dome, as the occupants of Matthew's house rise. Eric rushes in to see his dad and George awakens to the licking of his mates. All of George's mates are well and he tries to rise, but falls. The loss of blood will put him down for a day or two. Raquelle's screams are heard, even through her closed door. Matthew and Eric come into her room. Desiraa is beside the bed, sponging cold water over her head, which does seem to help. Matthew looks puzzled, "Who are you, and why is Raquelle not better?"

Desiraa speaks softly, "I am your caregiver. The Centurion only gave some of his leader's blood to you and Eric. He would not give it to a female, but he took George's blood and gave it to his mates. After he took the third pint of George's blood, he stopped, and the blood container spoke to him. Then he went to his ship and got five shots, and cured the rest of George's mates. The Centurion told you all this last night. Don't you remember?"

Matthew shakes his head. "It is a blur. Is George all right?"

"George will have to rest for the remainder of today and, tomorrow, he should be OK. Why don't you go to the dock and talk to the Centurion?"

Matthew and Eric walk quickly to the dock. The Centurion's ship is not at the dock and Matthew becomes concerned it has left. Elizabeth swims to the surface. "He is taking his ship on a test dive. He will be here about a week, which is all the time Raquelle has left. He is not a bad man. He has spent ninety-eight years in the military and is close to retiring. Only after he retires, can he have a marriage and a family. If he gives his leader's blood to Raquelle, he loses his retirement. Would you give up a future with Shalee, Eric and Raquelle for a strange girl, Matthew?"

Matthew's hands fly to his face, "Oh, God, Raquelle is going to die." Matthew unsteadily sits on the dock, with his legs dangling over the side. Eric puts his arm around his father and hugs him. Elizabeth's face rubs his other side.

"Dad, you can convince the Centurion to save Raquelle. I know you can. Dad, say something. You're scaring me, Dad. Raquelle is not going to die, is she?"

Matthew removes his hands to reveal tears, "Elizabeth's thoughts speak to my heart. I would not give up a future with your mother or you and your sister for a dying strange girl. How can I ask this man to do what I wouldn't do? And Eric, you cannot ask him either. He brought us the blood that saved our lives. Elizabeth, is there any way we can stop this poison?"

Elizabeth shakes her head slowly. "Even the Lake Guardians know that a bite from the black serpents is fatal, but it does take us three months to die. A Lake Guardian, that is bitten, will go out of the hole, to the Atlantic, and find the biggest Kraken it can, and attack with all its strength. Its goal is to take out a Kraken's eye before it is killed. The black serpents can't come in the salt water and we cannot attack them on land. I am sorry, Matthew, but the Centurion is the only key to a cure."

Eric smiles broadly, "We could pray for God to heal Raquelle."

Matthew rises, then he and Eric slowly walk to the temple to pray. They pray until Eric tires of praying. "Well, Dad, do you think Raquelle is healed?"

"Son, you can do everything right and still get kicked in the teeth. God is going to do what He wants to do."

"You mean, after all this prayer, Raquelle may die?"

"Yes."

Eric closes his eyes and thinks real hard, "Then why do we serve God?"

"Could you serve the Red Serpent? I hear he is a god to his followers."

"No, I couldn't serve that evil snake, that would eat Mom. His followers are the black snakes that bit us. How could I serve him?"

"So we have to serve our God by default. We can't serve the Red Serpent, so we pray to our God. Will He hear all our prayers? I just don't know. But He did have George call in some old life debts and saved us. We will do all we can to save Raquelle and your mom. Now, let us ride on the Lake Guardians." Matthew reaches over and tousles Eric's hair.

They have to pass by their home to get to the lake and Matthew strains to listen for Raquelle's screams, but doesn't hear any. His heart leaps, as he and Eric rush into the house, and into Raquelle's room. Desiraa is exhausted and asleep in the chair and Raquelle's body thrashes in the bed. She is worn out from screaming and her body rests, but not in peace. Matthew touches her forehead and it is on fire. Eric touches her hand and it is very hot. Matthew's shoulders sag; there is nothing he can do, so he and Eric go on to the lake.

Matthew and Eric approach the docks, as Elizabeth flies past them, through the water, with the Centurion on her back. He is tiring, but Elizabeth tells him to hang on for a dive. As she dives, some high-pitched sounds come from her throat. Almost immediately, two young male Guardians come from the depths, past Elizabeth, to surface and swim to Matthew and Eric. Matthew and Eric plunge into the water, then they ride the dinosaurs to the middle of the lake of life.

Eric challenges his father to swim to the shore, as he slides off his mount and starts to swim toward the dock. Matthew turns his head and tells the Lake Guardians to stay close so that, when they tire, they can ride to the dock. As he turns and slides off his Lake Guardian, he notices that Eric is already a sixth of the way to the dock. He starts swimming, with all his might. His strokes are clean, powerful, and so swift, that his body rises slightly out of the water. Elizabeth is beside him and they race to catch Eric. Eric has never been a good swimmer but today he feels like he could swim the length of the lake. His strokes are so easy and so powerful. Today he is going to beat his dad to the dock. Matthew and Elizabeth speed up their strokes. Alpha urges Elizabeth to go faster, so Matthew goes faster, too. The two young males are the first to give up the chase. Elizabeth keeps up with Matthew, but the Centurion feels her strokes slowing. Eric reaches the dock, then climbs up, and shouts victory. "Beat you, Dad!"

Matthew reaches the dock with Elizabeth a few feet behind. "Eric, I am so proud of you. How were you able to swim so fast and so far?"

"I don't know, Dad, but I feel I could swim the whole length of the lake of life. I am not even tired."

Matthew realizes he is not tired either.

The Centurion swims off Elizabeth's back, then climbs onto his ship, "It is the blood. It strengthens your bodies, but changes your muscles and skin first. My leader owed three life debts to A Slither's Nightmare, so he gave three pints of his blood as repayment. It was dangerous to take so much blood, but he did it to repay his debt. A life debt must be repaid when asked for, even by a leader."

"So what happens, if the life debt is not repaid?"

The centurion wrinkles his brow, "It does not happen often. If the life debt is not repaid, then the debtor must commit suicide.

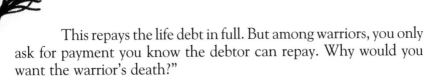

This repays the life debt in full. But among warriors, you only ask for payment you know the debtor can repay. Why would you want the warrior's death?"

Matthew walks up to the Centurion and looks directly into his eyes. "Do you hate your leader? Is that why you want him to commit suicide?"

His eyes narrow and his nostrils flare, "I am a Centurion from over one hundred generations of Centurions, and never have any of my ancestors betrayed their leader."

"So you will be the first?"

The Centurion reaches for his sword. Elizabeth bares her teeth, only inches from the soldier, "I will take you to a watery grave, before I let you hurt my friends, Matthew and Eric. Move your hand away from your sword and let him speak."

The warrior looks at the serrated rows of teeth and realizes he would be seized and dragged into the water before he could unsheathe his sword, so he moves his hand from his sword and crosses his arms in front of his chest.

Matthew seizes the moment, "When you return to your planet with a pint of your leader's blood, he will have to commit suicide, because a life debt was requested but remains unpaid. Is your leader's death your wish?"

A stunned Centurion stares back at Matthew. Only now, does he realize the consequences of his inaction. "I cannot let that happen." He pulls his sword, then quickly turns it toward his stomach. Matthew grabs his left arm and Elizabeth grabs his right arm. Eric seizes the man's right leg and lifts it, causing him to fall on his back. Elizabeth's teeth begin to bite into the Centurion's muscles. He fights to complete his task. Matthew shrieks, "I don't want your life, just give my daughter the blood. Give her the blood. Don't die. Give her the blood."

The Centurion releases his sword and flips Matthew and Eric off his body. Elizabeth brings a front flipper out of the water and comes down hard on him. An explosion of air leaves his mouth, as Elizabeth shifts her weight to this flipper. She appreciates the fact that too much weight will crush the man, so she applies just enough pressure to immobilize him. As Matthew and Eric rise, the Centurion is beginning to turn blue. Elizabeth releases some pressure, and informs him that she won't let him die.

A whisper escapes from the centurion, "Release me, and I will give her the blood."

Matthew picks up the sword. "You are a Centurion and a man of honor. I trust you to pay your leader's debt. Now, get the blood and give it to my daughter."

The Centurion hoists his sword, then goes into his ship to retrieve the blood. Matthew and Eric proceed ahead of him, to their home. George greets the trio of a smiling Matthew and Eric and a despondent Centurion, at the door. Alpha orders Desiraa to have ten buckets of ocean salt water put just outside the room. When the ten buckets are placed by the door, he enters Raquelle's room and removes the blood bag and places it over Raquelle's heart. The bag forms eyes and tells the dejected warrior that it is proud of him.

"Yes, you are pumping my retirement, future wife, and children into her heart. Her life is saved, while mine is ruined. A Slither's Nightmare, now is our leader's life debt paid in full. My father's debt is paid in full. I have no future."

George brushes against the Centurion, "Radio our leader and tell him that I require your services for six months and that I will pay for your services out of my own money. I used the leader's blood as I saw fit, and you are blameless. Take care of Raquelle, have the bites on your arm treated, then send the message."

"She has more poison in her system than all of you did, so the reaction will be violent. Matthew and Eric, you hold her legs; George, lay across her left arm; I will hold her right arm; have one of your mates lie across her stomach."

Before anyone can move, Raquelle's back arches straight up and the blood pouch, which has just emptied, flies to the ceiling with a loud splatter. She instantly snaps her arm and leg restraints; George jumps on her left arm, but is lifted straight up, as Raquelle's hands clutch his throat. His hind paws are off the ground, as her iron grip begins to crush his throat. Swiftly, Sonya covers Raquelle's left hand with her mouth, as she bites to tear the death grip from her mate. The Centurion wrenches Raquelle's right index finger back, with all his might, as Matthew and Eric try to hold down her wildly kicking legs. They both bounce off the floor, as Raquelle's legs send them flying.

Desiraa stands in the doorway, in total horror. That could have been her in George's place. Sonya's bite is the first thing to break the death grip and she savagely pulls Raquelle's hand from George's throat. Alpha frees Raquelle's right hand from George and yells to Sonya to not crush Raquelle's hand. George falls on her left arm, gasping for breath. George's right front paw pushes on Sonya's face, to make her release her bite on Raquelle's hand. She releases her bite, and she swiftly climbs on George's back. Her body continues to convulse, as a rumbling in her belly grows louder. Like an oil well hitting, Raquelle gushes black tar straight up, almost to the ceiling, and the Centurion orders her thrown from the bed and out the door. He grasps the back of Sonya's neck, too, and throws her, then George, off, as he pulls Raquelle off the bed and pushes Matthew and Eric towards the door. The black tar hits the floor, as George and Sonya are rising, and a tiny drop lands on Sonya's front paw. She instantly begins to howl, as the tar burns, like acid, into her paw. Alpha flings a bucket of salt water on her foot, and the pain stops. He races back and forth, dumping buckets of salt water on the black tar until the sizzling stops.

"The poison can kill its victim, as it exits the body. I am sorry that I was so rough on you, Sonya and A Slither's Nightmare but, if the poison hits her face, she dies. The salt water neutralizes the poison, but I would have this liquid mopped up, then sealed in a metal container and I would have a sub dispose of the contents in the ocean, at least ten miles from Atlantis. Now that the poison is out, she will heal within an hour. Give her salt turtle soup with a lot of salt."

Desiraa goes to the market to purchase some soup and she returns in a short time. Raquelle, now conscious, is in the tigers' room, on a bed. Her tongue extends as far as it can, "I feel like I ate tar." Desiraa quickly offers Raquelle the container of soup. She rips off the top, and quickly drinks the saltwater turtle soup. When the liquid is gone, she reaches for the turtle meat. No utensils--just fingers--appropriate the food, because Raquelle has not eaten in over a week.

Eric can't resist teasing his sister, "You know that is a salt sea turtle, and I wouldn't be surprised if it was an endangered species."

Raquelle just shakes her head, "Don't care, do you have any more?" Desiraa steps forward, "My name is Desiraa, and I have another container of soup."

Raquelle snatches the container, and rips off the top. She drinks the soup until she can drink no more. Then she puts the container at her side, to guard it, "George, you look terrible. You look like someone kicked your tail really bad. Who did that to you, George?"

George grins and bears the shame, "You kicked all four of our tails. I weigh over a thousand pounds, and you lifted me off the floor by my neck. If not for Sonya and the Centurion, I would be dead."

Raquelle looks at her father, to see if George is kidding. Her father nods, so her eyes turn to Desiraa. "What are you doing here, Desiraa?"

"I was purchased by George to look after your family until you died. But you got better."

Matthew looks at George, "Is this woman a slave?"

Chapter 15

Serpent's Mouth

The mouth is moist, and saliva flows from the rear of the mouth. Shalee touches the right fang. It feels like ivory, as her hand slides down its length. She stands tall, and stares at the cheering crowd. The side of the Red Serpent's mouth feels like old jelly, smooth but somewhat stretchy. She realizes that she can't break through the skin, so she sits down, surrounded by veins of poison. She is depressed. This was not in the escape plan. Could she die or go mad, if she spends a week in this hell?

Her mind clearly lays out the situation. Her family could be dying from poisoning, at this moment. Life without Matthew is unthinkable. If her family is dead, why go on living? Shalee feels a pinch at her waist and reaches under her covering to the bottom of her bathing suit. The green vial that Heather gave her was pinching her side. Heather had said that this substance made the Red Serpent sick for a week. Shalee opens the vial and dumps the contents as far back on his tongue, as she can. She places the cap on the vial and puts it under her cover inside the bottom of her bathing suit. The foulness is nauseating and Shalee squeezes her nose and breathes through her mouth. Still, the vile smell attacks her senses. She feels the Red Serpent lower his body to the ground and, involuntarily, he opens his mouth.

Shalee rushes out of the mouth, quickly turns, then points at the Red Serpent, "My God will make you sick for a week, you abomination of a Red Worm!"

The horrified crowd looks for the Red Serpent to strike her dead but, instead, they witness his stomach violently contract. His whole body turns pink, then a milky white. The Red Serpent turns and looks at the crowd and the priests for help, when his insides explode outward onto the crowd and the priests. Everything inside his stomach covers the crowd. Shalee sees the half-digested remains of five human babies, and so does the crowd, as the putrid smell fills the temple and their senses. Involuntarily, every person covered with these putrid smells starts to retch. Immediately, the floor is covered, and she staggers out the door and back to the black palace. She finds a corner and falls on her knees to pray, "God, why don't you just destroy this place. Even the women of this palace feed babies to that monster. I feel like I am dealing with the Gestapo. I have never felt so filthy in all my life. If my family is alive, please give me a sign. If they are dead, please let me follow them to You."

A hand touches Shalee's shoulder and she turns to see Heather and her sailor. "We can escape now, but it will take a week to get to Atlantis. Are you ready to leave?"

She stands and hugs them. Silently, she thanks God for an answer to prayer. The women dress in sailors' uniforms, and head for the dock. Some people stagger from the temple, but none stop them. A small sub waits at the dock. "Shalee, you will be in the cargo hold. There is food, but no light, and you can't communicate with the front of the sub, as we travel. So you will be in solitude for a week, but we will surface in Atlantis. Are you ready?"

Shalee climbs into the cargo hold, all smiles.

The sailor seals the hatch, as he beams at Heather, "Our freedom is assured, upon delivery of our cargo, in one week." Heather and the sailor enter the sub and he descends to guide the sub out of Abaddon. Shalee can feel the sub move, and her heart sings. As they pass the magma flow, the sub heats violently, but only for a few seconds, and then it cools. Krakens pass the Abaddonian sub, with little notice.

In one week, Shalee will be with her family. She wonders how Atlantis really looks. The ride is smooth for the first three days, but it is boring inside the cargo hold. On the fourth day, Shalee senses the sub rising and her spirits rise, too. Then it comes to a stop. The sailor opens the hatch and jumps onto dry land. The sun is just now rising and he breathes in the tropical breeze. Then, he turns and lifts Heather out of the sub. "This island is small but it has fresh water and food and we are free. Feel the warmth of the sun and smell the clean air. Now, all I have to do is to set the automatic pilot to return the sacrifice back to Abaddon. Our plan worked perfectly." Then the sailor picks up the intercom and tells Shalee of the beautiful sunrise and the clean sea air and that, by the way, she will be returning to Abaddon.

Shalee is thunderstruck, "How could you betray me? My husband will pay you whatever you want. Why return me to that hell?"

Heather grabs the intercom, "You consider us vile, and beyond redemption, and you are right. Do think that all the Gestapo came from Germany? The Red Serpent supplied many of Abaddon's finest priests to the Gestapo and, after the fall, many returned to be priests to the Red Serpent again. Your family is probably dead now, and the Red Serpent will conquer Atlantis so, by returning you, we stay on his good side and we are free. With his sacrifice returned, he won't send anyone to hunt us down and return us to Abaddon. I put a note by the controls and it reads, 'Her life for ours'. You have one frightful voyage coming up because you dealt with the Gestapo- and you lost! The Red Worm looks forward to tasting your flesh." Both Heather and the sailor burst out in maniacal laughter.

Shalee's stomach burns, as the sub sinks. She tries to open the hatch for a quick death, but it won't budge. This is some answer to prayer.

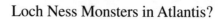

Chapter 16

Slavery

George shifts his paws, then he stands tall, "I did what I had to do. Slavery is wrong, but after the black serpents' attack, who do you think would care for you, but a slave? Matthew, you almost choked Eli to death in your fever. People were frightened of your family and of all the screaming in this house. People were also terrified that the priests would put black serpents in their homes. Atlantis was one ball of fear. Sonya and I attacked the priests, but we could have lost. Then the priests would have come here and slit Desiraa's throat, and let your family scream themselves to death alone. The actions I took were needed, at that time. Do you concur, Centurion?" George looked to him for moral support.

He nods his head and states matter-of-factly, "Three life debts are now paid by A Slither's Nightmare and only seven remain. Be thankful you are alive. Now, I go to have my wounds tended and contact my leader."

"George, I can't have slavery under my roof but, she is your slave, and only you can set her free. I ask you, as a friend, to give her her freedom."

George stands on his hind paws, and barely touches Desiraa's shoulder with his front paws, "You were purchased only to look after the Wolverines until they recovered, so you are free, but Matthew does need a woman to care for the house. Will five gold coins a week, paid by Matthew, be acceptable?" George is one sly War Cat; some people would claim he was born in Scotland, but he wasn't, though he has just transferred Desiraa's wages to Matthew. He wonders if Matthew picked up on his trick.

Desiraa counters with ten, but they settle on eight gold coins per week and twenty-five gold coins for the past week. Raquelle had immediately picked up on George's agenda, but she is so happy to be out of pain, she doesn't care, as she goes to the safe and brings the gold coins and puts them in Desiraa's hands. Desiraa shakes her head, "Freedom and money; this must be a dream." Desiraa turns and falls at Matthew's feet, "My lord, if ever you need anything, just ask, and it shall be done."

He helps her to her feet, "There is one favor--to care for this house and my children, until my wife and I return, or until they become adults." Desiraa studies Matthew, because she knows the implications of his trailing statement, if Matthew dies; then she looks at the children. She shrugs her shoulders, because freedom is never free. But, at last, she nods.

"With that covered, George, we have to plan the attack on Abaddon."

George is very blunt. "You have been unsuccessful in your attack on Abaddon because of your desire to rescue your wife. The Centurion and I will plan the attack. Your input is appreciated, but our decision is final. I have planned and executed hundreds of battles. Trust me. We can win.

Matthew doesn't like relinquishing power, but he needs George's help and this new Centurion may prove crucial in the coming battles, so he nods.

George walks in front of Eric and Raquelle. "Eric, put your arms under my chest and Raquelle, put your arms under my stomach, then lift my body to shoulder height, but remember to lift with your legs."

Matthew watches, as his children lift George up to their shoulders, in one smooth motion, and his mouth drops, "How, how are they able to do that?"

As George is set down, he clears his throat for effect, then he thinks, "My leader's blood has fused with your muscles. Look in the mirror, Matthew; you don't have any more wrinkles."

Raquelle walks to her father, and closely examines his face, "He's right, Dad; your face is as smooth as Eric's face. That blood was a fountain of youth for you."

Matthew's rubs his face, and it is as smooth as a baby's bottom, "How long will our increased strength last?"

George remains mysterious, "Until your wife is in your arms again--or you are dead. Now, you children need to leave, because your father must make a difficult decision." Eric and Raquelle walk to the dock to swim with Elizabeth.

George gravely thinks, "Now, that you have our strength, you can use our weapons--but only you and your children may. The other Atlantians are too weak. But do you want your children turned into battle-hardened warriors? As you know, there is no reversal of the process. I will ask the Centurion to teach them, but you must not interfere with any of his instruction. No matter what he does, you must not interfere. He is your warfare ace and his word is final. Go and talk to your children and let me know your decision. I will be at the

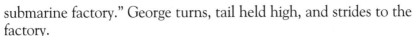

submarine factory." George turns, tail held high, and strides to the factory.

Matthew trudges to the dock, shaking his head. Raquelle and Eric turn their Lake Guardians toward their father and stop close to the dock, then they dismount and climb up on the dock. "Do you want to talk to us?"

Matthew looks into their innocent faces and breathes a heavy sigh. "Yes, we need to make a decision, because I wanted this year to get to know you better. To play on Caribbean beaches and just get really close. Well, that is not going to happen. Now, we have to make a decision about whether or not to sacrifice your innocence for your mother's freedom. Did you ever wonder why, in a movie theater, no one sits close to us?"

Eric tilts his head to the side, "Yes, I have, Dad. Why is it that they don't sit close to us?"

"Because I send out an aura, that says, "I am a trained killer, so don't get too close." Yes, the military trained me, many years ago, to kill the enemies of our country swiftly and efficiently. Only certain men and women can be trained that way but, once they are, then they do whatever it takes to protect our freedom. The Marines do such a great job, that they are never put in charge of our nuclear weapons because, if they are given the order to launch, they will carry it out. I never met a Marine I didn't like."

Raquelle challenges her father, "Come on, Dad, some of them are obnoxious and arrogant."

Matthew just smiles, "Well, the Marines have so much to be proud of, that they fight a constant daily battle to be humble. So, when I run into the person you described, I give them mercy and understanding, because they lost the battle to pride that day. Which brings me to our decision… I need your help and a big sacrifice from both of you. I promised that you could go into battle with me during the next attack. Raquelle, you will be a woman soon so, if you allow the Centurion to train you, you will promptly lose your innocence. He will teach you to evaluate all people as fellow warriors, to meet and conquer all challenges and to be self-reliant. You may not like what you see in most men, and I know that you will have trouble finding a mate. You will be too headstrong for most of them. Will you take the Centurion's training?" Matthew's eyes water; the last thing he wants is for his daughter to lose her innocence, but he loves Shalee with all his heart, so he asks.

Raquelle thinks of her mother and of how decisive and

strong-willed she is. She can charm or intimidate all men. There will be few men, beside her father, that could or would marry her. This Centurion will turn her into a battle-hardened warrior and, perhaps, an old maid, but she loves her parents so, very solemnly, she answers, "Yes, Father, I will help you rescue my mother and maybe become an old maid." Matthew hugs his daughter. He loves her melodramatic comment about the old maid. She will be a great movie actress, someday, because she already has all the right moves. Matthew squeezes her tighter, then releases his grip.

Eric is one big smile, as he blurts out, "Sure, Dad! I can't wait to get started."

Matthew hugs his children, and Elizabeth tries to be included in the hug. Soon, Matthew, Raquelle and Eric hug Elizabeth's neck and she smiles.

Matthew and his children go to the submarine factory and meet George and the Centurion. "My children are ready for the Centurion's training. When do they start?"

Alpha snarls, as he looks up, "The training is for all three of the Wolverines and it starts early tomorrow morning. Now, let me measure you for an individual sub." He roughly grabs Raquelle to take the measurement. Matthew has to fight not to take him down and he notices Matthew flinch. "Ok, Wolverine, do you want the training or not? You will all either die or you will become warriors. Those are the only options. Once the training starts, there is no quitting. I repeat, there is no quitting. There is only death or becoming a warrior. So, if your family can't become warriors, then quit now, and don't waste my time."

Matthew's ears smoked, but then he thought back to his old drill instructor. Tough jobs call for abrasive tactics. Matthew clenched his fists and forced a smile, "By your command, Centurion we will become warriors."

The Centurion grunts, then harshly measures Eric and Matthew. With the measurements taken, he dismisses the Wolverines.

After they leave, George speaks, "Centurion, you were really soft on the Wolverines. You are going to give them full combat training? No half-hearted training that gets them killed in the first battle. They will be fighting in water, so they need to be able to swim fast and be more lethal than the great white sharks of their oceans. Letting them sleep into early morning... What? You getting soft because you're getting close to retiring? Your dad never got soft. I will make up the diving lines, with depth marks, and I will have them ready in two hours, in the water, tied to the dock so, at midnight, you need to be with the Wolverines at the dock and diving. Start them off at fifty feet. Do I make myself clear?"

The Centurion's hand caresses the hilt of his sword, and George's eyes narrow, as he continues, "I have ripped warriors' hands off, as they reached for their swords. If you think you are faster than they were, continue, but I will have a hot iron to seal your severed hand and you will dive tomorrow. Give me the blueprints for the new subs and leave. The warrior releases his sword, then he gives George the drawings. A worker approaches and George gives him the new plans for the new individual subs. Can these subs be ready in one month? The man nods. Suddenly, he bursts out, "With two shifts, we need a café that always stays open and we need better food. If our families could eat with us, that would be even better. We would know that our wives and children are well fed. The old owner kept us hungry, because he felt our hunger caused us to work harder."

Alpha looks at George, then jumps on this opportunity to leave, saving face, "I will take care of the café and visit the wives and children." He goes and hires more cooks, so the café can stay open during both shifts and he secures fresh seafood for all meals. Then he visits the workers' houses. He does not enter any home, but informs the wives, from outside the houses, that they and their children can eat with their husbands, at the café, at any time. The wives are very thankful and gather their children to rush off to enjoy a meal.

George has seaweed ropes made, four hundred feet long, with a glowing sign at 100 feet, which reads 50, another sign at 150 feet, which reads 75, and another sign at 200 feet, which reads 100. He has three holes drilled in each sign and three glowing tags attached to each. He tells the workmen to hurry and take the ropes and attach them to the dock, a leg's length apart, close to the Centurion's sub. They finish their work, then attach the ropes to the dock. Their work complete, they walk past the Centurion, as he boards his sub, and inform him that the ropes are lowered and attached to the dock.

"The War Cat is efficient," Alpha thinks, as he climbs into his bunk. "More troops to train, then another war to win." He sets his alarm for four hours' sleep, then closes his eyes and dreams of retiring and holding his new wife in his arms. Yes, she will be worth all this agony. My Evita waits for me. Grinning from ear to ear, he falls asleep.

Chapter 17

Shalee's Inevitable Despair

Vipurr has all the Krakens looking for the small sub. After a few days, the people of Abaddon get over the sickness they felt in the temple, but the Red Serpent is still deathly sick. For three days, he can't keep anything down and his skin turns a dull maroon. His movements are sluggish, but his temper is quick. On the fourth day, he calls for Vipurr, to find out the status of the three escapees. Vipurr shifts from foot to foot, "The Krakens patrol as far as the statue of O, but we have no sighting of the sub. They seem to have vanished."

The Red Serpent's forked tongue barely comes out of his mouth, as he thinks, "I must have the green-eyed sacrifice to devour at the red tide, in front of all of Abaddon. The people know I am deathly sick because of that woman, so I must prove to them that I am the more powerful. Fear of me is slipping away from the people and we can never let that happen. Tell the Krakens that the one that brings in the sub will receive one hundred dolphins."

Vipurr protests, "We only have eighty dolphins in captivity."

The Red Serpent vomits in front of Vipurr, then his eyes narrow into laser beams of hate. "Krakens can't count; they are stupid; there has never been a Kraken born with the ability to reason, so lie to them. Just bring me all three. Now, get some priests to give me some medicine to make me feel better."

Vipurr goes to the dock to contact the Krakens, who are guarding the entrance to Abaddon, to give them the new orders. More than thirty squids bob in the sea water, off the dock. The water in this section of the dome is sea water, which mixes with the fresh water from the Red Serpent's temple. The Krakens have never entered the Serpent's fresh water pool, but they could sail into it, if they were ordered to protect their god. The colossal gray cone shapes and the monstrous eyes still unnerve Vipurr. He sees only cold, unmerciful death in their eyes and shivers go up his spine. He steadies himself, then he thinks, "A prize of one hundred fifty dolphins for the Kraken that brings in the small submarine. This is top priority, so spread the word to the others and I will have our submarines man the posts that guard Abaddon. So, go!" The squids bob in the water, as these thoughts permeate their brains. Tentacles rise, as they imagine grabbing the dolphins and eating till they bulge. Then one Kraken, which is twice as big as the others, submerges and jets out of Abaddon. All the other Krakens quickly follow, chasing the first one.

Vipurr breathes a sigh of relief. A big lie is always so much better than a small lie. Since Krakens can't count, why not one hundred fifty dolphins? The submarine fleet guards Abaddon, as Vipurr confers with the other priests on how to cure the Red Serpent of his sickness. Every priest is reluctant to voice a suggestion. If a cure doesn't work, the Serpent has a habit of crushing the priest to death slowly, just to let him experience his pain. Vipurr tells the youngest priest to feed the Red Serpent fish oil. That should work. The young priest grabs containers of fish oil, then proceeds into the temple and feeds the fish oil to his master. The Red Serpent drinks the fish oil, then slithers into the water. After an hour, the fish oil comes up, as he slowly crawls to the bottom of his gold statue, where he stays and suffers. His hatred for Shalee grows until his mind is filled with thoughts of how sick she made him. The young priest absconds into the interior of Abaddon. All priests vanish from the temple, as the Red Serpent suffers, but finally falls asleep.

Shalee is in pitch-blackness, wallowing in self-pity, so she has dark thoughts. The revenge on Heather and her sailor are tops on her list, as she cries out to God, "I know You said not to let the sun go down on your anger, but I am in total darkness. There hasn't been a real sun in months, and I want to spike those two bloodsuckers to a cross so bad, I can taste it. If I survive this return ride, I will nail them, if it is the last thing I do on earth." The bile burns in the back of Shalee's throat. She reaches for some food and takes a bite. It is sweet dried dolphin meat, but she doesn't care. It is pleasant and chewy. The acid in Shalee's stomach subsides and she nods off to sleep.

Krakens are scouring the seas to the south of Abaddon, when the leader spots the sub. He races toward it, and his tentacles encircle its front. Other squids quickly wrench the sub with their tentacles. A tug of war follows, with each creature imagining one hundred fifty dolphins, all for himself, so the battle is bestial. Shalee tosses from side to side inside the cramped sub. The Krakens crush the front of the sub, and water rushes inside. Heather's note is thrown outside the sub and shredded among the flying tentacles and legs. The Krakens' black "parrot" beaks viciously open and close, biting off legs and tentacles alike. Then, the largest one starts biting mantles as Kraken after Kraken dies until the five remaining Krakens flee in terror. The winner tows the semi-crushed sub toward Abaddon.

Shalee can feel the cold water on the control side of her compartment and she is happy there is metal protecting her from the cold water. Then a pinprick of a hole sprays a light mist of cold water on her back. She jumps, then tries to plug the pinprick with a piece of dried dolphin, but she just slows the spray to a few drops that roll down her hands. The water is chilly, and she knows that she can't hold the plug for very long. How far they are from Abaddon, she has no idea. Are they even going to Abaddon? The compartment's blackness and the days of isolation impregnate her soul. The chance to return to Abaddon drains the life out of her hands and she involuntarily drops the dolphin meat, then the spray continues. Shalee sits down, depressed, and feels the cold mist touch her legs. She considers Heather, the Red Serpent, Vipurr, the slime that lives in Abaddon. "I am a Wolverine and they are not going to beat me!" She grabs a dry piece of dolphin and slams it against the hole, pressing with all her might. The water stops for the moment.

The giant Kraken is jetting through the water at breakneck speed. He can see that the sub is damaged and he wonders if any humans inside survive. This Kraken has the power to reason, so he knows it is not the sub that Vipurr wants, but the occupants. He can taste the one hundred fifty dolphins that await him in Abaddon. He reasons that he can eat ten dolphins a day so, for fifteen days, he will be well fed. His muscles contract and relax at lightning speed, as he is propelled nimbly toward home. The damaged sub hinders his progress, causing his muscles to ache, but he concentrates on the dolphins and guts it out.

Shalee concentrates on pressing her weight to her hands and plugging the leak. Some water slowly coats the metal and collects at her feet. The crisp salt water covers her feet and they feel like they are encased in ice. She stamps her feet, splashing the water. It is getting deeper, but she will not give up to the slime of Abaddon. She draws on all her strength from deep within and doubles her effort to plug the leak. She can feel the sub speeding rapidly through the water.

Vipurr is hiding in the palace and he is worried. The Red Serpent will eat him, if he doesn't come up with a cure. Alexis steps into Vipurr's view. "I can cure the Red Serpent but, will you give me freedom and my weight in blue diamonds?"

Vipurr grasps at any chance for his life and he lies easily, "You can be as free as the Krakens. Do you wish to be put on a surface island with your blue diamonds after you cure the Red Serpent?"

Alexis's eyes flash at the prospect, "You can put me on a surface island with my blue diamonds?"

Vipurr gives his best smile, "Why, of course, only let us not let our god suffer another minute."

Alexis tells Vipurr to bring the Red Serpent to the dock by the salt water. She will meet them there with the ingredients for the cure. Vipurr rushes to the temple, then he and the Red Serpent laboriously proceed to the dock.

Alexis fills a bucket with the jelly lobes of dolphins, then she orders the cook to bring ten live sea turtles, and a sharp knife, to the dock. She looks out the palace door and sees the cook and the ten sea turtles on the dock. She struggles to carry the heavy bucket of dolphin jelly to the dock. The Red Serpent stares at her. Alexis swallows hard, "Cook, cut out the tongues of the sea turtles, quickly, and wash them in salt water, then swiftly mix them in this bucket of dolphin jelly and feed it to the Red Serpent."

The cook's shoulders tremble, as he hurriedly cuts out the tongues, washes them in the sea water, mixes them with his hands in the bucket of dolphin jelly and throws the contents as far as he can down the Red Serpent's throat. Then he backs to the end of the dock, on the pretense of washing his hands at the end of dock. Alexis forgets to tell the Serpent that the salt water will cause a violent reaction in his stomach, but it will be only for ten seconds, then his body will return to normal. Only a small piece of information, but so crucial, when dealing with a violently sick, short-tempered god. The Red Serpent sees the water break, as a gigantic Kraken bobs straight up from the water. The sub remains below. The Serpent's stomach feels like hot irons are fighting to burn through his skin and his eyes flare, "You poison me." With all his energy, he scoops Alexis up, in one movement, and swallows her whole. Vipurr and the monstrous Kraken remain frozen by the Red Serpent's atrocious action. Vipurr, fearing he will be next, slowly, involuntarily, quivers in place. The cook dives into the sea next to the squid, so the Red Serpent will not eat him. After a few moments, the sweetness of fresh mints fills the Red Serpent's stomach and the natural bright red pigment returns to his skin, starting at his tail. He shakes himself, then he raises up, "Vipurr, what did you promise that wonderful girl?"

Vipurr takes a moment to recover. "Her freedom on a surface island and her weight in blue diamonds."

The giant squid slowly bobs, as he focuses on every thought

the Red Serpent will broadcast because of the death of this woman, who just cured him. That bothers him, but he doesn't know why.

The Red Serpent looks at the cook in the water, then says to Vipurr, "So you offered her freedom on a surface island and eight blue diamonds? Well, that prize should go to this brave cook who delivered my cure. Get eight blue diamonds and hand them to the cook."

The cook is reluctant to leave the water, so the Kraken takes a tentacle and lifts him onto the dock. Since he is covered in salt water, Vipurr makes sure not to touch him. He drops eight blue diamonds in his hands, then tells him that this Kraken will accompany his sub to the surface island, along with a priest to guard him and guide the sub. The cook falls on his knees and thanks the high priest for his freedom. Vipurr thought the man would reject the idea of going to the surface, so he scowls at the man, then turns to the Kraken, "Why are you here?"

The loathesome Kraken's brain is processing all the events that just happened. He jets toward the dock and, a moment before he impacts the dock, he does a U-turn and flings the sub into the air. It sails out of the water for a second or two, then crashes into the dock and almost kills Vipurr. He trembles and his knees buckle, and he staggers to lean on his master for support. The Red Serpent just stares at the sub, transfixed by the Kraken's action, and he wonders how the creature reasoned that his move would beach the sub.

Other priests rush to open the hatch and drag Shalee out of the sub and onto her knees. She looks around to see the huge squid bobbing in the water, the Serpent flushed with new red color, and Vipurr still shaking from the sub's near miss. Her feet are numb after being submerged in that cold water, so she supports herself on her hands and knees. Dark thoughts rise from her stomach to her face and her scowl causes even the Red Serpent to recoil. Then, like a cobra, she spits out her words, "Red Worm, you will never capture Heather and her sailor on their surface island. I dropped them on the island and was headed for Atlantis, when this monstrous Kraken stopped my sub. So eat me now, because I know I won, and you will never capture Heather because you are dumb. But she is smart and free."

The rest of Abaddon has gathered around the palace and temple to witness the return of this sacrifice, who, while on her knees, stands up to their god. The Red Serpent senses the doubt running through the crowd's minds. Even if he eats this sacrifice, they will believe she won by freeing Heather. The two on the surface must be found and punished. Towering over the crowd, the Red Serpent booms out forceful thoughts, "Your god will show mercy to this sacrifice and spare her until the red tide. Priests, take her away to the temple and heal her feet. Vipurr will send every sub we have to the surface to hunt down that traitor, Heather, and her Judas of a sailor. They are the ones that caused my sickness and they will pay. Now, my worshipers, disperse and go back to work. Vipurr, follow me into the temple." The Serpent slithers into the temple, with the high priest close behind.

The Kraken submerges and jets into the lake inside the temple and rises. The Red Serpent is alarmed to see the Kraken in his lake, "What do you want?"

"I want my one hundred fifty dolphins, but spread out over fifteen days. So will Vipurr feed me my first ten dolphins now?"

The Red Serpent can't believe that this Kraken can count, "He will feed you in a few minutes. Now, leave my fresh water lake and don't ever return to my temple." As the giant squid sinks, the Red Serpent turns to Vipurr, "Feed him the eighty dolphins over ten days, then send him out on patrol. Send him close to Atlantis's navy; because he can reason, he needs to die. Do you understand?"

As Vipurr nods, then turns to leave the temple, the water behind the Serpent ripples, as the Kraken now leaves the fresh water lake for the salt water. So the Red Serpent is out to kill him. The creature bobs beside the dock, as Vipurr approaches, and he prepares to hear more lies. "Your dolphins will be released in the feeding pond. Feed quickly and follow the sub that carries the cook and the priest, to the surface island, then return here to finish your meal. After you finish feeding, proceed to the waters around the statue of O. The Red Serpent must know when their navy moves. Now, go to the feeding pond."

The Kraken goes to the feeding pond and hurriedly eats his ten dolphins. He would have liked to take all day to enjoy the meal, but the sub is preparing to leave. So he jets to the dock, and sees the cook fill a sub with his belongings and get inside the storage compartment. The priest, with two daggers at his side, enters through the hatch to guide the sub to the island.

The trip takes three days and the Kraken gets hungry. As the sub surfaces near the shore of the island, the squid surfaces next to it. The priest exits and scans the horizon. There is smoke on the far side of the island. The Kraken sees the smoke and asks the priest to check it. Could it be surface dwellers or Heather and her sailor? The priest hears the cook banging on the hatch and opens it. The cook breathes in deeply and sings, as he emerges from the sub. The priest tells him to be quiet, until he checks out the smoke. He leaves and the cook unloads his supplies and belongings.

The Kraken bobs beside the submarine and he fills the cook's mind with pleasant thoughts, "This is a great island. Just look at that sunrise. You made a wise move, escaping from the Red Serpent; but I don't trust that priest. I think he may murder you and take your blue diamonds."

The cook jerks back and abruptly stops unpacking, "You think he would kill me? I am not a fighter. What can I do?"

The Kraken weighs his thoughts, "I could help you, but then you would have to be loyal to me instead of to the Red Serpent. Whom do you think ordered your death, the Red Serpent or Vipurr? Do you want to stay loyal to those betrayers or have me as a protector?"

The cook looks worried, as he stammers, "Why would they want to kill me? I am no harm to them. I have always been loyal to the Red Serpent and he is my god."

The Kraken enjoys reasoning with humans, so he tests the limits of this new power, "Alexis was loyal to her god, and where is she now, but inside the Red Serpent's stomach? After the dagger enters your back, I hope you will live long enough to admit you were wrong. I will stay by the sub until the priest kills you, so I can hear your apology."

"No, help me to live. I will be loyal to you; just don't let me die."

The Kraken raises one of its huge tentacles out of the water and lightly touches the cook on his left shoulder, "I will protect you; only stay close to the water and the sub. The priest will try to get you to go deeper into the island so he can cut your throat, but don't you do it. Now, start cooking one of your finest meals, and make it enough to feed four."

The cook gathers some brush and starts to cook. As the smell of the food wafts through the air, the priest returns. "Heather and her traitorous sailor are on the other side of the island. What a reward the Red Serpent would give for their capture! That smells so tasty. Is it ready to eat?"

The Kraken looks at the cook, then stares at the priest. "Why not invite Heather and her sailor to eat with you and tell them the Red Serpent is so pleased with their returning his sacrifice, that he wants to present Heather with a three-strand ruby necklace. After the ceremony, they can return to their island, because all is forgiven. Oh, yes, and allow the cook to live, because his eight blue diamonds are nothing, compared to the reward that the Red Serpent will give you. Now, go invite them to eat with us."

The exposed priest looks at the cook, who holds a knife and has backed into the water, and knows his plan is revealed, but this Kraken's plan can work. The priest turns and walks to the site of the other fire and approaches Heather and the sailor from behind. In his happiest voice, he says, "Come join me for a meal, because the Red Serpent is so pleased with you, that he sent a cook to prepare you a real feast."

Heather and the sailor jump up and whirl to face the priest. The priest stands with open arms and a grin from ear to ear. "How did you find us?"

The priest sighs and prepares his best lies, "When the Red Serpent found that his sacrifice had been returned, he was so pleased, that he had his jeweler craft a three-strand ruby necklace for Heather. He wishes to honor you in Abaddon, and then you can return to this island because your loyalty to the Red Serpent is true. There are only the cook and I in our sub. The cook has prepared a magnificent feast, but I see you are disturbed, so I remove my daggers and lay them at my feet, as I step back."

Heather and the sailor watch the priest lay his daggers at his feet and step back. When the daggers are safely in the sailor's hands, the priest turns to go to the beach and the feast.

Heather softly speaks to the sailor. "Do you think we should return to Abaddon?"

"They know where we are and they would not have sent one priest and a cook to capture us. The Red Serpent would have sent a full crew, so the priest must be telling the truth. Let us eat the meal and then decide if we will return or kill the priest and the cook." Heather takes one of the daggers and nods.

The Kraken bobs in the sea, enjoying the sunshine and how easy it is to deal with humans. "Our honored guests came for their celebration. Priest, did you tell Heather of the sparkling ruby necklace that Vipurr wishes to drape around her neck? The Red Serpent was so pleased that you returned his green-eyed sacrifice. But, enough talk! Savor your delicious feast."

Heather clutches the hilt of the dagger, as she glances at the feast, the cook, then her sailor. The sailor is still suspicious, "It could be poisoned, so Cook, you try it first."

The cook is famished, so he grabs a large bowl and fills it to the brim, then quickly wolfs down the soup. He is going for his second bowl, when the sailor stops him and takes a bowl for himself and Heather. It is dried sea turtle soup, with Sargasso sea weed and Atlantic eels for flavoring. The cook got the fresh water from the sub. Both the sailor and Heather devour their soup. The cook asks them where there is fresh water, on the island, and they point back to their fire, where there is a stream. There are fruit trees on this island, beside the stream, and the sailor built a bungalow, where he and Heather live. There is a small lagoon, where the fish get trapped, when the tide goes out, so food is plentiful. This is their dream come true.

At this point, the priest interjects, "It is so beautiful and peaceful. But admit it, you miss the food of Abaddon, so that is why the Red Serpent sent the gift of your own cook. He will live with you, and cook your meals, which will give you more free time. My job was to deliver the cook to your island and our master told me that, if you decide not to return for your reward, then I get the ruby necklace, and that gift will buy me years of pleasure at Heather's old palace." The priest plays his part to the max and gives a dreamy sigh, as he closes his eyes. After a few minutes, he opens his eyes, "I know you don't want to leave your dream island, and I totally understand, so I will cast off for Abaddon. Cook, you stay on the island and treat these people like royalty. Many nights of pleasure await me." The priest is up like a shot and starts to climb into the sub.

Heather jumps up and grabs the hatch, "No! That necklace is mine and I forgot the rest of my clothes and treasures in Abaddon. We will pick that up before we return to this island."

The sailor shakes his head, "Heather, let him have the necklace. Please don't leave the island."

Heather braces herself as she turns, "We have his daggers, the Red Serpent sent a cook for us, and I want the envy of all the other women of Abaddon, as I parade my jewelry and bask in the praise of my god. He has his sacrifice, so what have we to fear? Do you really want to remain with this cook, when you could be honored in Abaddon, in front of your fellow sailors?"

The sailor looks at the cook, then at Heather. He orders the priest out of the control section and into the cargo section. The priest looks at the Kraken and tells it to go ahead and make the preparations for their return. Then he enters the cargo section and the sailor closes the hatch. The squid motions the sailor away from the sub, and into the water, with the wave of a leg. He cautiously follows. The creature gently thinks, "There is a deep sea cave, a day's journey from here, and I want you to go into the cave and wait for my return. Some of the Krakens are still looking for you and the sacrifice. They don't realize that you sent her back to the Red Serpent. I will follow you to the cave, then I will go to Abaddon and collect more Kraken and inform them of your arrival. This is for your safety—or, if you prefer, we can proceed to Abaddon. But, if more than five Krakens attack the sub, I am gone. What is your decision?"

The sailor looks at Heather, who is climbing into the sub and motioning him to hurry. He thinks they should wait in the cave, until the Kraken returns. He agrees and the sailor enters the submarine and dives. The squid waits a full five minutes after the sub leaves before he thinks to the cook, "Surface ships pass by this island, so signal them with smoke. Escape to the islands to your west, as soon as possible, but keep your blue diamonds concealed from the surface dwellers and live a long happy life."

As the Kraken submerges, he realizes that he should have killed the cook, but he feels pity for the human. What a strange new emotion is this clemency! Krakens are born killers, without the emotions of love or pity or the ability to reason with humans, but he feels emotions other than hate. He is evolving into something new and he likes this devious new nature, even if it does have pity mixed into it. He speeds up and, after he catches the sub, he swims beside it. After a day, they approach a large wide ledge with a small hole in it, in the side of a mountain and the creature motions the sub into the cave. The sailor cautiously enters the cave and steers into the interior until he can surface. As the sub rises, he switches on the lights and finds there is air and a beach in the cave. The sub glides toward the beach and docks. Now, they can stretch their legs. Heather is the first one out of the sub and she lets the priest out. They explore the cavern, as they walk. The air is stale and musty, but breathable.

These humans are so trusting of what they consider inferior life forms. The Kraken moves up above the cave to a pile of boulders, and wraps his tentacles and all his legs around the largest of the boulders and starts to shake it. It is very heavy and, for a while, it does not move but, by using his will power and by forcing water through his jets, it starts to move, and then tumbles for the ledge. The other rocks holding the pile slide down to the cave's entrance and quickly fill the ledge and seal the cave. The Kraken surveys the sealed cave and feels much better. Mercy is nice, but malicious killing is to be savored and relished on the quick trip back to Abaddon and a feast of a hundred forty dolphins.

Chapter 18

Breaking the Spirit

The Centurion's alarm goes off, and he hits it with the side of his right fist. The alarm is built into the side of his ship and is built to take the ramming of a charging bull elephant. There were always rumors of a Centurion breaking his alarm by smashing his fist through the ship's hull, but this one never has. He rises and dresses in swim shorts, then grabs some towels and checks the seaweed ropes. They are secure, so he lays the towels beside them and heads for Wolverine's house. He enters without knocking. George sleeps in the hallway, and when he hears the noise, his eyes pop open and his muscles involuntarily prepare to launch an attack but, when he sees the Centurion, he rolls over and goes back to sleep. The soldier spits on the wall, then enters Raquelle's room, "Up, Maggot!" He flips her bed over, then heads for Eric's room. "Up, you worm!" Eric's bed tumbles over and the Centurion heads for Matthew's room. Matthew is in the hallway, with his sword in his hand. He shouts at Matthew, "So, you want to swim with a sword? Strap it to your back, and get a swimsuit on now. That goes for all of you maggots. Outside, now!" Eric and Raquelle scramble to get on swimsuits, and Matthew changes, while the Centurion swears at his slowness. Their clothes changed, the Wolverines race to the dock, with their Drill Instructor shouting at the top of his lungs, what maggots he has to train.

He switches on the lights on his ship to full illumination. Matthew has the sword strapped to his back, as they stand beside the seaweed rope. Elizabeth and a few of the Lake Guardians surface to see why the lights are on, and why their sleep was disturbed. The Centurion's voice blares over the water, "You maggots will dive to the first glowing signs and bring me back the glowing tags. Now, worms, don't fail me! Dive!"

Matthew dives into the water, traveling down beside the rope. Eric and Raquelle dive into the water, kicking as fast as they can, beside their ropes. They keep looking for a glow, as they go deeper. Eric's lungs start to burn, but he keeps descending, to find the glowing sign. Off in the distance, he sees a faint glow, but he is suffocating, so he turns, kicking as hard as he can, for the surface. Raquelle sees Eric turn, and her chest hurts, but she goes deeper, until she sees the glow of the sign. It seems so far away, and she turns to propel herself to the surface. Matthew can see the glow and it is close,but fire is consuming his lungs, and he turns toward the surface. Matthew, Eric and Raquelle break water at the same time, gasping for air. They crawl up on the dock and lie on their stomachs, each fighting for more breath.

The Centurion shouts that none of them returned even one glowing tag. They cannot even make it to the first marker. He keeps shouting until each Wolverine stops gasping. Then, he shows them how to take ten deep breaths and he swims to the marker, in one long steady dive, unlocks the tag and swims to the surface. He shows it to the trio, then dives to the glowing sign and clips the tag back on. He surfaces, then climbs onto the dock. "Can you maggots do that? You must learn to control your air and your swimming, to conserve energy." The three reluctantly dive into the water and head down the ropes. Matthew is determined to make it to the marker and grab the tag. As precious seconds slip by, he swims and swims. His muscles burn, and so do his lungs, but he keeps descending. Matthew can clearly see the marker, but that is as far as he can go, and he turns for the surface. When he comes up, Eric and Raquelle are on the dock, gasping for air. Matthew hates failure and he just failed twice. He pulls himself up on the dock.

The Centurion is livid, "You scum can't even make the first marker! Now get back in the water and dive. Matthew, remove the sword from your back and bring me a tag."

Elizabeth swims beside Matthew, as he dives, the next time, and she encourages him down to the glowing markers and he removes the tag, then speeds toward the surface. He comes out of the water and throws the tag at the feet of the Centurion. He stoops to pick up the tag and holds it over the side of the dock for Eric and Raquelle to see, "The first tag is returned. Where are your tags, Scum? One maggot has succeeded, now you return this tag to its marker and you other scum dive."

Elizabeth swims beside Raquelle, as she dives but, as they approach the marker, the girl appears ready to turn back. Elizabeth swiftly swims to the marker, then she stops and looks up at Raquelle. Raquelle continues to swim toward Elizabeth, then she swiftly removes the tag and swims for the surface. She makes it to within ten feet of the surface, where she blacks out and releases air bubbles. Elizabeth immediately uses her back to bring Raquelle to the surface beside the dock. The Centurion, in one motion, has her off Elizabeth's back and performs mouth-to-mouth resuscitation on her, until she coughs up a little water, and opens her eyes. Raquelle lifts the glowing tag for the Centurion to see. He smiles and gives her a hug, and puts his mouth close to her ear, "Good. I knew you could do it." He raises her to her feet, as Eric and Matthew climb up on the dock.

"Are you all right, Raquelle?"

"Yes. I just took in a little water, but I got the tag. Did the Centurion show you my tag? Did you get your tag, Eric?"

Eric hangs his head. "No, I just get to where I can see the glowing sign clearly, and I feel like I am suffocating, and I turn back. I'm not as brave as you."

Raquelle smiles, "Take Elizabeth with you. She helped me, and she can help you. I believe in you, and I know you can get the tag. Now, let's get back to diving."

Raquelle stands up and dives into the water, kicking with all her might, to reach the glowing marker. Elizabeth, with smooth clean strokes, swims ahead of her, to the marker, then she turns and stares up at her and waits. This reminds her of teaching her babies to swim into very deep dark water. They were afraid that the darkness contained horrors like Krakens and, sometimes, it did, but their mother taught them to go into the darkness and to not be afraid. Elizabeth is proud of Raquelle for returning to the water so quickly. She has her mother's courage. Elizabeth smiles. Raquelle reaches the glowing sign, head first, and attaches the marker, then flips her legs downward and darts for the surface. Not one expended ounce of energy was wasted. Raquelle now knows that she can make a complete dive. As she grows close to the surface, she sends all her energy to her legs, keeps her arms at her sides and breaks the water with a splash. The Centurion helps her to the dock and she rests until her father returns with a glowing tag. Eric surfaces slowly, and without a tag. He slowly crawls onto the dock. "I just can't make that last few feet to the tags."

The Centurion is in his face, "I don't have time for scum or little babies that need their mommies. Do you want to crawl back to your house and go to bed or do you want to dive?"

Eric's nostrils flare, "I am not a baby and I can make this dive. I'll show you!" With those words, Eric takes ten deep breaths, then plunges over the side and speeds for his glowing marker. Elizabeth swims by his side, as he goes deeper and deeper. The marker glows in the distance and Elizabeth races ahead to turn and encourage Eric to go further down. He reaches his usual turn-around, as his brain slows nis swimming, and he prepares to turn, but Elizabeth releases a loud roar. Eric can clearly hear the roar, because sound travels four times faster in water than in air, and he reaches the glowing marker in record time. He fumbles with the tag, as he unlocks it, but it slips through his fingers. It drifts toward the lake's bottom, as Eric heads for the surface. The current from his feet kicking speeds the tag toward the bottom. He can see the lights from the Centurion's ship, but he can't get through the water to break the surface and his lungs have never burned this badly. He needs air now, and he puts all his strength into his kick, then he realizes that Elizabeth is gone. There is no safety net. He feels so alone and he mentally calls for his dad to rescue him, as he draws strength from deep within and pumps his legs harder. As he breaks through, his strength fades and he lays face down in the water. Four powerful arms snatch him out of the water and pull him up on the dock. The Centurion pushes Matthew out of the way, as Eric coughs. "I did get the tag but I dropped it."

The Centurion snarls, "If you don't have the tag, then you didn't retrieve it. You failed."

Eric looks to his dad, and Matthew thinks he is going to cry. He holds his son tight. Just then, Elizabeth surfaces and flings the glowing tag onto the dock.

"How do I know that *you* didn't remove the tag?"

Elizabeth tilts her head, as she looks into the Centurion's eyes, "I have flippers. Even you are not dumb enough to believe that flippers can remove a tag. Where did you come from, Planet Stupid?"

Alpha roars with laughter. It is contagious, and Eric begins to laugh, then Raquelle and finally, even Matthew laughs. Their laughter fills the dock, as George strides up to them. "So, you think this training is funny? Well, Centurion, it is not supposed to be funny. Did each of them make it to retrieve the first tag?"

The Centurion is now sober, as he replies, but he exaggerates, "Yes; it took them quite a few attempts, but each recovered his tag and then replaced it."

George fills his lungs ten times, then he races over the side of the dock and plunges like a boulder to the bottom of the lake. The stunned audience takes a few seconds to react, then the Centurion orders Elizabeth to dive after the War Cat. Elizabeth's powerful fins take her down quickly to the first marker. George is methodically doggy paddling, as he inspects each marker, then he wraps his paws, with his claws retracted, around Elizabeth's neck and orders her to quickly rise to the surface. After they surface, George releases his grip and puts two paws on the dock. Elizabeth uses her head to push his rump up on to the dock. The tiger walks to the Centurion and says, "Only two tags were replaced and one is missing. I am not pleased." George turns and walks back to the Wolverine house.

Matthew has to ask the Centurion, "I didn't think cats could dive. How did he reach the marker so fast--and how did he plan to return to the surface?"

"The War Cat sinks fast and, when he reached the marker, just tread water, to inspect my results. He knew I would send down the Lake Guardian to rescue him. What do you think, I was born on Planet Stupid? Get in the water and swim to the other side of the bubble and back. I will tell you when to stop your laps." He dives in to replace Eric's tag.

Matthew, Raquelle and Eric enter the water and start their laps. Elizabeth goes beside them, and it is artificial dawn, before they stop for breakfast. The trio can barely climb up on the dock. The Centurion races them to their house, where Desiraa has breakfast ready. He slowly looks her up one side and down the other. She does not notice the hunger in the Centurion's eyes, but Raquelle does. He suppresses his passion and barks, "Eat fast because we need to run along the streets until lunch. Your muscles are soft, but I will make them as hard as blue diamonds." George and the Centurion exchange a glance, as they remember their basic training, and they smile at the term "blue diamond". It is a military thing.

The Centurion runs the Wolverines until lunchtime and Eric, Raquelle and even Matthew drag aching muscles to the table. Eric's leg muscles cramp and Matthew gives a deep sports massage to his legs, but his hands begin to cramp and he has to stop. The Centurion has the trio lie face down on the ground, and he starts to massage Raquelle's legs. "I have to massage deep into the muscles, and it will hurt, but we have to get fresh blood to the muscles to flush out the toxins and heal them. I start at your feet and massage each toe, then move to the calves, up to the hamstrings, the butt, the lower back, the upper back, the shoulders, and I finish with the arms. Give Raquelle a piece of cloth to bite on for the pain."

Raquelle bites on the cloth, but the pain soon has her growling. The Centurion takes a full hour on Raquelle. She staggers to her feet, dog-tired, but the pain in her muscles has gone. He tells her that her training is done for the day and she slowly shuffles to her room and falls into her bed. She is sound asleep, as Eric bites the cloth then growls in pain. He is only given a half hour and dismissed. He trudges into his bedroom and flops across his bed, his feet almost touching the ground and he goes to sleep face down. Matthew places the cloth in his mouth, as the Centurion goes incredibly deep into his muscles. His goal is to reach the bone. Matthew swallows hard, and bites down hard. He knows that, the deeper the Centurion massages, the quicker his muscles will heal, so he bears the pain. He grabs the legs of a chair to occupy his hands. He fights not to mutter with pain, but it slips out. The Centurion appears not to notice, because he kneads the muscles deeper. His hands feel knots in Matthew's shoulder muscles, and his thumbs dig into the knots, to break them up. Suddenly, he uses the point of his elbow to burrow into Matthew's shoulder muscles and he really leans into the movement. It is like having a bull elephant step on his shoulder, and the pain flashes across Matthew's brain. His knuckles turn white, as he fights not to react to this assault on his body. The Centurion finally rises, "Do you feel better?"

Matthew glares, "Oh, yes! Like being beaten by a hundred baseball bats, one swing after another." He plods off to his bed and falls in. It has been years since he has gone through such brutal training. He knows it is needed, but that doesn't make it any less barbaric. He mentally apologizes to God for putting his children through this training, then he drops into an exhausted sleep.

Chapter 19

A Reasoning Kraken?

Shalee is carried into the palace and placed in hot water. Her feet hurt, but the warmth of the water causes the feeling to return. She trusted Heather, so she now wonders if any of these women can be trusted. Are they all as rotten to the core? Escape, without their help, will be next to impossible, but whom can she trust? For the next hour, Shalee sits in the hot water and contemplates her escape. Amber breaks into her thoughts with a question, "So, Heather and her sailor really escaped?"

Shalee plays the role, "Why, yes, they are on a desert island that the Red Serpent will never find. It was just my luck to be recaptured by that gigantic Kraken, but you can now see that escape is possible."

Amber beams, "We need to plan to get the rest of us out of Abaddon. I am astonished that Heather did not betray you, because she was so two-faced, but I must have misjudged her. She is free and in no danger of being eaten by the Red Serpent. With Alexis and Heather gone, only one person left in our group would betray us."

Shalee's forehead furrows, as she mentally notes that Amber believes there is still one traitor in their midst, "What happened to Alexis?"

Amber becomes very somber, "She made the mistake of curing the Red Serpent and he ate her, for her good deed. In Abaddon, no good deed goes unpunished. You were inside the sub, being pulled by the Kraken, as she was being swallowed. We need to escape immediately. I shake at night, in fear of waking inside his belly. Please, Shalee, I don't want to die that horrible death!"

Shalee looks into Amber's eyes, and there is real terror. She is so scared she would be a danger to any escape plan. If the priests see this fear in her eyes and confront her, she will confess in an instant. "It is best if I keep any escape plans to myself, so as not to endanger you. I will tell you only the portion of the plan that is your part. Remember that we still have one traitor in our midst."

Amber appears satisfied with this explanation, and Shalee leaves the whirlpool to be rubbed down with Dolphin Oil. After the massage, she goes to bed to get a restful sleep. For the next five days, Shalee gets the strength back in her legs and body. She takes long

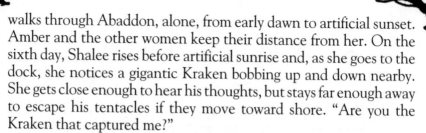

walks through Abaddon, alone, from early dawn to artificial sunset. Amber and the other women keep their distance from her. On the sixth day, Shalee rises before artificial sunrise and, as she goes to the dock, she notices a gigantic Kraken bobbing up and down nearby. She gets close enough to hear his thoughts, but stays far enough away to escape his tentacles if they move toward shore. "Are you the Kraken that captured me?"

Its large eyes focus on Shalee, "Yes, you are worth one hundred fifty dolphins to me. I am glad you survived. I was afraid that, if you died, Vipurr and the Red Serpent would cheat me out of my prize. That would be unwise on their part. I have eaten ten already and they owe me one hundred forty more, at ten per day, for the next fourteen days."

Shalee realizes that this Kraken can count. Then she looks for the sub with the priest, which she had heard that he guarded, "Where is the sub with the priest and the cook?"

The Kraken bobs, as his body changes to bright silver, and his eyes sparkle, "That sub was attacked by an enemy sub and sank. The three were lost."

Shalee seizes this last statement, "But only the priest and cook were on the sub. How did they become three?"

The giant squid needs to polish its lying and it fumbles for a thought, "I was mistaken; it was only the two."

"No, you can count, you can reason, and you can lie. You fit right into Abaddon. So, I know you don't trust Vipurr or the Red Serpent. Are they going to give you the full one hundred fifty dolphins? I know they will cheat you so, when you know that they have cheated you, we can talk, and you can tell me who the three were, who perished on that sub. Enjoy your ten dolphins today, if they actually give you ten dolphins." Shalee turns to walk back to the palace. She planted seeds of mistrust inside this Kraken and he may be her future confederate on an escape. As she enters the palace, Vipurr emerges from the temple and sees the Kraken. He cautiously approaches the dock, "Where is the sub with the priest?"

The Kraken remains a bright silver color; it will not make the same mistake with him. "An Atlantian sub destroyed our Abaddonian sub, with the cook and the priest on board. It crept up from behind and fired lasers, then it quickly fled. I am starved and need ten of my dolphins."

Vipurr's face turns a bright red, "It was your job to protect that sub! Krakens are dispensable, but submarines are not." As soon as the

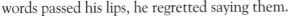

words passed his lips, he regretted saying them.

The squid changes to fire engine red, but continues to bob. "So you feel all Krakens are disposable. We fight and die for the Red Serpent but, since we are nonessential, it does not matter to you or to him. Now, for my ten dolphins." What Vipurr did not see were the Krakens just below the surface, that also turned a bright red after this statement sunk into their brains. The gigantic creature, as he passed the streams of molten lava, contacted the Krakens on guard, and told them he would share his dolphins, if they remained concealed in the water and listened to Vipurr.

The high priest spits out his words, "The dolphin pool has released your ten dolphins, so go there and eat." He turns and hurries into the temple.

The huge squid leads the others under the water, to the dolphin pool, and his sensors detect only five dolphins. His tentacle reaches inside the pool and he grabs a large one. He signals to the other Krakens that all the rest of the dolphins, today, are theirs. They cram the pool, as tentacles snatch the four remaining dolphins.

The largest Kraken enjoys his dolphin, but he is still hungry, so he proceeds to the entrance of Abaddon, just inside the streams of molten lava, as the others group around him, to go back on guard duty. He is furious at being cheated by Vipurr and the Red Serpent. "Vipurr only gave me five dolphins, instead of the ten he promised." The others stare blankly at the huge squid. They cannot count, so his thoughts form no pictures in their minds. The calculating Kraken changes his tactics, "Are you hungry? Well, I am hungry because Vipurr did not give us enough dolphins. He keeps us hungry. He does not feed you, but I will feed you. Vipurr is bad, but I am good."

This concept of hunger and being underfed, the other Krakens' brains can embrace. They are hungry and their brains associate this hunger with a bad Vipurr. The huge squid tells them that he will bring them food, so they are to stay prepared, by the entrance, and grab the food, as it enters. All the other squids cluster around the entrance, as the giant one jets through the hole to search for a school of large fish. After about three hours, a large school of tuna swims toward the streams of magma. The massive Kraken shows his mantle, as he fans his two tentacles and eight legs as far from his body as possible. The tunas panic at the sight of death and race ahead of the horrendous beast. He keeps after them for ten minutes and the fish begin to tire. He steers them toward the streams of magma, jetting first to the their right, then to their left, to keep the tunas in a tight school. They now swim sluggishly, as they head for the opening between the streams of magma. The tunas pass the opening and are immediately gripped in the tentacles of the waiting Krakens. The giant squid jets into the opening, with all limbs extended, as every limb seizes a large tuna.

The monstrous Kraken has never held so much food in his limbs, at one time, but he draws his limbs into his beak. His two-foot tongue, or radula, with its backward teeth, slices the tuna into mush, as he stuffs himself. He eats so many tunas, he can't eat any more, so he calls to the other squid to take them from him. They quickly consume the free tuna until they, too, are stuffed and they can eat no more. Some tuna escapes into the lake, but the Krakens just let them go for another meal. As the stuffed squids float in an enormous circle, one thinks, "Since my first thought, I have never been full. Always, under the Red Serpent, I have been hungry but, under our new leader, I am full." The other Krakens' thoughts agree that they are full and that it is because of the giant Kraken, and they acknowledge him as their new leader.

He chooses his thoughts carefully, "To the Red Serpent, your lives mean nothing. He does not care for you, but I do. I have fed you to fullness. Follow my commands and we will be full, most of the time." The rest of the group takes a minute for their brains to absorb the change in leadership. Then their new leader continues, "Stay on guard and I will search for a new home for us."

The Kraken leader jets out of the opening, past the flow of magma, then goes to the nearest mountain range, to search for caverns. He finds many caverns, but not the one he is seeking. A shark comes out of the side of the mountain and the Kraken stops. He had not even seen the hole, so he goes closer to the mountain's side, to inspect. There is a hole that his mantle can fit through. He goes back outside and measures the hole, with one leg, and it is half the length of his leg in circumference. That is too small for a whale to fit through, so he proceeds back into the hole and it opens into a wide cavern. He moves along the wall, and it goes for miles. He finally circles the entire cavern, then he goes down to the bottom and his huge eyes scan the darkness. There is something on the rock floor and he reaches out with a tentacle to feel the object. It is in the shape of a "T" and his tentacle goes over every inch of it. This is made out of metal; it is a pick. This cavern must be one of the first mines of Bluegreen, that flooded. It can hold a thousand Krakens and no whale can get through the opening. It is a safe haven. He rests on the floor to work out the rest of his plan.

Early the next morning the Kraken floats in the water, beside the dock, and waits for Shalee to come out. As the rest of the palace sleeps, she quietly rises, dresses and heads for the dock. She sees him bobbing up and down. Is he waiting for her? She proceeds with caution, as there is a guard at the dock, but he is asleep. She sits by the dock, closer to him than yesterday. He softly thinks, "You were right. Vipurr only gave me five dolphins. The Red Serpent wants me killed, as I patrol Atlantis. Any suggestions?"

Shalee studies the monstrous Kraken's shape and eyes. She had heard tales of giant squids, but this one has a huge mantle, but only slightly larger limbs, than other Krakens. His eyes show intelligence and a killer's stare. This thing can turn malignant in a heartbeat, so she must proceed with caution. "Now, that we have established that I tell you the truth and the Red Serpent and Vipurr lie to you and want you killed, can you help me escape?"

The Kraken's mantle throbs, as he assimilates all of Shalee's information. He tells her that he will submerge and remain under water, at the end of the dock. She should go to the end of the dock to hear its response. Cautiously, she rises, then checks the sleeping guard. The squid appears to head for the opening to the sea, as he submerges, but he turns to glide under the water to rest at the end of the dock. Shalee goes to meet him there, then sits down, dangling her legs over the edge. She can see the gray mass, just under the water, and realizes that she may have walked into a trap. Well, no guts, no glory--and she needs a way to escape.

Soft thoughts from the Kraken enter her mind, "I cannot help you escape from Abaddon, but I can contact someone in Atlantis to help you. We have spies in Atlantis and know they prepare to attack Abaddon before the red tide. A War Cat builds strange new subs and I heard that they are Kraken killers. So my species will be the first into battle and the Red Serpent considers all Krakens to be expendable. The Atlantians are in subs, so how will I know who to contact?"

Shalee sees the Kraken's problem. "Is there any way to get a message inside Atlantis?"

"No. It is guarded by the statue of O and, beyond that, is the opening to Atlantis, which is patrolled by the Lake Guardians. I could not just swim into Atlantis and deliver a message."

"What is this statue of O?"

"It is a memorial to Atlantis's founder, O, and it is a naked figure of her with her arms extended."

An idea flashes in Shalee's mind. "Are the fingers on the statue open?"

The Kraken must remember the shrine and this takes a few minutes, "Yes, the fingers are open."

"Good, I will get the bathing suit I wore when I was captured, and send it, with a message to Matthew Wolverine. Place the bathing suit in the fingers of O's right hand, then wait for an answer."

"Since Vipurr is cheating me on the number of dolphins he promised me, I don't know when I will leave for Atlantis."

"I will sit at the end of the dock early every morning, with a red eel skin bag containing my bathing suit with the message to Matthew. I never thought I would trust a Kraken, but I am trusting you." Shalee rises from the dock, quietly strolls past the sleeping guard, and enters the palace. The other women are just getting up. She goes to her room to hunt for her surface bathing suit, but she can't find it. She rummages through all the clothes in her room, but the bathing suit is not there. Shalee sits down on her bed, as Amber walks into the room. The girl looks around. "What are you looking for?"

"The bathing suit that I was wearing, when I first came to Abaddon. Do you know where it is?"

Amber turns and leaves, but returns in a few minutes, with the bathing suit, which she hands to Shalee. She looks puzzled, as she takes the suit. Amber admits she took it, just to try it on, but says she prefers the dolphin skin bathing suit next to her glossy skin. Shalee has to admit that the dolphin skin is much smoother next to her skin. She asks Amber to get her some breakfast. Amber smiles, and leaves for the kitchen.

Shalee must get a message to Matthew on her bathing suit. She is trying to come up with a solution, when Amber brings a tray of breakfast into the room. Amber and Shalee begin to eat. "Amber, does Abaddon have a written language?"

"Of course, we have a written language. Would you like me to teach you to write it?"

"You don't have paper, so what material do you write on?"

"We write on eelskin with a mixture of Kraken ink and Sargasso seaweed juice, mixed one part ink to ten parts seaweed juice. This ink dries quickly, so you must know what you are going to write on the eelskin, because it is waterproof and, once it is written on, it is very hard to erase."

"Amber, could you get me some of this ink and some eelskin.

I would like to start practicing today."

   Amber is more than happy to fetch some ink and eelskin but, what she fails to tell Shalee, is that the priests control the ink. She goes to the temple to ask for some ink and eelskin. The priests carefully question Amber about the ink. Vipurr listens intently, then gives Amber the ink. "Now, let me know how her learning progresses." Amber nods and leaves.

Chapter 20

Centurion's Love Letters

The Wolverines are all asleep, so Alpha goes to the factory to talk to George. The tiger carefully monitors the progress on each sub and they are being built twice as fast as normal. He is very pleased with the progress. The Centurion's right hand rubs his temples, "I don't know if their bodies can adapt to my training quickly enough for the coming battle. Do you have any suggestions?"

George appraises the Centurion, and wonders why he has to do all the planning. How did these humans survive before War Cats? Then he realizes that they were in slavery to the Slithers before Patton the Liberator, so he gently guides the Centurion to the answer, "In your ship, you sleep on what type of bed?"

The Centurion's forehead furrows, "Standard issue magnetic bed. You know that is code issue for all combat ships, and has been, for over ten millennia."

George flexes his front claws, as he thinks that this is like teaching a cub to reason, and it takes all his patience, "Yes, I know but why does the High Command have magnetic beds installed?"

"Warriors' muscles need healing after a battle and the magnets cause new blood to flow into damaged muscles while we sleep, so our muscles remain pliable."

"What type of beds do the Wolverines sleep on?"

The light bulb goes on in the Centurion's eyes, "I don't know, but they need magnetic beds. So I need to build some magnetic beds for them to sleep on?"

"Yes. Take five of my employees and build the beds immediately, then wake the Wolverines and exchange their beds for the magnetic healing beds. Then have magnetic beds built for me and my mates."

The Centurion hurries off to get the beds completed within the next two hours.

George considers sleeping on a magnetic bed again, and what effect this will have on his mates. Females are only allowed to sleep on magnetic beds after they are married, though the reason eludes him. But he will figure it out.

The Centurion completes all fourteen beds and has the workmen haul them to the Wolverines' house. Two tigresses guard the door, so their beds are installed first. Then the Centurion pounds on Matthew's door, "Up, Maggot!" As he enters the room, Matthew is on his feet, at attention, but sleepy. The Centurion picks up Matthew's mattress and throws it out the door. Two workers immediately place the new magnetic mattress on the bed. "Sleep, you maggot!"

He does the same to Eric's and then Raquelle's mattresses. Desiraa stops the Centurion in the hallway, "What are you doing?"

He scans every inch of Desiraa's body, and she becomes very uncomfortable. "I am changing their beds to magnetic beds, to heal their bodies for swifter training. Would you like a magnetic bed? It would heal the tightness in your shoulders." The Centurion reaches to take Desiraa's left hand and place it on the right side of his neck. She pushes downward, as soft pliable muscles allow her fingers to go to the bone. She drops her hand to her side, "I know men demand payment for every gift, so what is your payment?"

The Centurion takes in a deep breath, then turns to the workmen, "Build and deliver to her a magnetic bed, at no charge. Deliver it before you quit tonight. Now, go!" He doesn't even look at Desiraa, as he leaves to return to the dock.

When he arrives at his ship, he changes into a bathing suit, then swims beside the dock. Elizabeth surfaces and challenges him to a race. The Centurion thinks, "to the other side of the dome," and starts to swim. She uses slow, steady fin strokes and swims under the water, so as not to beat him too badly, but then, she raises her head and neck and sees that he is way ahead of her. She pours on the speed, but she still can't catch him, and he reaches the side of the dome first. Elizabeth is amazed, "How did you beat me?"

Alpha gives a wide Texas grin, "I knew you would underestimate me, so I swam with all my might and, of course, I won. You had better get used to losing because, soon, the Wolverines will be beating you."

Elizabeth splashes a deluge of water, with both front fins, on him, as she loudly thinks, "I am going to beat you, Maggot." She is off like a shot. Every fin is whirling through the water, and her head is held just above the surface. Twenty other Lake Guardians surface, and they mentally cheer their matriarch. Elizabeth gains strength from their cheers, and increases her speed. The Centurion is swimming at full speed, but he can't gain on her, and she reaches the dock first and slaps one of the pillars. She turns, "Who is Slither dung now?"

The Centurion pulls himself up onto the dock, then turns to look at the Lake Guardians. "Great race! You are in top form. Are all of you in such great shape?"

The others nod their heads, and he challenges them to race from the dock to the other side of the dome. For the rest of the day, they race back and forth. The Lake Guardians tire and, one by one, they submerge and don't surface. At last, only Elizabeth and the Centurion watch the artificial sun set. He sits on the dock and Elizabeth places her head in his lap. As he rubs her head, he asks, "Are all these Lake Guardians your offspring?"

Elizabeth enjoys the head rub. "Most of them are my children or are mated to my children. That is what one thousand years of breeding can accomplish. Yes, God has a sense of humor and I don't age. I have watched five of my mates die of old age, but I don't grow old. Do you have any children?"

"No, I do not have a wife or any children. That can only happen when I retire. Our lives start only after our military service is completed, but that is the price of my peoples' freedom. I do appreciate your assistance in teaching the Wolverines to dive. You encourage Eric and Raquelle to become warriors. You are a good friend to them and you give me someone to talk to on this planet. Space travel is so lonely."

"Raquelle would make you a good friend. She is coming into womanhood and her body is changing. Encourage her in your training and share your heart with her. You both need a confidante."

"Now, I need to get some sleep, so I can continue training the Wolverines. I hope the magnetic beds rejuvenate their muscles. Sweet dreams always, Elizabeth." With that, he gives her head a gentle rub and pushes it off his lap. She submerges, and the Centurion enters his ship, strips naked, and goes to bed.

The alarm screeches, the Centurion pounds the side of the ship and rises. He swiftly dresses, then races to the Wolverines' house. As he enters the door, he shouts, "Up, Maggots!" but there stand the Wolverines, in bathing suits, staring at him. Eric, Raquelle and Matthew push past him to race to the dock. The Centurion is thunder-struck. In all his years of training, he has never been met by recruits, on entering their barracks. Is this his leader's blood, the magnetic bed, or Matthew Wolverine's old military nature returning? He isn't sure, but they are eager to learn. When they reach the dock, he orders them to retrieve the first tag from its marker. The whoosh of air entering and leaving the Wolverines' lungs reverberates on the dock, then three splashes are heard, as the trio descends. As Alpha waits, George appears by his side. They wait for the first splash, and Matthew surfaces with a glowing tag, followed by Eric and Raquelle each holding glowing tags. The tags are held up for the Centurion and George to inspect. "Good job. Now replace those tags, then surface for further orders." The three trainees fill their lungs ten times, then dive into the water. George returns to the Wolverines' home, as the Centurion stands on the dock. For the next four hours, the retrievals and replacements of the tags continue. Then, two hours are dedicated to swimming the length of the lake of life and returning to the dock.

Eric feels something brush against his leg and he looks to see that, swimming beside him, is an eel. Eric speeds up the pace and the eel speeds up its pace. Eric passes his dad and his sister, but the eel beats him to the dock. Eric is the first to climb onto the dock. The Centurion is impressed, and Eric winks at the eel, as it goes back under the water.

They head back to the Wolverine home for a late breakfast. The scent of maple syrup fills the air, as they enter the front door. There are no tigers guarding the front doors and this concerns the Centurion and his recruits. High pitched roars come from George's room and the Centurion rushes to open the door. Desiraa places herself, alluringly, in front of the door. She informs him that those sounds are George and his mates procreating, and that they want privacy. She grabs his right arm and holds it close to her, as she guides him to the breakfast table. He sits down and she runs her hands up his arms, then massages his shoulders.

Matthew and Eric are filling their plates with what resembles pancakes, then covering them with thick syrup, to savor this delicious breakfast. Whether it was all the diving and swimming that gave them a healthy appetite, or the delicious meal, who knows? But they are enjoying every bite. Raquelle glares at Desiraa, as she atomizes each bite of food. The Centurion smiles and enjoys the attention, as he eats the meal. She continues to massage his shoulders and neck. The tension in his back and neck vanishes. The magnetic beds are healing, but a woman's massage truly relaxes a man. He closes his eyes and envisions marriage, with a wife, like Desiraa, massaging his neck. He is lost in euphoria, as Raquelle blurts out, "We need more syrup."

The moment is lost, as Desiraa scurries for more syrup. The Centurion opens his eyes and continues to eat. The roaring of the tigers gets louder and Alpha is envious of George and his mates. "Up, you scum! We run twenty miles today!"

The Centurion pushes his chair out and bolts for the door, with the Wolverines following close behind. He takes off at a brisk pace, then speeds up. They run through Atlantis's streets and through the air locks between each dome. After about five miles, they stop by the lake of life for water. They all kneel and place their faces into the lake and gulp the water. An eel comes up to Eric's face and watches him drink. He opens his eyes and sees the eel filling his cheeks with water, then spitting it out toward him. The eel thinks, "I am helping you, Eric. I am helping you."

Eric jerks his head out of the water and the eel rises to the surface. "What do you think you are doing, spitting water at me?"

The eel shifts his head to one side, "I was helping you get more water. What? Don't you know that all the water in the lake of life goes through each aquatic creature in one way or another, and gives you life. Come back here after your training and we can swim together."

The run is hard, but the trio keeps up with the Centurion. Matthew judges the mileage to be closer to that of a marathon, 26.2 miles, than to twenty miles, but he keeps that to himself. When they finish the run, they walk to Matthew's home and, after the meal, Matthew goes to the sub factory and Eric goes swimming with the eel. Raquelle wants to talk with Desiraa about her chest pains but she brushes her off with, "It means you are becoming a woman. It is normal." Then, Desiraa rushes off to find Joshua.

Raquelle sits in her room, but the roaring of the tigers finally drives her out of the house and down to the dock.

Raquelle sits on the dock with her head in her hands. The Centurion comes out of his ship, and walks to the end of the dock, and sits beside Raquelle, "The training got you down?"

"No, women's issues and no one to talk to!"

"Well, I can't help you there. I've got men's issues and I can't talk to anyone. George is in kitty heaven with his mates, and that is driving me nuts. I can't even write a love letter, so how am I going to get a wife?" The Centurion's shoulders slump, and he shakes his head.

Raquelle puts her hand on his shoulder, "Why is it so important for you to write love letters?"

"The really good marriages I've seen, when I go on shore leave, have husbands who write weekly love letters to their wives.

This does something to the women that I don't understand, but they are so happy to receive these letters. I've tried to write love letters to some of my girlfriends, but they only laugh at them, and that is not the response I intended. I tell them they are efficient and can bear ten children easily. What more do they want?"

Raquelle shakes her head. Just this past spring, she had gotten into her mother's dresser drawer, and found a stack of well-read love letters from her dad, so she read them. They were so hot, they almost burned her hands. The seduction of Irish charm permeated each word. They were calculated to enchant the woman, setting her passions aflame. On rainy days, her mother would retreat to the bedroom and read these letters and, when she came out, she was flushed and looking for Matthew. Raquelle knew this flush and disappeared into the woodwork, then went outside with Eric for an hour or two. It reminds her of George. She snaps back to reality, "I will teach you to write seductive love letters. But these are only for your wife?"

Alpha looks puzzled, "Who else would I write them to?"

"You are not going to find a wife, the first time you meet a woman. So you need to be careful, because when you write a very seductive letter to a woman, she will hunt you down. Now, what can we write on?"

The Centurion goes back into his ship and brings out two small ebony boxes. "Think your words toward the red glow, and they will appear on the screen. Then think, to send."

Raquelle looks at the red glow, then thinks. Instantly her thought appears. "First lessons-- never speak of a woman's efficiency. That is a big turn-off. We will start with Scottish love writing. You do know a woman gets sick and has pain, once a month?"

The Centurion swallows hard and his face flushes. These are areas that he never, in his wildest dreams, thought of discussing with a young woman. He looks down, then shifts in his place.

Raquelle grows impatient. "I need to know what you know about women. You have to know her needs, wants and desires. I am going to assume you know nothing about women. This story is about one of my dad's friends. His wife is raising six children. She gets the flu and is sicker than a dog, so she escapes to their bed. Her husband calls a neighbor and pays her to cook the meal at his home and have it ready when he gets home. The neighbor watches the children for pay, as he serves the meal to his wife; they eat together, alone. He massages her feet for two hours, while he listens to her talk about her pains and troubles. He does not give any advice or opinions. Then, he takes the dishes to the kitchen and, as the neighbor washes them, he writes his

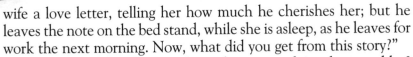

wife a love letter, telling her how much he cherishes her; but he leaves the note on the bed stand, while she is asleep, as he leaves for work the next morning. Now, what did you get from this story?"

"Why didn't he give her advice on solving her troubles? That's what I would have done."

Raquelle shakes her fists and growls, "Typical man! A woman does not want advice, so you don't give her advice! She just wants her man to listen, and not to talk. This man is easing his wife's pain, by having the neighbor feed and watch the children, and by massaging her feet. The note, the next day, totally thrills her because she knows she is loved by his actions and by his love letter."

"What did he write in the note?"

Raquelle is becoming exasperated. "This is so clear to women, and such a mystery to men. I need terms you can understand. When you order troops into battle, and they do nothing, are you happy?"

The Centurion looks bitter. "No, because I have failed."

Raquelle brightens, "So, it is their actions that make you happy?"

"Yes."

"A woman feels the same way. The fact that this man took action and wrote the letter is what's important. The contents of the letter are irrelevant. She knows she is loved, because he took action and wrote the letter. Now, if your troops become sick what is your response?"

"I get a healer or, if no healer is around, then I make sure they get medicine. I need my troops ready for combat, so I must do whatever it takes to keep them healthy."

"Will you concede that loneliness is very painful?"

"Yes."

"Then you are the healer that will cure the woman's loneliness through your love letters and your actions. Now, I am going to massage your back, then you write to me about how it makes you feel--everything--especially my touch. I will analyze your letter and we will go over better responses, but you will write and send that letter to me, tonight, before you sleep." Raquelle gets up and gives him a fifteen-minute sensual back rub, then goes home and goes to bed.

Afterward, he goes to his ship and tries to compose a letter on the ebony box. His forehead begins to drip sweat, as he thinks a sentence, then erases it. Hours slowly tick by, as he struggles with the letter. Finally, he is so tired, he can no longer reason, and he thinks,

"Your hands on my back brought me such pleasure, that I did not want you to stop. They felt so gentle and sensual, on my skin, and I dreamed of returning such pleasure to you. The Centurion" He sent the letter, then fell into a deep sleep.

The next sound he hears is the pounding on the side of his ship. The Wolverines stand on the dock, ready for training, as a bleary-eyed Centurion exits the ship, "What are you doing here so early?"

Matthew looks puzzled, "What? Did you oversleep? It's past training time."

The rest of the day, the Centurion pushes the three to their limits then, that evening, he stands beside Raquelle on the dock, anxiously awaiting her critique.

She bends her knees, then reaches behind his back and legs and picks him up. His hands immediately encircle her neck. "Actions are the seeds of future dreams. I have swept you off your feet, and that is what you want to do to a woman." She sets the Centurion on his feet, then places both hands around the Centurion's right biceps. "There is power in your muscles, so your lift must be done in one smooth motion. Now, you try it."

He stoops to lift Raquelle, but fails to support her back and she slips off his right arm, then dangles, with her legs crooked around his left arm, and her head almost touching the dock. She shoots her arms to the dock and flips to her feet. "Look, bend and lift with your legs, while supporting my back and just above my knees. If I can lift you in one smooth motion, why can't you do the same with me? Now, try it again."

On the first few tries, his movements are jerky but, with Raquelle's coaching, his lifts become smooth and gentle. "That is the basis for your actions. Now, when you write a letter, you are selling yourself to the woman. Every woman has one thing about her body that she feels is her best feature. It is your job to find that feature and glorify it in your letters. My hair is my glory. It is jet black, with a blue tinge, and only my mother has hair like it. Also, my green eyes are rare. So, you center your love letters on these two attributes. Take some of my hair so you can feel the silky smooth texture. Maybe that will inspire you. Oh, and end your letters with 'Your loving Centurion,' 'Your teddy bear Centurion,' 'Your dreams come true Centurion'--any way but 'The Centurion." He draws his sword and cuts off a lock of Raquelle's hair. She leaves to go home; as the Centurion enters his ship to compose his love letter, he softly caresses her hair.

Chapter 21

Trust a Kraken?

Shalee takes the ink from Amber, and Amber starts to teach her the Abaddonian alphabet. Over the next few days, Shalee develops a basic understanding of Abaddon's written language. Early each morning, she goes to the dock to communicate with the Kraken, then she heads for the pens where they hold the dolphins that are to be fed to it. She communicates with one of the few remaining dolphins, and asks it to take a note to Atlantis. The dolphin agrees, if it can escape from this pen. Shalee comes up with a plan, and tells the dolphin she will release him tomorrow.

Vipurr is making preparations for the ceremony of the red tide, which will be next month. The Red Serpent is as giddy as a schoolgirl. "So, you gave her the ink, and she thinks she can get a note to Atlantis. Great, when the anticipation of escape is high, the sacrifice tastes so much sweeter. She is being watched every day?"

Vipurr smiles, "Amber watches her inside the palace and I have priests watch her when she leaves the palace. She has gone to the dolphin pen, several days in a row, but there are only a few dolphins left in the pen. We can stop her before she releases any of the dolphins."

The Red Serpent rises and sways back and forth in front of Vipurr, "No, let her release the dolphin, but have our Krakens stationed just outside the pens and have them slowly eat it in front of her. Contact me, when she goes toward the dolphins' pen, because I want to see her spirit shattered. This sacrifice is turning out to be very entertaining."

Shalee sends Amber for some food and scribbles on her bathing suit—"Trust this giant Kraken. Love, Shalee--Texas Freedom," then she rolls up the bottom of her swimsuit and writes on eelskin, to Matthew, to hurry and rescue her. She also signs that note, "Love, Shalee". The eelskin and the bathing suit are hidden, just as Amber arrives with the food. "Some nice dolphin soup… but this will be the last, for a while. Our subs are not gathering any dolphins to replace what we are using. Most of our subs were lost in the battle with your husband, and our factory is working day and night to replace our fleet."

Shalee keeps her head down, as she assimilates this news. So

Matthew was able to wreck Abaddon's fleet. He must be rebuilding the Atlantian fleet; that is why he has not rescued her but, with the red tide coming within a month, he needs to hurry. "When is the sacrifice of the red tide?"

Amber jumps. "Why, at the end of the month, so you have thirty more days of freedom."

The next morning, Shalee rises very early and quickly proceeds to the dolphin pen, with the eelskin and her bathing suit in a bag. Just as the artificial sun rises, she sees the dolphin and calls him over to her, and takes out the eelskin and ties it around his lower jaw. The dolphin can still open and close its mouth, so this will not interfere with its swimming. Shalee releases the gates to the dolphin cage, then races for the dock. The Red Serpent and Vipurr are hiding in the shadows, but they are perplexed by Shalee's actions. The dolphin splits out of the opening and right into the tentacles of a Kraken. It slowly raises the dolphin high out of the water, turns upside down, with its tentacles and legs straight up and its mantle in the water. Its beak is snapping open and closed. The squid slowly lowers the struggling dolphin to its beak, where it takes large chunks from its stomach. The Red Serpent and Vipurr both lick their lips, and they are so mesmerized by this performance that, for a few minutes, they forget about Shalee.

She sprints to the dock, runs to the end, and leaps into the water. While diving deeper under the water, she reaches into her bag and removes the bathing suit, as the pad of a giant tentacle appears. She rams the bathing suit into the center of the tentacle and, as it closes, she kicks hard for the surface. There is a one-man sub docked nearby and she swims to it, climbs the dock and gets in the sub. She starts pushing buttons and the sub starts. The jets of water from the sub are on full and the surge of power breaks the cords holding it to the dock. She is headed for the Red Serpent's temple and tries to get it to dive. It will not cooperate. As she frantically pushes levers, the side of the temple rushes toward her sub. Her death is certain.

The Kraken surfaces and sees the run-away sub, then sticks the bathing suit into its beak. It uses all its power to swim after the sub. The water speeding through its jets has the creature literally skimming the top of the water, when it catches the sub. Shalee's face contorts, as she prepares to be crushed. The squid makes a gigantic effort to propel himself more forcefully, and he sails out of the water, landing on top of the submarine and forcing it under the water but, as he does, he scrapes his mantle and the pain is intense. He steers the sub to the right and it plows up onto the beach, inside the temple. Priests rush upon the sub and roughly haul Shalee out. She snaps at the Kraken, "If it hadn't been for you, I would have escaped!"

The Red Serpent and Vipurr enter the temple and the Serpent is furious to see the Kraken in his pond, because the taste of ammonia lingers for days. "I told you never to enter this temple again. Now, go to Atlantis and station yourself just beyond the statue of O, until I send for you."

The Kraken, still in pain, submerges and proceeds to the outer entrance. The creatures guarding the hole gather around to ask their new food supplier where he is going.

The giant squid conveys to them that the Red Serpent is sending him to his death because there are no more dolphins to feast upon; therefore, he must go to Atlantis. This most intelligent animal lets that idea sink in before he shares his next thoughts. The others turn bright red. They are hungry and they see their new leader leaving. One of them thinks, "I could kill Vipurr and the Red Serpent." The others nod their heads. The giant Kraken tells them that he will return, then he streaks through the hole, and is gone. The seeds of rebellion are planted. Now, for Vipurr and the Red Serpent to water them, so they can grow. He tastes the outworld material in his beak and spits it out. His tongue, with its downward-pointing teeth, has ripped holes into Shalee's bathing suit, but he doesn't notice, as one of his legs clutches the suit, and he swims for Atlantis.

Meanwhile, back at the temple, Shalee is dragged in front of the high priest. "Another failed attempt at escape. When will you ever learn that escape from Abaddon is impossible? I had one of the girls brought from the palace. I don't know her name. You priests hold her tightly, so she must watch, as the Red Serpent coils around this slave girl and slowly crushes her to death. This is all because of your actions, Shalee."

Shalee had never had much to do with this girl, and she can't even remember her name, but she watches, as the girl violently kicks, bites, and scratches the priests, as they bring her to the Red Serpent. This is anything but a willing sacrifice. She screams at the top of her lungs, and a crowd from outside enters the temple. They sneer at the girl and cheer when the Red Serpent slowly coils around her body. She faints, and the crowd's cheers turn to boos, so the priests throw cold water on her face to awaken her. She thrashes, as her screams reach the heights of the temple, then echo back to mix with her current screams.

Shalee turns her head, but a third priest forces it back, and makes her watch the torture. Hour after hour, the torment continues, until the crowd tires of watching and the Red Serpent releases his coils and drops the panting girl on the floor. Vipurr helps her up and he tells her all is forgiven. She hugs him in gratitude. Then, she staggers over to kneel in front of the Red Serpent. His fangs draw out a pint of her blood, then inject a pint of his venom. She shakes violently, then flops on the floor, until her eyes protrude and her tongue swells and chokes her.

Shalee sags in her captors' arms, as the Red Serpent swallows the girl. The crowd has swelled to fill the temple, and they go wild with enthusiastic shouts. Then the Serpent hisses to Shalee, "Go ahead and try to escape again. There are still seven or eight girls left and my worshipers love watching me torture or kill someone."

The priests hold her arms tightly, as they drag her back to the palace and throw her on the floor. They spit on her, as they leave. The room remains empty, as Shalee stands and strips off her clothes and steps into the hot water. No help can be expected from these women or the people of Abaddon. The vileness of the Red Serpent and the priests has reached a level of depravity that she didn't even know existed. Her hope depends on a hideous giant Kraken. Her laughter fills the empty room, as her hope of a rescue fades.

Chapter 22

The Rage

The Centurion trains the Wolverines, each day, until their muscles ache from the diving, swimming, and running but, each day, they can dive deeper, swim farther, and run faster. They are so accustomed to passing George's room, and hearing all the growls that come from inside that, on the fifth day, the silence that greets them upon entering their home catches them off guard. Eric opens George's door, and a bedraggled War Cat slowly crawls out. He can see George's ribs, as the tiger makes his way toward Eric's room. "Eric, bring my magnetic bed and some food into your room, then shut the door. No more females."

Even though he is very tired, Eric races to get George a basket of fresh fish. Just as the tiger makes it into Eric's room, Matthew throws down George's magnetic bed and he crawls up on it. Eric places the basket of fresh live fish close to George and his right paw spears a fish, which he quickly consumes. The Wolverines eat their evening meal, then Eric quietly enters his room. The basket is empty, but one live fish sticks out of George's mouth. He is fast asleep. The fish's tail slaps the floor, so Eric removes it from the exhausted cat's mouth, and walks to George's room and opens the door. All the female cats have broad smiles on their faces, as they groom their fur. He throws the half-dead fish into the center of the room, and closes the door. The boy goes to his dad's room, but Matthew is fast asleep. He returns to his room and goes to sleep. Raquelle is reading a letter from the Centurion and she mutters to herself, "This is good; this is very good." She was going to go to bed, but she goes, instead, to the dock to encourage Alpha on his writing.

He is petting Elizabeth's head. Raquelle sits beside him, and she starts to stroke Elizabeth's head, too. The water around the dock begins to splash, as her fins quiver. One hand, petting, is good, but two hands are better. Raquelle continues to pet Elizabeth, as she speaks, "That last letter was very good. I was blushing, as I read it. The woman that you romance with that letter will totally blush, but I want her panting. We need to go for heavy panting."

Alpha looks confused, and even Elizabeth raises her head and thinks, "What are you talking about?"

Raquelle yawns, "Oh, I am helping the Centurion compose

love letters, so he can win a wife after he retires. His letters now arouse passion in me, so I know he is close to being able to write truly great love letters."

Elizabeth shakes her head. "I will never understand you humans. Two of our bulls fight to see who becomes my mate but, if I don't like the winner, I kick his tail and wait for two more challengers. That is our courtship." Elizabeth turns and dives under the water.

Raquelle looks stern, "For your next assignment, you need to put your whole heart into your letter, because we are going for heavy panting. I want her panting like a dog, after it has chased a pheasant for a mile. Take a week to write the letter. The setting is a Scottish stone cottage, built in the 17th or 18th century, with two chimneys, so there are nice roaring fires blazing inside. It is spring, and flowers of many colors are blossoming, but there is still a chill in the air. You walk your love out of the forest, onto a stone walkway, which reveals this breath-taking cottage. Your words should make her pant heavily with desire." Raquelle pats him on the knee and leaves for home.

The Centurion enters his ship, to think into the black box. He comes up blank. He accesses his database of great Scottish and Irish writers of love poetry. The screen has tens of thousands of references. He redefines his search as "extreme passion," "heavy panting," "love letters or poems". The screen shows hundreds of listings, which he starts to read.

Shouts of "Up, maggots!" fill the Wolverine house. Eric is already in his bathing suit. George growls quietly. Eric thinks to George, "Such language, George! Clean it up, if you want to sleep in my room."

The tiger staggers up onto his feet and immediately goes to the salt pile. He shakes his head, as the Centurion enters Eric's room, then he gives him a dirty look. "Don't you ever sleep? Some of us are retired and like to sleep in till dawn." Before the Centurion can answer, Sonya comes into the room, followed by all of George's other mates and they sit directly in front of him. Sonya growls low and long, as the Wolverines and Desiraa enter Eric's room; then she looks deep into George's eyes and thinks loudly, "Guess who is pregnant. All of us!"

George rises, as if the ground is on fire, "How do you know so soon?"

Sonya waves her front right paw. "We just know, so we need to start thinking about larger quarters and a place of our own."

George puffs his chest out and struts around the room, "Yes, we will talk about that later. But, now, Centurion, let us get on with the training. George races out the door and down to the dock, in front of the Centurion and the Wolverines. After they have been diving for hours, the sun rises and the Lake Guardians surface close to the dock. The expectant father is calling each of them over to tell them the all-powerful news. Alpha determines that his heart is going to go into his next love letter. He needs to be married.

George goes to the factory and is surprised that the four subs for the Wolverines and the Centurion are finished. He slips inside the first sub and mentally works all the controls. They work perfectly, so he has the sub launched, then heads out into the lake of life. Soon, he is surrounded by a group of Lake Guardians and is forced to surface by the dock and open the hatch. "This is one of the new submarines for the Wolverines, so get accustomed to seeing them patrol the lake of life."

Elizabeth surfaces to inspect every inch of the sub. "I called all the Lake Guardians in from patrol in the lake of life and just outside, because I thought we had an enemy sub inside Atlantis. Inform me before you launch any more subs. And, yes, we all know that all of your mates are pregnant. Now, you Lake Guardians that were patrolling around the statue of O, go back on patrol."

Just outside the entrance to Atlantis, the Kraken has been waiting for days to deliver Shalee's message. Finally, when all the Lake Guardians rush back into the lake, he makes his move. Shalee's bathing suit is wedged between the fingers of the statue's right hand. The squid jets away, as fast as it can.

George slips back into the sub, and guides it through the entrance, to test its speed and maneuverability. It handles like a dream but, as he banks to come back to Atlantis, he notices something fluttering from the statue of O. He maneuvers his sub inches from the hand and sees that the item is man-made, so he orders one of the Lake Guardians to gently remove the item and bring it to the submarine factory. He docks the sub, as the Guardian lays the item on the dock and disappears. George grabs the item in his teeth and takes it to the Wolverine's home. The Centurion and the Wolverines are eating lunch, and George lays the item on the table. Matthew snatches the item. "This is my wife's bathing suit." He tries to read the message, but the holes in the suit make it difficult. Raquelle makes out a few words, "Trust, Shalee, Texas." Eric chirps in, "Kraken? Trust giant Kraken? Can that be right, Dad?"

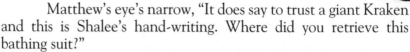

Matthew's eye's narrow, "It does say to trust a giant Kraken and this is Shalee's hand-writing. Where did you retrieve this bathing suit?"

"Between the fingers of O's right hand. It must have just been placed there today, because that area is patrolled constantly."

Matthew takes the new sub and heads out of Atlantis, past the statue of O. The nude statue causes his heart to ache. He has been obedient to George and to the Centurion because he needs their help to rescue his wife, but he is at the end of his rope. A gray blur, off to his right, disappears into a gorge, that is part of the mountain range, and Matthew guides the sub into it. Upon entering the gorge, his sub is seized by giant tentacles. Instantly, a thought flashes into his mind, "Did you receive your wife's message?"

Matthew thinks, "Yes," and, quickly, his sub is released. He turns the sub and faces a gigantic Kraken. The creature's eyes give Matthew chills, and he involuntarily shivers. The Kraken thinks, "The Red Serpent sent me to Atlantis so you could kill me. I can reason, so I am a threat to him. Shalee understood this and sent you a message to trust me. Did you receive and understand the message?"

Matthew places his weapon's sights on the giant squid. "We could not read the message because of the holes. I know it is from my wife, but the message is unreadable."

"I am sure that you have your weapons ready to fire. That would make the Red Serpent very happy and it would be your wife's loss. Your last attack on Abaddon was a disaster because you were betrayed on two fronts--by the priests and by the Royals. We received word that you have wiped out the priests, but that the Royals remain in power and, when you leave to attack Abaddon again, you will be betrayed a second time and the Royals will take Atlantis under their control again, just after you sail."

"How could you know the Royals' plan?"

"I patrol close to the Red Serpent's temple and, when I saw the high priest enter with an Atlantian Royal, I went into the lake in the temple to listen, but I remained invisible, under the water. Vipurr informed the Red Serpent that the Royals would tell them when you launch your attack, in exchange for his leaving Atlantis to them. Then they will resume control of the city. The Red Serpent agreed, but after the Royal left, the Serpent informed Vipurr that, after you are defeated, the Abaddonian fleet will attack Atlantis, and capture it, before the red tide. The Royals will make wonderful sacrifices. There is less than a month before the Red Serpent eats your wife. Do you want my help?"

"What reward do you want for your help?"

The squid's eyes brighten, "Do not attack with the whales. My Krakens are terrified of the whales. I will lead them into an undersea cavern, and we will wait there, until you have defeated the Abaddonian fleet and secured the temple. When I am sure that the Red Serpent is dead, I will lead my people into the ocean's depths. Yes, I will be their one and only leader. Do you agree to these terms?"

Matthew never thought he would deal with a Kraken, but the news of the attack by the Royals makes sense. They control Atlantis's fleet, and they will not support Matthew in his attack on Abaddon. They have been ghosts since the Ghouls were killed. Their plan makes perfect sense. Matthew tells the squid that he will attack Abaddon in one week. The animal speeds back to Abaddon to tell the Red Serpent.

Chapter 23

Poison

Shalee rises before anyone else and dresses. She walks to the end of the dock, sits down, and stares at the water. She has performed this routine daily, since the Kraken left, but today her tears fall into the water. Depression clouds her mind and her hope is almost gone. Where is Matthew? Why doesn't he attack? Was the gigantic Kraken killed by a whale? Why don't you answer my prayers, God? Shalee gazes into the blue water.

Evil eyes watch Shalee's every move. From the palace and from the temple, they watch her. This sacrifice has no hope of escape and they smile to see her depressed and crying.

The explosion of water in front of her startles everyone. She is drenched. That same Kraken bobs only an arm's length from her. She quietly thinks, "My message got to Matthew?"

The squid's mind is blank, as Vipurr and the Red Serpent hurry down the dock. The Red Serpent rises high above the Kraken. "Why are you back?"

It thinks loudly, as a crowd of priests and others gather, "Your plan worked. Matthew Wolverine will attack in six days. Your fleet can destroy his fleet, then you can occupy Atlantis, and still have your sacrifices before the red tide."

The Red Serpent's tongue flicks out, as he smiles at Shalee. "You have no hope, Sacrifice, so continue to cry. I do like my meals with salt. Vipurr, gather all the people, so I can inject my evil into them. You can watch, Sacrifice."

The entire population of Abaddon is summoned to the temple and they form a line. One by one, the Red Serpent injects his venom into their backs. The people's eyes change to black slits, and they have permanent scowls. Evil and hostility radiate from the people after the poison enters their bodies. All sailors are given a triple dose of poison, so that their tongues are now forked and their speech is slurred. The shadow of evil completely covers Abaddon and Shalee trembles. The Red Serpent is drained of his venom and filled with the blood of his people. Shalee leaves the temple and goes back to the dock, where the giant Kraken still bobs. She marches down the dock, and says, "So, even you fooled me. Well, Matthew will still win this battle and I will be free."

The Kraken quietly thinks, "We will see." Then he submerges and gathers the other creatures, which are on guard. He orders them to follow him and they drive school after school of fish through the small hole, to the undersea cavern. He places a guard just inside the cavern entrance, right above it, to stop the schools of fish from returning to the sea, but to allow fish to flow into the cavern. The guard can eat as many fish as try to escape. He is very happy with his job. Next, the giant Kraken has his band corner and eat two large schools of fish. Now that they are all stuffed, they return to guard duty, happy and knowing that this new leader feeds them very well. He is firmly in control.

Chapter 24

A Father's Rage

For the next week Eli, Joshua, the Centurion, George and Matthew spend one hour a day going over their battle plans. The subs are ready, but there are fewer than they had wanted. The Royals order the Atlantian fleet to protect Atlantis and not to participate in the attack. They are showing their true colors by making it clear that they don't care about anyone except themselves. When Matthew leaves, Atlantis is theirs to rule, as they desire.

The Centurion completes his final love letter, and then he carefully reads it and checks for mistakes.

Dear Raquelle,

I dream of you always and my imagination runs wild. Come with me, Raquelle; let our imaginations travel together.

Come back to the inviting cottage in the hills of Scotland. Our romantic refuge from this maddening world. The fragrance of wildflowers greets us on the dirt pathway, where the forest shrouds our cottage. Their intoxicating aroma weakens our knees. The bouquet goes to our heads, and we lean against each other for strength. Drawing strength from each other's bodies, we press on. The pathway becomes stone, as the forest slowly unveils our enchanted cottage. Three hundred year old stones built this cottage and they stand strong and proud, even today. Its alluring beauty leaves us breathless. Sighing, you put your arm around me. In that magical moment, we stop to savor its beauty, as the last kisses of the sun embrace the forest, before it sleeps.

Then, we stroll to the left flowerbed on the stone pathway. I ask you to sit, while I create my angel a halo of flowers. Mixing just the right amount of blue, with pink, and some yellow, your crown is created. I gently place it on your head, as I kiss your cheek. You radiate beauty. As we rise, I sweep you into my arms. We laugh, as you lower your head and rest it on my shoulder. I carry you to the door. Slowly opening it reveals a small table, with piping hot homemade bread, steaming mashed potatoes, vegetable beef soup, roast lamb, hot chocolate, apple pie and Scottish shortbread. There are two brightly blazing fires. Our caretakers have sprinkled enchantment into every corner of this cottage. Now, that seduction tempts us. Willingly, our bodies submit, and I gingerly sit you down and we enjoy a long lingering kiss.

I escort you to the table and hold your chair for you but, as I finish seating you, I nuzzle your neck and caress your body. We say grace, then enjoy our meal. The glow of the fires, dancing off your hair, is arousing. You sense my need. A sly smile crosses your face, and you tease me, by seeming to take forever to finish your meal. Finally, you finish, and we relax on the couch, where my arms enfold you.

Love,
Your Centurion teddy bear
PS How soon can we make this a reality?

Well, that was the best he could do, and he hoped it was panting material for Raquelle. He sent the message with a prayer, then he headed to the church to pray, before the coming battle.

Raquelle reclines on the bed, as she checks her black box, then slowly reads the letter. She becomes flushed and her palms sweat. Is it getting hotter in the house? She puts down the letter, and swallows hard. She is only critiquing this letter. It is not really written to her. Gingerly, she picks up the black box and carefully rereads every word. She joins in the Centurion's imagination, and she can see the stone cottage and feel his arms around her. Eric enters the room and immediately notices a red-faced Raquelle. "Are you sick?"

She doesn't answer him, but bolts from the room and heads for the dock. Eric looks at the black box on the bed, picks it up and begins to read. Matthew is in the hall, walking to his bedroom, when he notices Eric, "Whose black box is that?"

Immediately, Eric hides the black box behind his back. Matthew enters the room, "That's Raquelle's black box, isn't it?"

Eric nods his head and hands the box to his dad. A quick glance reveals the passion in this message, and Matthew's face turns fire engine red. "That snake in the grass!" He bolts to his room, grabs his sword. With the sword held high, he sprints for the dock and the Centurion.

Raquelle can't find him, so she checks the church. He is praying aloud, and George stands guard in the back of the church, as Raquelle silently enters the building. "I want to be married and raise a family. I know I sinned by giving Raquelle my leader's blood. You have the right to take my life under our law. I was born free and I die free. That is all I can expect from my God and I appreciate my years of freedom. I cannot ask for forgiveness, because to know Raquelle is to love her, and I do. She is the type of perfect woman I wish to find and marry. If You take my life for her life, then know that I freely give it. I only ask that a woman give three days of tears for my death. If You deny me a wife and children then, at least, give me three days of tears. Until the final victory, bless the God of freedom."

As the Centurion finishes his prayer, Matthew bursts through the church door. Eyes on fire, he races to kill the man who would steal his daughter. He barely gets his sword unsheathed to deflect the strike. Matthew rains down blows on the Centurion, with the force of an unrelenting hurricane. "Swine, I trusted you!" The Centurion switches to attack mode and, now, Matthew is deflecting blow after blow. The warrior's sword pins Matthew's sword to his chest, then he uses his right leg to sweep Matthew's right leg into the air. Matthew slams to the floor, on his back, knocking the wind out of him. The Centurion's sword is at Matthew's throat. He leans forward, just as Raquelle yells, "Stop!"

The Centurion is livid. A church is sacred ground, and there is to be no human combat, ever. "I helped you at every turn, and my reward is death by your sword. Well, I return to my post. The battle is all yours, Wolverine." The Centurion sheathes his sword, turns to go to the dock, boards his ship, and speeds away, under the water.

George and Raquelle are stunned, and just stare, as Matthew rises. As he walks up to the pair, Raquelle lays into her dad, "What got into you?"

Matthew roars, "Were you having an affair with the Centurion? I read the black box, so don't lie. That letter was written for a woman, not a little girl."

Raquelle charges her father. George gets between them, but she erupts, "No, I did not have an affair with the Centurion, but I wish he would pursue me, because I want a husband like him. I am sixteen, and a woman, but you didn't even remember my birthday. Your woman is being held captive, and that is all you care about. Well, this is a good man, and he is willing to die for me. He listens to me and, I was helping him learn to write love letters, so he can find a wife after he retires. I told him to use my name. So, because of your temper, Mother and the rest of us may die. Why didn't you just talk to me, Dad?" Raquelle doesn't give her father time to reply, and she turns to walk out of the church. A crowd of the Royals gathers outside the church. They see the Centurion leave, then Raquelle and then, disgusted, George leaves. The Royals smile to each other, as Matthew roars out of the church. "We will attack tomorrow and we will defeat

Abaddon." The Royals' smiles grow, as they nod their heads.

When Raquelle enters her home, she immediately tells Sonya that the Centurion has left. She is furious with her father, but she strokes Sonya's head, "If we don't survive the battle, then you and George's other mates must get to the surface world. I don't trust the Royals. They have their own fleet of pleasure submarines and I'm afraid they will kill you." Sonya puts her paws around Raquelle's neck and they hug; then Raquelle goes to her room.

She is in her room, when George enters the Wolverine house. He walks into the room. "That prayer was not for your ears. What is said in a worship center is between God and the originator of the prayer."

Raquelle cocks her head, "What is the three days of tears?"

George nods his head. "That, I will tell you. If I die, then my mates will cry three days for me. A warrior needs a female to weep three days for his death, but only three days, and then she stops. Grieving must have a final closure. We leave for battle tomorrow, so get some sleep."

George goes into his room and talks with his mates. Sonya and the other tigresses look concerned, as they gather around George. "The Centurion left, so will you still go into battle with the Wolverines?"

George looks down. "I owe Wolverine seven life debts and, by the warrior's code, I must fight at his side until my debt is repaid. Matthew's temper may have sealed all our fates, but I cannot abandon my code."

Sonya growls viciously, "I want to tell you how I was captured by a Siberian Russian. He trapped me, put me in a cage, then read the Bible to me. That was supposed to calm me down. Well, I listened to all the stories, but one caught my attention. God was bragging to his archenemy about the integrity of his servant Job. Not another righteous man like Job in all the earth. The enemy tells God that the only reason for Job's worship is because of the wealth God has given him. So, God turns the righteous servant Job over to His enemy, to prove a point. Job's wealth is stolen, his children are killed, then boils cover his body, but Job does not give up his integrity, and he still worships God. His friends and his wife turn on him, but he keeps his integrity. In the end, God blesses him with twice the wealth and more children. My point is, Job was too righteous and so are you, George. We are your pride, and we don't want you to fight and die with the Wolverines."

George smiles, "No War Cat in the universe could have a better pride than I have. I want to be there to raise our cubs. I will fight with all my strength in the coming battle, because I cannot change who I am. I serve the God of light, live by my codes, and I die free. Let us get some sleep before the battle." George's mates snuggle beside him and go into a deep sleep.

Matthew finally enters the house, totally disgusted with himself. With his head down, he drags himself into his bedroom, then quickly goes into a deep sleep.

Chapter 25

Terror and Refuge

The Red Serpent's poison slowly transforms the people into beasts. Each day, the snarling, clawing, and biting at each other increases in intensity. They are ready to tear all invaders to shreds, when they attack tomorrow. When some of the women in the palace start to snarl at her, Shalee decides it is time to hide. She packs a bag of dry food and two large containers of water, then she stealthily leaves the palace. Keeping out of sight of these beasts, she makes her way to the mines. As she opens the hatch and proceeds into the darkness, her mind screams, "You are trapped. These miners will rip you apart. Run from here."

She fights her fear by opening her bag and eating some food. The taste is sweet. She hears the sound of a dumper on the rails and her heart sinks. As the sound gets louder, she gropes for a rock to use as a weapon, but she finds none. The dumper is very close and a voice cries out, "Who are you?"

Shalee swallows hard. "I am Shalee."

The figure pushing the dumper surges forward and Shalee clenches her fists. She will go down fighting. The form stops only an arm's-length away, "I am Jon. We met before. Is it time to rebel?"

Shalee's mind whirls. "Weren't you injected with the Red Serpent's poison? All the rest of Abaddon was injected."

Jon snickers, "No, the production of blue diamonds must never cease. We die too quickly in the mines, from the dust, for the Red Serpent to want our poor blood. Now, I have contacted other miners that want freedom, so we will kill our overseers on your word. But, once we murder them, there is no turning back. When does your husband attack?"

Shalee breathes in deeply, but she chokes. Jon smacks her on the back. "He attacks tomorrow."

"Then we will kill them tomorrow and join in your husband's attack. There is a platform higher up in the mine, with a hole where we can see the outside. I will take you there, and you can tell us when the attack starts." Shalee grabs her food and follows Jon to the platform.

The giant Kraken has the lesser squids drive school after school of fish into the cavern. His plan is in place and he swims to the dock in Abaddon. Vipurr tells him to station his Krakens in a group, down in the depths, and that he will send a sub to give him instructions for the attack. Krakens are the first wave of Abaddon's attack, and Vipurr expects him to lead this one. The giant Kraken repeats back the plan to Vipurr, then slips below the water. A sub passes by his side, while all the Krakens are assembled, then dive to await the attack.

Shalee goes to sleep and waits for Matthew to attack tomorrow.

Chapter 26

Attack?

Matthew wakes Raquelle and Eric. George stands in the hall, then turns and goes back in to his mates. Matthew doesn't say a word as he, Eric and Raquelle leave for the subs. The word that the Centurion has left has spread throughout Atlantis. George is not at Matthew's side and the odds against winning now seem insurmountable. The subs load as many solemn troops as possible. The Royals have activated all sailors and warriors for duty and they are aboard the Atlantian subs. This dodge works perfectly to deplete all warriors from the city. The fleet patrols from just outside the statue of O, around the entire perimeter of Atlantis. Eli commands the fleet that will attack Abaddon. The Royals dress for battle, as they watch from their homes, for the subs to submerge.

Eli sails his fleet to a nearby undersea trench where they stop. The Atlantian fleet join's Eli and they all wait in the trench for a signal. George and his mates, with Desiraa, race through Atlantis, communicating that there are leaks in some of the domes and that all must flee to the farthest dome from the docks. The women and children fear an implosion, so moms grab their children and race for the farthest dome from the docks. They pack in shoulder-to-shoulder and Desiraa stands by the hatch and tells them not to leave until the leaks are fixed; then she locks the hatch. She runs to a nearby transmitter and contacts Joshua, who contacts the fleet. Eli orders the fleet to move out, as he broadcasts to all subs that the Royals have joined with the Red Serpent and that they are the ones who butcher their wives and children. This news spreads through the subs like wildfire, and it ignites all warriors for battle.

Even the royal children and women carry swords and knives, and hatred covers their faces. Now is the time to kill any Atlantian that ever slighted them. The massacre will put Atlantis under their authority forever. They charge out of their homes, and head for the Wolverine home. They smash the furniture, but they find no tigers. Someone shouts that the tigers fled in fear. This draws laughs from the crowd, as they hunt for people to slay.

The Trader comes out of his compound to join in the hunt, but they can't find any people to kill. It is like the sea has swallowed up all the Atlantians. They go to the next dome, but it is empty.

There are doors open and there is even clothing in the streets. The Royals are perplexed, as the subs dock and the crews pour out, seeking revenge. The hand-to-hand fighting is so intense that the sailors are slipping on the blood of the Nobles. Then George and his mates attack from the rear and they are caught in a vise. Some of them flee to their subs, as a huge hole develops around Eli and Matthew. Now, more Royals see the hole and they sprint for their subs. George and his mates join Matthew and Eli at the front of the line and they block the warriors from pursuing them. Sub after sub submerges and speeds through the opening, past the statue of O, toward Abaddon. Strangely, there are no Lake Guardians on duty.

Matthew sends a message to Desiraa to release the wives and children, and send them to the docks. When they arrive, there are hugs and kisses awaiting them. Matthew shouts, "Sorry, for this deception, but we know the Royals informed the Red Serpent about our last attack and they had to be driven out of Atlantis. You'll do a great job. Now, go home to your families; eat, drink, and rest, because tomorrow we destroy Abaddon!"

From the crowd, someone yells, "What about the fleeing noblemen? Will you let them escape?"

Big Texas smiles appear on Matthew, Eli, Joshua and George, "They are being rewarded for their service to the Red Serpent, as we speak. Now, go home and show your wives and families how much you care for them." The crowd slowly breaks up, clutching their children tightly. Matthew pulls Raquelle and Eric close to his side.

The fleeing subs form a ragged fleet, as they dash for Abaddon. Their sensors detect one ship, as a torpedo detonates just behind them. The explosion pushes the fleet to maximum speed. The Royals assume that this is the lead ship of Eli's fleet. They hastily contact Abaddon and inform them that they are fleeing Atlantis. As the transmission ends, two torpedoes blaze past their subs, and each person breathes a sigh of relief. The entrance to Abaddon is close. Once they enter the city, they will be safe.

The Abaddonian fleet commander receives the message, but he doesn't trust any Atlantian. The detonation of two torpedoes in front of his sub spurs him into action, "Fire until nothing remains." The fleet unleashes a stream of laser blasts and the noblemen's fleet shatters. The pieces sink, hitting the waiting Krakens. The giant Kraken orders the others to feast on the dead, then to proceed to the cavern and celebrate by eating their fill of the fish inside. The squids rush to the cavern entrance and attack the fish inside. They have never had this much food that couldn't escape. They stuff themselves until they sink, lethargically, to the cavern floor, to rest. The cavern's floor now has a carpet of mantles, tentacles and legs everywhere. It will be a week before they have to eat again--or even desire to move. The gigantic squid enters the cavern, and his eyes brighten at the carpet below. These squid couldn't fight a battle and won't even want to leave the cavern for the next week or two. He is their new leader, and his plan is playing out.

The subs dock in Abaddon, and the Red Serpent, Vipurr, all the black snakes, the priests and the people celebrate their victory. The poison has transformed some of the people into violent beasts and they attack some of the others who are at the celebration. The serpent rises to full height and telepathically stops these attacks with the threat of being swallowed whole. Shalee can see the celebration, and she fears that Matthew has been defeated. She shouts, "Attack, Matthew! Where is your attack?"

Just then, an overseer enters her chamber. "What have we here, but the green-eyed sacrifice to our god?"

The next instant, his head twists violently to the right, and he falls dead on the floor. Jon's bulk fills the entrance, "The other workers are killing the rest of the overseers, as we speak. When do we break from the mines and join your husband's attack?"

Shalee's stomach tightens, as bile fills the back of her throat, and she thinks fast. "Tomorrow we attack. My husband let a small group of Atlantian subs be destroyed, so the people of Abaddon would celebrate and be in no condition to fight. Yes, Matthew will attack tomorrow. Definitely, he will attack tomorrow. What weapons do you have in the mines?" That is the biggest lie Shalee ever told, and she waits to see if Jon will buy it.

Jon's mouth drops almost to the floor, "But we killed the overseers today! We have their swords and daggers. Every miner has a pick and shovel. But we killed the overseers today! If we are discovered, they will send the black snakes into the mines. In the pitch black, the snakes are lethal, and it takes two weeks, in excruciating pain, to die. I will not die in the mines, but in the sunlight. You keep watch, to see if we are discovered. The shift changes at dawn, so we will be discovered then. I will assemble the miners at the main cave entrance to attack tomorrow at dawn. My beautiful woman, you have sealed our fate." Jon turns to go, leaving Shalee to stare out the window, watching the animalistic celebration of the city of Abaddon.

Chapter 27

Deception

It is still the middle of the night, as the combined fleets set sail for Abaddon. Matthew, Eric, Raquelle and George are in the subs George built. Matthew contacts Eli about the captain's concern that they are not taking any whales with them, but only dolphins, as scouts. Matthew is blunt, "We either trust this squid or we don't. It was truthful about the deceit of the Royals. Now, I trust that they are all dead and will burn in Hell for eternity. If he betrayed us, then we are sailing into a trap. Atlantis is defenseless. We have every Atlantian warrior on board our subs and victory or death are our only options. Every person among them will fight like a War Cat to save their families and they realize they will receive no mercy in Abaddon. My children and George and his pride fight at my side. George has the subs he built loaded with salt, and each ship has a weapon that sprays the salt in a stream up to thirty yards long. George's subs will be the first to land, and we will spray the docks. The black snakes will fry, as our troops debark the subs."

Eli is just as abrupt, "Trusting a Kraken… I will never trust a squid. They are food for the whales and for humans to eat." Eli ends the transmission.

At Abaddon, Shalee witnesses the drunken orgy that lasts all night long and, even in the dark, she can make out drunken bodies lying in the streets. Even the black snakes sleep in the street. It is very unusual that the snakes are not hiding. Shalee thinks that, maybe, they did destroy Matthew's fleet. Well, before the sun rises, they need to prepare to attack, so Shalee calls aloud, "Jon, it is time."

Jon appears in the entrance, with two short swords, and hands one to Shalee. "We need to attack in a few minutes. The priests will notice that the overseers are missing, if we wait for sunrise. Any sign of your husband?"

"No, but these people are so drunk that, maybe, the miners can overthrow Abaddon by themselves."

Jon smiles, "Once we killed the overseers, our fate was sealed. We dumped their bodies into the lava flow that separates to form the Tears of Lucifer."

Shalee's head snaps around. "Those are the lava flows that conceal the entrance to Abaddon. Show me where you dumped the bodies."

Jon walks Shalee downward, into a tunnel that opens onto a huge ledge with rows of tables and piles of blue diamonds. "We mine the eggs and bring them here to crack them and remove the diamonds. The shell is thrown into the lava, far below, and the blue jewels are placed in a pile. That other tunnel is the exit back to the mines. It is more than a mile to the lava flow, so we are safe."
Shalee rubs her hands together. "How many miners are ready to fight?"

"There are 253 miners. Why?"

"Station 13 miners on this ledge, and give them half a shovel handle, so they can knock out the drunks your miners bring here, then throw their bodies into the lava. Leave picks, shovels, and weapons by the main mine entrance. Let us see how many drunks we can kill, before we are discovered."

Jon and Shalee hurry to the main entrance and the large hatch is wide open. The miners are becoming accustomed to the light, as Shalee explains her plan to them. Jon inserts a twist to get the drunks into the mines. Tell them their god wishes them to have one handful of diamonds from the mines to celebrate the victory. That draws a laugh from the miners, and they leave in groups of two, to haul the drunks into the mines.

Shalee stays in the shadows and watches drunk after drunk descend into the mine. The artificial sun is beginning to rise, when a black snake decides to follow the parade and, just inside the mine entrance, it sees Shalee. Terror of this green-eyed monster grips it. With a lightning U-turn, it slithers, for all it is worth, to the main body of black snakes. In mass, the black snakes rise to assault the main mine entrance. Shalee sees them coming and yells to the miners to race back to the mine, so they can shut the hatch.

Miners drop their prey and sprint for safety. Unfortunately, the black snakes are quicker and they strike the men numerous times. The men take a few more steps, then they drop, as scaly bodies cover them, and only humps in the sea of black reveal where the men fell. Jon closes the hatch and locks it. "It is only a matter of time, until they get in, so we retreat to the ledge above the lava. Given a choice of the serpent's belly or the lava, I choose the lava."

A priest tells Vipurr that the miners are revolting, and that Shalee is leading the revolt. The high priest bites the air and grinds his teeth, "That sacrifice needs to be eaten today." He turns and rushes into

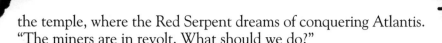

the temple, where the Red Serpent dreams of conquering Atlantis. "The miners are in revolt. What should we do?"

The forked tongue extends and licks Vipurr. He is very calm, "At the top of my gold statue is a lever that shuts off the lava. I will shut off the flow, and the heat inside the mines will cook the miners. Recall all the black snakes to the dock, so I am protected, and station troops at all mine entrances. Those that come out, we capture alive. Those who have been boiled in the mines—have the troops bring them to the temple, so that I may eat their cooked flesh." The high priest leaves, as the viper climbs the golden statue and wraps its body around the lever, then moves it to the closed position.

The flow of lava from the Face of Lucifer ceases. The crews of the three Abaddonian subs that are patrolling the entrance to the city are in total shock. In their memory, the Tears have never stopped, so they investigate. The three subs converge and shine beams of light on the face, where the lava once flowed. Two gigantic metal discs block the flow of lava. Their god has thought of everything. At that instant, the first sub explodes, sending shards of metal against the left disc and, before the second sub can react, it explodes, sending more metal against the left disc, causing pin-hole punctures. Lava begins to slowly trickle out. The third sub cuts its lights and scans for the enemy, then launches two torpedoes, as they communicate to the city, that they are under attack, and need immediate reinforcements. Their torpedoes make a U-turn to chase two high-speed torpedoes, which were fired by the enemy. All four explode into the Face of Lucifer.

Chapter 28

Confusion

In the mines, Shalee and Jon notice the river of lava is rising. All the miners have picks and shovels for weapons. Jon ponders the situation, and shouts, "The fact that the new overseers are not in the tunnel suggests that they will sweat us to death with the lava. The Serpent has stopped the Tears of Lucifer, and the lava is backing up into this valley. Within a quarter of a day, the heat will rise above one hundred fifty-degrees in every mineshaft, and the lava will only rise halfway up this valley. We will all be dead, and the serpent can open the Tears of Lucifer and recover his diamonds. I want to die in the sun, so I suggest we open the hatch, and fight the black snakes in the sun. Who will join me?"

All the miners remain very still for a few moments then, one-by-one, they shout, "Yes!" Shalee steps forward, "I got you into this mess. I will be the first one out of the hatch. These black snakes know me as a green-eyed monster and it may cause them to freeze for a moment, so rush out of the entrance and kill them quickly."

They reach the hatch, and Shalee tightens her hands' grips on her sword. She mentally tells Matthew she loves him, then nods her head to open the hatch. The hatch swings wide open and she races out. As the miners pour out of the hatch, they stop in disbelief because there is not a warrior, a black snake, or a priest at the entrance to the mine. And there are no bodies on the streets. In fact, it is a ghost town. Shalee and the miners cautiously move toward the dock.

All of Abaddon's subs gather behind the last patrol sub, and their sensors pick up an enemy ship, almost out of sensor range. The fleet pursues this sub, and they fire torpedoes and lasers at it. The laser blasts and the torpedoes can only come close to the ship, because it swiftly maneuvers out of their range. It lights up, like a neon light at midnight, and its glow interrupts the Abaddonian subs' sensors, but they target the light. The Abaddon fleet is closing fast on the light, with all lasers firing.

The brilliant light blazes through the hole, into the side of the mountain and into the cavern. The light stings each Kraken's eyes, and they all turn bright red. The carpet of squids mutates into red beasts that feel caged, and they want out, to extinguish that light.

The giant squid tries to keep them in the cavern, but in vain, as they pour out of the opening and into the middle of the Abaddonian fleet. The Kraken leader is the only squid left in the cavern, and he is sulking.

The light switches off, as the Atlantian fleet pours lasers and torpedoes into Abaddon's subs and the Krakens. The squids turn scarlet and race to attack the enemy. Before they can reach their enemy, the fleet races at full speed for the entrance to Abaddon, with Matthew, George, Raquelle, Eric and the ship with the bright light leading the way. As the trailing Atlantian fleet reaches the entrance to Abaddon, Eli turns his fleet to protect the entrance. Blast after blast pours into the Krakens, but they continue to come, and some of them make it to the subs and wrap their tentacles and legs around many of them.

The waters violently vibrate, tossing subs and Krakens end over end, then the left eye of Lucifer explodes, sending a stream of lava out a mile horizontally, over the Abaddonians, who are trying to regroup. The submarines glow red, from this encasing lava. The water quickly cools and hardens the molten rock. As the subs find that they can't navigate, they sink. In the confusion, the giant Kraken slips past Eli's subs and into Abaddon, where he stations himself beside the temple.

They have had enough of all these lights, lava, and lasers. They flee into the depths. Eli leaves three subs to guard the entrance, and sends the rest of them to help Matthew defeat the city of Abaddon.

Chapter 29

Can you kill a God?

Shalee and her band of miners cautiously make their way to the dock. The stillness is frightening, as the group looks for an enemy. There are no warriors, priests, slave girls, or black snakes. Shalee and the miners stand on the dock, and Jon asks, "What do we do now?"

Before she can answer, the doors of the palace open wide, and floods of black snakes pour out. A strange ship surfaces behind Shalee and her heart sinks, because they are trapped. The ship sprays a fine white powder, in a stream, over the band of miners. As it filters down, it stings her eyes. It has no odor at all, but it tastes like salt. In the next instant, four more subs surface, and the white shower intensifies, since it now comes from all the ships. The wave of black snakes has momentum and it can't stop. As the first of the black snakes slithers over the white powder, they wriggle in pain. The serpents continue to pour out of the palace, and the current carries them over their dead comrades and onto more salt. The crackles and hisses of serpents fill the air, as the salt stream ends, and an enormous man emerges from the ship, with his sword drawn. From the other subs step Matthew, Raquelle, Eric and George.

Shalee rushes toward Matthew and bumps into George. She hesitates, as she expects the massive tiger to attack her, but he simply passes her to survey the scene of the deaths of the black snakes. Matthew grabs Shalee in his arms, and Eric wraps his arms around both of them. She has to push Matthew away. "It is not over. There are warriors, priests, slave girls, and the Red Serpent. I don't know where they are, but they will attack soon. Where is Raquelle?"

Matthew's head turns to the right, then Shalee turns. Raquelle is hugging this massive man and he is returning her affection. Shalee tries to break Matthew's hold, to stop her, but he holds tight. Other subs surface and, as more troops disembark, from the temple and the surrounding domes, comes screaming, and men and women with snake eyes are charging toward them. The Red Serpent's poison has transformed these people into bloodthirsty creatures.

The Atlantians form a circle, protecting the dock and their ships. The charging hordes did not count on salt so, as they race toward their enemies, they hit the salt, and slip and fall. The Atlantians immediately kill the first wave but, even as bodies pile up, the enemy keeps charging. The Red Serpent raises himself up and controls the battle from his temple. The Centurion and Raquelle fight side-by-side, moving toward the temple. Matthew, Shalee, Eric and George fight, heading toward the palace. Another sub surfaces, and releases George's mates into the battle. George is one big smile and is very happy to see them. Hour after hour, the battle rages. The warriors of Abaddon, little by little, push the Atlantians into a tighter circle on the dock.

The sun is beginning to set, as Jon shouts, "I will die in sunlight." Jon cuts through warrior after warrior and the other miners follow. The Abaddonian line breaks in front of George and his pride. The tigers kill with efficiency and their line collapses. The remaining warriors of Abaddon turn to flee, with the Atlantian warriors chasing them, seeking revenge.

Some of the priests in the temple throw down their weapons to run, but the Serpent's strike leaves them wriggling in pain, as they slowly die. The Red Serpent is shocked that his poison does not kill instantly but, since he gave so much to the people, his poison sacs are depleted. The other priests stand their ground, as the Centurion and Raquelle hack their way into the temple. Priest after priest goes down to defeat, and the Red Serpent realizes that he may lose. The Serpent mentally calls all the Krakens to help him. He turns and, almost instantly, sees the gigantic Kraken bobbing in the lake, but it is just bobbing. The Serpent orders it to attack the enemy on the dock, but he continues to just bob.

The enemy has penetrated the temple. Vipurr draws his sword and, screaming, he charges Raquelle. He is fresh, so his blows rain down on Raquelle's sword with the power of sledgehammers. She weakens under his blows, and sinks closer to the floor. The Centurion sees that she is in trouble and cuts through the priests, to get a clear shot at Vipurr. He throws his sword sideways. The blade whirls like the rotor of a helicopter, then it buries itself into the neck of the high priest. The man quivers in excruciating pain. The Red Serpent strikes, as the Centurion reaches for a weapon, but the Serpent's fang slices down his back, and poison squirts from the fangs.

Raquelle screams, "No!" as she leaps at the Serpent's neck. She buries her sword to the hilt in his flesh. The whipping of the Serpent's head throws her outside the temple. The Serpent smiles at the dying Centurion, then he feels something in the water touch his tail.

The long tentacles wrap around the Red Serpent's tail. The chitinous circles in the tentacles bite deep into his skin and the Kraken attempts to submerge. The Serpent snatches wounded priests to add weight to his body, in a futile attempt to keep himself in the temple, but the squid forces more water through its jets and, inch by inch, the Serpent slips under the water. The Centurion opens his eyes and smiles. This wriggling god is being pulled behind the giant squid, like a baby rattlesnake on a fishing hook, fighting for air. The Kraken quickly swims through the entrance to Abaddon, into the sea. He purposefully slows to cruising speed, as he passes close to the three Atlantian subs, where Eli sees chunks of the Red Serpent separate from his body and fizzle away in the salt water. The squid just keeps going deeper, dragging the disintegrating body into utter blackness. Now that the Red Serpent is dead, Eli orders his ships into Abaddon.

As the Serpent is slowly dragged into the water, the priests flee. Raquelle's shoulders ache, as she stands and struggles to enter the temple. She finds the Centurion and cradles him in her arms. He agonizes and slowly opens his eyes, "I was born free and I die free. That is all I can expect from my God. Weep for me, my beloved." The Centurion closes his eyes and his body goes limp. Raquelle begins to weep.

The other Atlantians and George's pride hunt down the remaining enemy and they show them no mercy, but give them quick deaths. Matthew, Shalee, Eric and George enter the temple. Raquelle's tears drop on the Centurion's face and Shalee puts her arms around her, to pull her away. George's roar reverberates inside the temple and Shalee jumps backward, as Matthew raises his sword. George places himself between Raquelle and Shalee. His expression turns bitter, as he stares directly at Matthew. "Wolverine, my debt to you is paid in full. This woman gives three days of weeping for my fellow warrior. If either of you touches her before the three days end, I will tear your guts out. If you wish to fight now, then keep your sword raised and your woman can weep for you for three days." George prepares to leap.

Shalee looks at Matthew, but he is in deep thought, mentally replaying the current battle and how George sliced the warriors and priests to shreds with his claws. Shalee is beside him, and he can see that she is not physically hurt. As his eyes shift back to George, he lowers his sword, pulls Shalee close to his side and squeezes her, as they walk out of the temple. Shalee and Matthew step over body after body of priests and warriors, "So much evil in one place. I am glad I married you, Matthew Wolverine. No one else would have paid such a price to rescue me. Please, let's get on a sub and leave this awful place."

Matthew gets in his sub and moves the seat as far back as he can. Shalee slides in and sits on his lap. The silky smoothness of her hair against his cheek stimulates him, and he squeezes her tightly around the waist. "I need you too, Matt, but not here." Matthew grabs the controls and submerges the sub and steers it out of the entrance to Abaddon. They only go a few miles toward Atlantis and his hands are all over Shalee. The smell of her skin is driving him wild. He puts the ship on automatic, and she turns to face him. Her hands encircle his face as she kisses him deeply. Her tongue searches his teeth for an opening and, finally, she is rewarded. The kisses become deeper and longer, and the passion builds in both of them, until Shalee rips Matthew's shirt to get it off. Her wetness soaks him, as she, in a series of acrobatic movements, and with Matthew's help, removes her clothes. Their satisfaction is quick and she collapses on top of him. "I needed that so badly. Maybe I am just a wanton woman."

Matthew feels Shalee's naked breasts against his skin, so he pulls her to him and drives them deeper into his chest. "I love you so much, I hurt inside. Life without you is hell."

George orders that the bodies of the slain Atlantian warriors and the Centurion be taken back to the temple in Atlantis, to make sure that they are loaded on a separate sub from Matthew and Shalee, then to leave for home. Eli enters the temple and George orders him to police the slain Abaddonian population, and pile the bodies on the dock. He is to order his submarines to strap five bodies to cords and drag them out to sea, behind them. When the squids see the bodies, the subs are to lead them back to the dock and let them feast. Also, have five men remove all the blue diamonds from the wall and place them in boxes, because this is George's reward for fighting. The gold statue of the serpent is Eli's, and can be melted down into coins.

Eli's face wrinkles, "All these blue diamonds are yours? Why?"

George sits down and patiently explains, "I built the subs for Matthew. I recruited the Centurion. The plan to flush out the Royals was mine, and my pride and I put our lives on the line for Atlantis in this battle. The gold from this hideous serpent statue will mint you enough coins to inspire the Atlantians to elect you as their first President. Inscribe, on the coins, Texas Freedom--on both sides, so they won't ever forget this battle and you leading the Texans, the War Cats, the Centurion and your navy to victory over Abaddon. What will be your first priority after election?"

Eli hesitates only for a moment, "To find the passage that the Red Serpent took in the lake of life to get back to Abaddon, then build subs to ferry people between our two cities." Eli is very proud of himself and immediately orders five warriors to strip the walls of the blue diamonds, box them and ship them to George in Atlantis.

Chapter 30

Weeping

The subs with the dead warriors dock in Atlantis, with Raquelle on board one of them. Desiraa and the other women clean the dead, and they are placed in the temple. Raquelle and the other women weep for them. Some of the fathers of the dead weep but, when the Atlantian fleet returns, the docks burst into cheers of victory and Atlantis is in a party mood. George, with his pride following, goes directly to the church and orders the men to leave. Sonya is commanded to allow only women into the temple, to weep for three days. Food will be supplied, at the back of the temple, for the weepers, and fresh fish for the pride. She rubs her cheek on George's cheek and softly thinks, "We survived the battle, and I am happy, but Atlantis is too small for our cubs. We need the mountains and hills in which to roam. I want to go to Argentina."

"I will work that out but, did you see the Trader? Was he killed with the Royals? I don't know, so I will go to inspect his compound."

He walks to the Trader's compound and all the doors are open. Cautiously, he enters. The safe is open and empty. He left in a hurry, but where did he go? He did not go to the dock, so how did he get out? George goes into the next dome. Unicorns are standing in a group, as George approaches. "My name is George, and I am looking for the Trader."

The leader of the Unicorns steps forward. "Who will feed us? The Trader had a sub hidden in our pond, and it was able to get out to sea. He loaded cases of blue diamonds, then he yelled, 'Starve to death, unicorns and tigers. I hate you!' Then he left. Who will feed us?"

George senses anxiety in the unicorns, "The people of Atlantis will feed you, but we need to get you all out, so the people can see you. Bring the tigers into your dome and we will go into the streets of Atlantis." The unicorn gets the tigers and the group leaves the Trader's compound. The tigers ask George if the Centurion will still take them to training, now that the Trader is gone?

"The Centurion is dead. I wish I had remembered that you were in the Trader's compound. We could have used your help in the battle with Abaddon. Yes, we did win the war."

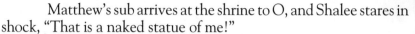

Matthew's sub arrives at the shrine to O, and Shalee stares in shock, "That is a naked statue of me!"

"That is O, but she could be your twin. She and the Red Serpent caused the sinking of Atlantis. I have stopped the sub because, every time I see that statue, I long to make love to you. Let's make love before we dock." The sub spends an hour, just sitting in front of the statue of O. Elizabeth and other Lake Guardians eventually surround the sub, and she tries to sense mental communication. She succeeds, blushes and has the other Lake Guardians keep their distance until the sub starts to move again. At the dock, Matthew opens the hatch, and Elizabeth licks Shalee, as she exits. She dives into the water to clean up and Matthew dives in beside her. Then they climb onto the dock, to Eric and Desiraa. Eric hugs his mother. "I knew you and Dad had to be alone in his sub, so I piloted my sub back to Atlantis.

Most of Atlantis is partying, and they cheer Matthew and Shalee. For the next three days, Eric spends most of his time swimming and riding on Elizabeth's back, because his mom and dad are hugging and kissing and just want to be alone. At the end of the third day, Raquelle is exhausted from weeping and she falls into a deep sleep in front of the Centurion's body. The Centurion appears to Raquelle in a glowing light. "Bless you for your tears. God has seen your tears and grants you the husband of your dreams. From faraway, he will travel and capture your heart. He is a man of honor and of light but, he is a man, and you will date no boys until he comes. If you wait for him, then you will be cherished as your father cherishes your mother. Take my blue diamonds as my wedding gift. Wait, wait, wait for him."

Raquelle awakes with a start, and George is standing over her. "Did you see the Centurion?"

"Yes. He was glowing and he thanked me for my tears. God promises me a husband of honor and of light from faraway, but only if I date no one else."

George presses hard on the next point. "Did he say any thing else?"

Raquelle's shoulders sag, as she drags herself to her feet. "Yes, he said to take his blue diamonds, as my wedding gift."

George becomes very formal. "His share of the blue diamonds will be prepared for you and put on your sub before you leave. On the surface, you will contact the Swiss Cayman Bank in the Cayman Islands and talk to Hans Luther and tell him a Slither's Nightmare recommended you. I will add some blue diamonds, as my wedding present to you. Now, go to your parents and tell them about your vision, but eat and take a shower first."

Raquelle leaves for home, and George has the Centurion's body transported to his ship and orders the ship to conceal the warrior's body deep in the ocean. The ship verifies that the warrior is dead, then automatically streaks through the entrance of Atlantis and dives into the blackness. About three hundred leagues down, it almost collides with the gigantic Kraken, but it swerves to miss the beast. It shoots laser beams into the side of a mountain, steers into the opening, then closes the shaft behind itself. The Kraken recognizes the ship and knows it is the Red Serpent's final victim come to rest--and he is happy.

Raquelle finishes her shower, then eats with her family, as she relates her vision. Matthew is concerned about the vision, and that his daughter may wait her whole life for this stranger, and voices his doubts. As has happened in the past, Shalee anticipates an explosion of anger, but Raquelle remains very calm, as she speaks, "Father, you expect us to believe you went back a thousand years to rescue Mom from dragons. I believe that story as much you believe my vision, Father, and no more. So, it is you who determines how much I believe." Raquelle continues to eat, and Matthew knows he has been had.

Chapter 31

Return

Eli comes to Matthew's home with George. The War Cat and his pride are leaving for Argentina in the next few days. Eli wonders if Matthew will return to Texas. "Yes, we want to go back to Texas. The secret of Atlantis is safe with us."

Eli grins, "The people of Atlantis want to make me their first President. The Red Serpent's statue is now processed into gold coins, with the inscription Texas Freedom. Here is the first one for you, Matthew. And Shalee, we are melting down the statue of O and making it into coins for you and Matthew. That statue has been a hindrance to us for millennia. We will store the coins here, until you need them, but take a box full with you, when you leave."

Shalee learns to pilot George's sub, and the four subs are loaded. After the good-byes have been said to Elizabeth and the other Lake Guardians, Matthew bids good-bye to George. "It was good fighting beside you." Eric is stroking Sonya's head, but Raquelle is anxious to leave. The four subs dive, and the automatic pilot takes them back to the mine where the whole adventure began. They see the bottom of the pristine white ship and know Scotty didn't move. They come out through the same entrance Shalee originally used to go into the cavern and they park the subs. Then they hunt for their scuba gear.

"When we get on board ship, Raquelle and Eric, come back with balloons for the two boxes. When they surface, we will bring them on board with hooks. Now, let's go back to Texas."

The Wolverines surface and climb on board the ship. The captain is flabbergasted. " You are dead."

"No, we are very much alive. Help my family retrieve two boxes, then pull up anchor and head back to Texas. I will talk to Scotty."

As Matthew descends the stairs, he is met by a ghost-white Scotty, "Yes, I am alive. How is my business?"

Scotty stammers but, when he gets the words out, you can hear Matthew five miles away. Shalee, Raquelle, Eric and the captain pull the boxes on board.

"You borrowed money from the oil cartel? Are you nuts?! Those tree huggers did what? They won in a federal court, by blaming all the air pollution on the oil companies? We are talking hundreds of billions of dollars in punitive damages. First, the cigarette companies; now us. Show me how bad it really is." Raquelle immediately gets on the radio to the Swiss Cayman Bank. They agree that the bank will have a ship to meet them, and they will transfer her blue diamonds, as they pass by the Cayman Islands. Hans Luther will have all the paperwork on board.

Shalee has her arm around Eric, as they stand by the boxes, looking into the sea. Raquelle joins them. Matthew's screaming has subsided, and Raquelle speaks, "We could go back to Atlantis but, then, a Texan doesn't run away from a fight." Shalee just pulls her closer, as the ship heads for Texas.

THE END

visit
WWW.DANIELJASON.COM

Listen to confessions of a Texas golden retriever, in front of the air conditioner.
Also, order a personalized copy of this book online, as a Christmas or a Birthday gift for a friend or a special family member. Or start the series with *"The Ultimate Dragon"*. Both make perfect gifts and both are available to order online when

you visit
www.danieljason.com